ALONE
IN THE
CLASSROOM

ALONE
IN THE
CLASSROOM

ELIZABETH HAY

MacLehose Press
New York • London

MacLehose Press
An imprint of Quercus
New York • London

© 2011 by Elizabeth Hay
Family tree © 2011 by Emily Faccini
First published in the United States by Quercus in 2014

ISBN 978-1-62365-104-6

Library of Congress Control Number: 2013913489

Manufactured in the United States

10 9 8 7 6 5 4 3 2 1

www.quercus.com

For my mother and father

Nothing would give up life:
Even the dirt kept breathing a small breath.

—Theodore Roethke

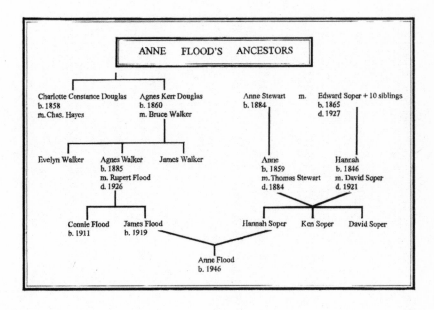

ANNE   FLOOD'S   ANCESTORS

Charlotte Constance Douglas
b. 1858
m. Chas. Hayes

Agnes Kerr Douglas
b. 1860
m. Bruce Walker

Anne Stewart   m.
b. 1884

Edward Soper + 10 siblings
b. 1865
d. 1927

Evelyn Walker

Agnes Walker
b. 1885
m. Rupert Flood
d. 1926

James Walker

Anne
b. 1859
m. Thomas Stewart
d. 1884

Hannah
b. 1846
m. David Soper
d. 1921

Connie Flood
b. 1911

James Flood
b. 1919

Hannah Soper

Ken Soper

David Soper

Anne Flood
b. 1946

1

CHOKECHERRIES

Other children were out picking that morning, but she passed them by in her light-blue dress and sandals. "Ethel," they called, and she gave a quick smile and went on up the road toward the woods and fields at the top of the hill. She had an empty kettle in each hand and was alone, despite having three sisters.

They were a family of bright solitaries, studious, quiet. Unlike anyone else in that town in the Ottawa Valley, she had been conceived in India, born in India, and raised there until the age of three. Her earliest memory was having warm water ladled over her hot head from an earthenware jar. For five years her father served in the British Army, then he left that parched and dusty land for the woods and rivers of Canada. In their apartment on the third floor of the Stewart Block adjoining the Rover Garage, there were a few keepsakes from that time, small ornaments, lacquered boxes, a monkey carved in ebony. Had they lived in a house with a veranda and a grassy yard, she might not have been so inclined to stay away for hours at a time.

Her mother, waiting impatiently for the plums to ripen, was no great admirer of chokecherries. Nevertheless, she simmered a second batch in a big preserving kettle and strained it through cheesecloth, then added four cups of sugar for every two cups of cherry juice and let the liquid boil until the flow of juice off a spoon turned to slower drips that came together in a sheet and broke off, at which point she removed the pot from the fire.

Ruby-sweet jelly was the ultimate goal, manufactured in summer kitchens for winter mornings. Pickers were out every day that summer, mainly children, the fruit uncommonly plentiful in a year that also saw a heavy growth of plums in gardens and fields. Blueberries had given promise, too, but in the hot, dry weather of late July the blue gold suffered a setback, and some were going as far away for them as the mountains of Pakenham.

Chokecherries merit the name, puckering one up even more than green apples. Held aloft on low and spindly trees, the size of peas, almost black when ripe and almost edible when black. Shiny black. Prune-black. *Prunus virginiana*. Not a name children knew, but they knew the word *astringent*.

Roads were narrower in 1937, more shaded. Cars less common and slower. Summer feet were bare and tough, or shod in old leather. Faces were careless of the sun. Noses burned, and children aided the peeling by picking the skin loose and giving it a fascinated tug. As many peelings per summer as there were pips in a winter grapefruit.

In a dress you were one flitting color among many in a landscape that mobilized its colors into a procession of ripening—from wild strawberries in June more potent in flavor, more fragrant, than twenty garden berries put together and reason for kneeling on the grassy verge, your face inches above your prey, your fingers gently grappling to dislodge the firm, pale, tiny necks from their leafy hulls—to raspberries in July that raked your hands and arms as you grabbed a thorny cane and swung it back like a throat about to be slit, the soft red fruit like gobbets of blood—to blueberries in August abloom with ghostly light that erased itself in your fingers. The whole landscape was a painting come to life, and not a Canadian painting (no figures allowed), but a European painting, peopled and unpeopled, storied, brazen.

A deer came out of the bush. Hardly a sound. It was there, a tawny pose and wet eyes. They absorbed each other's attention. The deer lowered its head and nibbled, Ethel moved closer. Around them was birdsong, breezes. One small branch of a leaning maple showed the first touch of red.

Early August. The jewelweed was in blossom, tomatoes were ripening, the morning became increasingly hot. Summer held. But school was in the air. Every child felt it. She was aware of precious time running out.

The search for the lost girl started at suppertime and spread rapidly. First, family and neighbors, then the police and Boy Scouts combed the Opeongo Road where she had been seen walking that morning. They moved out through the fields and along the creek, the Scouts blowing horns to communicate their whereabouts far and wide. Bugling criss-crossed the evening and gave the impression of a summer fox hunt. The sun began to go down.

Crows, not quiet before, were quiet now. A breeze picked up and stirred the leaves. Shadows deepened, but fields and woods were still clear enough to an accustomed eye. And a shout went up. A young man had stumbled over a body.

Word circulated through town, and an hour before midnight a ghost appeared. It lingered in front of the Argyle Hotel on Argyle Street, then continued on past Russell's drugstore and Barker's shoe store and over to the baseball diamond and the railway tracks in a slow, footless sort of swoop, a strange white moth involved in dusky explorations. A traveling player was drumming up an audience for the midnight "Ghost Show" at the O'Brien Theater. He drew an overflow crowd. Many had to stand in the back, others were turned away. It was the summer equivalent of Santa: children were up way beyond their bedtimes and even more suggestible than usual.

By then everyone knew that thirteen-year-old Ethel Weir had been found at sunset in the bush on Ivey Hill. Her battered head lay in a pool of blood. Four feet away were two kettles, one of them partly filled with chokecherries, the other empty.

This part of the world is where I live now. At least in a general way. It contains the stream in which my grandmother washed herself in dumb panic upon finding a large red stain in her underwear— a motherless child raised by a Scottish grandmother who told her nothing. She passed on the favor, telling my mother nothing, even though they shared the same bed, and my mother passed this abashed ignorance on to me, asking me after the fact if I knew what to expect. It's hard to credit in this age of palaver that people used to say so little about sex. Until it exploded in their faces, that is, at which point newspapers told all.

Two days after the murder, a name floated up on the front page of the *Mercury*. John Coyle, not an official member of the search party, "almost stumbled" over the corpse in a bush next to a grain field. Very quickly, suspicion veered from marauding cattle and prowling degenerates to the lone young man who had nearly tripped over the body. The hot breath of the newspaper. "Police are working on the theory that some local person committed the deed. Some questioning has occurred. It is felt that at any hour the mystery may be solved."

The old seesaw from horrified belief to dizzy disbelief to entrenched belief. The town was busy weaving a story, meting out blame, finding symmetry and plot and motive. Johnny Coyle's fascination with his crime, went common opinion, reflected the old desire to return to the scene—as I am doing right now in returning to this time and place, in revisiting my mother's childhood in the valley.

Stories from her past draw me on. The shadows and underbrush, the evening light and imminent sorrow, until I stumble over what I've been looking for without quite knowing what it was, and look up. How dimly quiet the library is, how industrious the other researchers as they, too, ruin their eyes in moonlit woods of microfilm. Let's not kid ourselves anymore about new technology.

In Ethel's clenched hand were some fibers of green and yellow, light blue and rose, also dark blue, evidently wool, and some "pointed" hairs of a golden hue.

My mother knew Ethel's sister, who was too shy to be a close friend. "I was shy," my mother said, "and she was shyer."

Toward suppertime I leave the library and step outside into a haze of twenty-first-century sunshine and wind. Wellington Street in Ottawa. Behind me the Ottawa River flows east, and upriver, sixty miles from here and a bit inland, is the town I have been reading about, my mother's hometown. I bicycle south, heading home through a flood of April light, and nothing around me is as clear as the colors and threads in Ethel's hand, those makings for a tiny nest. Birds everywhere, but no leaves, not yet, though the red maple at the foot of my garden earns its name by staining the air dark crimson with minute, discreet blossom. In the morning, taking my pillow with me, I lie at the foot of the bed in order to see the color through the upstairs window.

We have the most beautiful tree in the world. It turns my head every spring and again every fall when I step into this second-floor study and receive a bouquet the size of my window. Our house and garden used to belong to a botanist who was fascinated with orphan plants, waifs, like the Kaladar cactus first discovered a two-hour drive west of here in 1934, then lost from view and subsequently rediscovered in 1947, an isolated and vulnerable plant six hundred miles east of its Wisconsin home. The botanist used to sit on the front porch in a white chair and when he went inside he left a sign on the chair saying OPEN FOR BUSINESS. You could bring him any flower or leaf and he would identify it. My study used to be full of plants that he watered in the nude. I am sorry not to have known him, though very probably he was best in small doses, because there are so many things I would like to identify and because the story I'm telling now is another story of discovery and rediscovery, not botanical but personal. Perhaps every family tale falls into this category: a child discovers something the parent has neglected to tell her and brings it into view again, naming it and locating it and establishing its importance.

What happened that August Tuesday in 1937 lived on in my mother's mind, not that she ever mentioned it to me until long after I left home. Nor did she temper any of my own youthful wanderings with a warning. I went out into the world as free of apprehension as was Ethel Weir on the day she went to pick chokecherries, wearing a blue dress of synthetic silk and a green slip underneath it.

Birds compete for the berries. Robins peck the guts out of strawberries. Finches, robins, blue jays, kingbirds, cedar waxwings—all of them go after the chokecherries that favor fencerows and roadsides and the edges of open woods. Crows fancy the metallic glints of the kettles and pails children carry as they wander into the open center of wild plum thickets, or into the grassy meadow next to a little-used airfield, or into an abandoned orchard on a southern slope, or along the railway's right-of-way, or down a path skirting a grain field toward the straggly, ragged chokecherry bushes above the creek, or into the woods for shade and rest.

Murdered in the morning, it was thought, for by the time they found her body, it was stiff. Dead eight to ten hours, the coroner said. They carried the body on a blanket out of the woods and transported it by car to the funeral parlor on Argyle Street. Three days later, several hundred people, mostly women and children (though not my mother and grandmother, they were at the lake), gathered at the Presbyterian church for the morning funeral. A closed white casket. And afterward, interment in the Angusville Cemetery.

Another funeral took place in the afternoon, another instance of sudden and perplexing death. A doctor had died on the operating table. On Tuesday evening (as the search was on for Ethel) Dr. Thomas entered the hospital, and on Wednesday morning his heart gave out. An apparently rugged man with a heavy practice and a long history in the town.

Some who went to the first funeral attended the second, among them a reporter for the *Ottawa Journal* and the source of much of what I know. Connie Flood stayed on in the cemetery, notepad against her propped-up knees and her back against a tree, a young woman who made a desk for herself wherever she went. The cemetery was on a grassy hill half a mile from town. A white fence separated it from the road, and the large swing gates were open.

The second funeral came through the gates, a somber parade led by a firing party of the Lanark and Argyll Scottish Regiment with arms reversed. From a curious distance, Connie noted the contrast with the earlier scene of mothers holding their children by the hand, the bereaved family bent-shouldered and willowy, the sisters bare-armed in summer dresses and flat, flowered straw hats, purchased for Easter probably, the mother in black, the father in black, the ceremony at the graveside drenched in tears and formality beside the point. Afterward, the mourners left the baked cemetery for more of the noonday sun, some walking, some in cars.

In the second case, all the motions mattered. The regiment fired three volleys over the grave, then the pipe major played the customary lament and a comrade sounded the last post. A prominent citizen was being buried and prominent citizens were in attendance. Connie lingered on the edges. The dead man apparently had no children, no wife. It was hard to say. Two women seemed front and center, aunts perhaps or sisters. And men in dark suits and hats, older men, established men, and suddenly the air went funny and the ground shifted. She drew near to make sure.

He was still impeccable, immaculate. Still given to wearing the shade of gray that matched his iron-gray hair. She had known him seven years ago in a town thousands of miles from here—far enough away and a long enough interval that it took a moment—but then she was back in that appalled place he had created and fled from.

She waited until people started to file away, drew closer and said his name.

He turned and stared, then smiled a smile that finally made sense: he bared his teeth and clicked upper teeth against lower in an extended grimace expressly made for this cornered occasion. "Miss Flood."

The sun beat down. The grass under their feet was dry. The same weather that was withering the blueberries.

Her voice came out higher than normal. "I've been to France since the last time I saw you, Mr. Burns."

They were facing each other like a bride and groom on a funeral cake, wrong for each other, but too late to escape.

"I take it you know the deceased," he said.

"No. I work for a newspaper now."

He looked over at the grave. "That gentleman was a school trustee. I knew him reasonably well."

"Then you're still teaching."

"Less than I would like." He was the principal of the local high school, he said. Administration took up much of his time. It was always the way.

"Did you ever teach her?" She pointed to the other fresh grave two hundred yards away.

"Her sisters."

She was silent. Then, "I always wondered."

There was more silence. He had looked away in irritation. A weak word choice, *wondered*. "Finish your sentence. Wondered what?"

"If I'd see you again," she said, and left it at that.

An hour later, and on the other side of town, she walked from the road to the site of the murder, that spot in the near woods on the other side of a fence, and why on the other side of the fence unless enticed by someone she knew? Then down the wild slope to a lazy brown creek with ferns and cedars and sumac all around. Paths trodden out by children and animals. The deep summer smell of childhood, a tangy, fermented, woody smell fragrant with wild flowers and water.

The bank of the creek looked open and wide and mowed. A breeze stirred all the smells in the hot air—flies buzzed—cattails and marshiness off to the right—a little dock at the water, and lower than the dock, just above the water, a wide flat black rock offered a perfect place for entering the tea-colored creek.

Connie turned and saw a deer in a haze of brightness. Liquid movement. Dainty spots of light. The heat.

The deer was joined by another; they drank and blended back into the shade. She noticed the low tree on her right. A few choke-cherries hung by a thread, disemboweled, red around the pit. Nature wastes. Birds don't finish their plates. Neither do slugs, mice, raccoons, deer. They semi-devour berries, tomatoes, corn. Thoughtless and prodigal and against the Scottish grain.

In France the tapestries she had seen of unicorns and knights and ladies and spears and birds and flowers had pulled her back into a muffled, faded past. Then in Italy she had come upon a small oil on a wooden panel of a man being scourged. She looked straight through the dark centuries into bright sunlight, into the color and line of punishment, and it moved her to tears, a painting small enough for a child to carry around.

He had inspired her to go abroad, she had to give him that, the man who smiled like a fox.

The next day, wanting a quiet place to assemble her notes, she went into the Argyle Public Library and took a seat at a long table occupied by a few other readers. She saw the copy of *Nicholas Nickleby* lying there and picked it up. Across the table a bony, pale, well-dressed woman leafed through a magazine. "I couldn't read it," the woman said. "I couldn't stomach the cruelty." The woman continued to flick from photograph to photograph. "School isn't like that," she said.

The elderly librarian chimed in. "And you should know, Mrs. Burns."

So this was his wife, a woman older than he was, which made a kind of sense, who couldn't bear to read a book about children abused by a Yorkshire schoolmaster. Whom did she think she was married to? And how did Dickens bear it, except by making his characters colorful and comical in their cruelty, and by pounding them with his indignation.

"Mrs. Burns, I used to work with your husband. I taught under him."

"In Niagara Falls?"

"Saskatchewan."

"He talks about Niagara Falls."

But not about Saskatchewan. He wouldn't talk about Saskatchewan. "I lost track of him after he moved away," Connie said.

A girl of seventeen was at the far end of the table, half reading, half listening. She had a wonderful head of curly brown hair. The girl's name was Hannah Soper. Her mother, Anne, was the one who had washed her bloody underwear in the creek, uncertain what else to do. I was named after Anne, my grandmother.

On that day in the library my mother was reading Stefansson's account of his life among the Eskimos. The library was warm and dusty with light pouring in through high windows. She borrowed Stefansson's book and bicycled the six miles back to the lake, thinking less about Ethel, perhaps, than the famous explorer—tall, handsome, imposing—who had come as part of the summer chautauqua of music and lectures and marionettes and shown his slides of Arctic flowers in twenty-four-hour daylight that were never to leave her painterly mind. "*Ex*-quisite," my mother would say of them, stressing the first syllable as she had been taught to do by her very good Latin teacher. "I loathe ex-*quis*-ite." Her loathings, like her loves, were emphatic.

How tender it is sometimes to know the future. To know, for instance, that when my mother became very old, she turned up the heat, finally, and even then, in that over-warm house, she could not get warm. She lay in bed with her cherished hot-water bottle filled to near-scalding perfection and carefully positioned on her lower belly, while in her mind she painted and painted.

You touch a place and thousands of miles away another place quivers. You touch a person and down the line the ghosts of relatives move in the wind. In the library that day, hearing Connie in her stylish brown dress ask about renting a room, my mother lifted her head, offered up her mother's boarding house, and in this way opened the door to meeting my father, who was Connie's youngest brother. So interwoven are the strands of human life and so rich is the loam in which we lie that the same cemetery holds my grandmother and Ethel Weir and the man accused of her murder and the principal who knew them all, the bane of Connie's existence and therefore an abiding interest of mine.

2

JEWEL

He had entered her life on the last day of September in 1929. Tweedy, sophisticated, perverse; an excellent teacher who doubled as principal. He arrived three weeks late, an otherwise punctual man. Jewel was the name of the town in the southwest corner of Saskatchewan.

Before he arrived, and desperate, she had written *la fenêtre* on a piece of paper and taped it to the window, *la chaise* to the back of a chair, *la porte* to the door. But how could she teach French when she didn't speak a word?

The Ontario High School French Reader, edited in 1921 by Ferguson and McKellar, those two fine Frenchmen, and reprinted nearly every year thereafter, was the only text she had. It included a long passage about Jeanne d'Arc's great victory at Orléans. The story carried her into the France of 1429, exactly five hundred years ago, an easy sum, where word by word she deciphered how Joan was wounded and fell off her horse and taken for dead, how her followers fled until she pulled the arrow out of *la plaie*—wound, feminine—got back on her horse, inflamed her soldiers and drove the English out.

Connie made the story as hair-raising as possible. Her success as a teacher would rely on these basics. She could throw a ball, catch a ball, smack a ball with a bat. She knew some bloodcurdling poems more or less by heart and recited them out of the blue when restlessness overcame her. *Sennacherib came down like a wolf on the fold / And his cohorts were gleaming in purple and gold.*

Left hand on her hip, "Tell me three things about Lord Byron. All right, tell me one thing."

A hand went up.

"Tula?"

Big brown eyes in a small, fine-boned face. She slipped out of her desk and stood beside it. "Miss, who was Sennarib?"

Connie went to the blackboard and wrote, *Sennacherib. King of Assyria. 681 BC.* "How many years ago was that? Work it out for me. Take your time."

She dropped to her knees beside floundering students and head to head they solved the problem; flicked sleepy skulls into pained consciousness with her lethal middle finger; twisted your ear if she lost her temper and never felt bad about it.

One morning he was there, a bachelor of thirty-five with dark hair turning gray at the sides and eyes that undressed a woman, clinical, dry, chafing, light-brown eyes that plumbed the depths of female inadequacy. He came into her classroom and sat at the back and observed. No chalk on his clothes, no ink stains. A marbled fountain pen, purply mother-of-pearl, jutted out of his breast pocket.

And one day he took over her class and talked about *Tess of the D'Urbervilles*—the French influence, the Gallic strand through everything we say and feel.

"You're standing on French soil," he said. "Remember that." *Prairie,* from the French for meadow.

A door swung open for her then and it opened in that small town in the West, thanks to Ian Burns. Ian "Parley" Burns.

* * *

He liked to enter her classroom without warning. A curt nod in her direction, and her hand went to her throat and the students rose in a single swoosh, a covey of grouse flushed by a gunshot, but no escape, no sky, for there was the peeling *plafond* above their heads. He swept the class with his pale eyes, then proceeded to a straight-backed chair in the corner in the back. He sat down and the children followed suit.

A school with a classroom on either side of the hallway on the first floor, then a flight of stairs to a landing that functioned as a library of two bookcases, then the rest of the stairs to the second floor of two connected classrooms and the principal's office. On the first floor were the lower grades taught by ancient Miss Margaret Fluelling and the middle grades under young Miss Connie Flood. On the second floor were the upper grades shared by Miss Mary Miller and Mr. Ian Burns, neither young nor old, either of them. Whenever Parley patrolled the halls or visited the other classrooms, Miss Miller supervised his pupils.

Parley. It was pronounced behind his back with the derisive respect reserved for the overeducated. Oh, he was aware of it. But that was nothing, nothing to how aware the three women were of him.

They formed a classic school harem. Mary Miller, thirty-six, a plain woman but she dressed well, a different dress each week, usually navy with white piping or some white lace, four dresses in all rotated through the months. Very sensible shoes, owing to a back problem. Whenever Parley came to the door of her room, she blushed a most beautiful blush from the base of her throat to the roots of her hair—a surge of crimson, the rolling-out of a red carpet that ebbed not in reverse, but all at once, if gradually. What fun it was to follow it with your eyes.

Downstairs, Miss Fluelling, fifty-three, like a man wore the same suit day after day, a mustard-colored wool suit with wide lapels and a straight skirt. Her thinning gray hair made a ratty bun. She scratched her head with the point of a pencil so frequently that you could see scribbles all over her scalp.

Across the hall, lanky, athletic Connie Flood, eighteen, loped when she walked and dropped into a chair as if her limbs had given way. Five foot eight in high heels (she changed into flats at recess). White tailored shirt, straight black skirt, long wavy dark hair in a ponytail. The same build as my father, the same loose-limbed physical grace.

The town doesn't exist anymore. It rose overnight from whole grass into wooden sidewalks, railway station, grain elevators, houses, stores, churches, school. Then life rubbed the other way and the pattern disappeared. Nothing is left save a tiny chapel and the remains of a wooden sidewalk hidden by weeds. The buildings went to make granaries in the 1950s after the crops came back but not the people. A hundred years ago, however, they came from all over, from Ontario, the United States, Britain, Scandinavia, Central and Eastern Europe. Foreign tongues abounded. A child born in Ontario could grow up in Jewel, Saskatchewan, and travel the world and feel oddly at home. (The same child could go back to Ontario, an adult, and find herself crossing paths time and again with people she had known in the West.)

Given what Parley Burns did and what happened to him in the end, Connie never tired of mulling over what kind of person he was deep down. He wasn't handsome, she told me, but he was distinguished and very attractive to lonely women. Something fashionable, almost feminine in his manner unsettled and excited them—a sensitivity channeled into the dry-bed of bachelorhood. Yet he was far from dry. He was an intricately wired man. The smell of eggs turned his stomach.

He smiled (when he smiled) by baring his teeth, then holding the grimace to a count of five. A long time; a very long time if you were suggestible.

I picture them in the schoolyard, him and Connie, side by side. They're watching the best-looking boy play ball and play well, but Parley accuses him of making a feeble throw. "From *faible*," he says to Connie, "meaning weak."

She would have returned his unnatural smile with something natural and he would have felt encouraged to go on, to
say that the English *forget* that starting in 1066 the Court of England was a piece of France for three centuries. "Almost a thousand years have gone by and it's as hard for the English to learn
French as it ever was. Only an unusual person will take the neces-
sary pains."

Her eyes had a way of crinkling when she saw through you.
Parley reminded her of Jane Austen's Mr. Darcy, the same vanity
and self-importance. She asked him where he had learned French,
and he told her he had perfected his command of the language in
la belle France. She egged him on. She asked about Paris. The shin-
ing city, he called it, a cultured world of paintings, bridges, parks,
long walks in the rain. He had worked his way over to France on a
freighter and worked while he was there on a farm, and the labor
came easily, because he was one of six children raised on a rough
and stony farm in Quebec near a village where everyone spoke
French. "All six of us," he said, "were raised to ask what we could
contribute to the world. And so two of us are doctors and two are
ministers and two are schoolteachers." When he spoke about Paris,
the stiffening went out of him, and when he spoke about contribut-
ing to the world, the stiffening went back in.

They were Mr. Burns and Miss Flood to each other—again with
the echo of Darcy. Not that Connie had ever been convinced. Oh
yes, the wealth. But Darcy had no sense of humor. How could Lizzie
be happy married to a prig? In her opinion, Lizzie was by no means
wrong in her first impression and by no means entirely right in her
second. Would Mr. Darcy really make her happy? And by *happy*
Connie meant in bed.

October. With Indian summer came the last gasp of sundresses and
bare legs. A girl brushed her hair at recess—a few long black loose
hairs collected on the back of her yellow dress, looping lines, like a
butterfly. Susan Graves. The brush twice the size of her hand. Her
yellow back, and the long hairs shedding as she stroked, until six of

them drifted in uneasy decoration. The power of hair to unsettle. Her legs with their soft nap of fine hairs, her arms.

In the hall, as she passed under his eye, Parley Burns touched the strap of her sundress—an intelligent man. *Strap,* he said, and the word in translation, *la bretelle.*

Susan was not the prettiest girl in school, but there was something about her that struck him. Nervousness, willowyness, shyness, apartness.

Beige walls and chalk dust. Enclosed air, the quiet of students writing, and suddenly, in passing, the sound of crows.

The final class of the day. He lingered after Connie dismissed her pupils—they were gathering up their things when he came forward, not to speak to her, Miss Flood, but to Susan. He asked the girl to stay behind at her desk. The pupils left. Connie took her papers and left, too. Susan was alone with Parley Burns.

3

Michael

Susan Graves had a brother, the good-looking boy who liked baseball. Michael was a year older, but three grades behind her. The physical resemblance was strong, the same dark hair and blue eyes and high color in their cheeks. Outside, Michael's glance was full of amusement, mischief, secret ambition. His voice was loud and undiminished: hear me roar. In a classroom, he was pitiful.

After Parley Burns took over the school, he released Connie from her valiant efforts on behalf of *la belle langue* and she concentrated on English grammar, on assertive, interrogative, imperative sentences. Example of the latter? The house is on fire! Run! Run! Parley moved Susan into his own class and deposited fourteen-year-old Michael with "capable Miss Flood, who will take you in hand."

Parley was not the only one who claimed the boy was unteachable. None too bright, said Miss Fluelling, who had watched his lack of progress from the age of seven. A boy who read and wrote laboriously, grindingly, though memory work was no problem. Poems and songs he recited without effort, and numbers in his head were a snap. But they all did a strange soft-shoe when he wrote them down. He survived because so many others were behind, too—children who arrived not knowing English and were removed at regular, arbitrary intervals to help with the seeding and harvesting. He survived because at recess he ran and ran and shook off the hounds of learning. His father was a man of standing from Ontario. Owner of the hardware store in the center of town and the big white frame house across the road from the school.

Michael interested Connie from the first moment. She was intrigued by his cockiness in the schoolyard and by his affection for his sister: he teased, admired, listened to her. In her own experience brothers and sisters were close when the parents were not, and she wondered about Mr. and Mrs. Graves, the former bull-like in appearance and the latter the most attractive woman in town.

She had also wondered about Parley alone in her classroom with Susan and had paused on the way down the front steps, unresolved. Then she had turned and gone back up the stairs and into the school.

She waited in the hallway near the closed door, moving her load of workbooks from one arm to another. The young Prince of Wales kept her company, his framed likeness on the wall beside the door. In those days nothing animated her mind more than fantasies of rescue, and of those fantasies, the most vivid involved rescuing not a friend, but an enemy. To rescue a lamb has merit; to rescue a wolf quickens the pulse. She was anxious on Susan's behalf, but her inner dramatist leapt forward to Parley behind bars, and she was visiting him, bringing books into his pale, tormented, despicable life.

The door opened and she was the guilty party.

"Susan has agreed to help out," he said. "We're forming a drama club and she's going to help me organize it."

Nothing bad about that, although the play in mind gave pause. Scenes from *Tess* starring Susan as the ill-fated beauty. But he was a staple of the curriculum—pessimistic, erotic Thomas Hardy.

* * *

They were halfway through October. At midday Connie sat on the back steps of the school paring an apple with an old penknife when around the corner came Michael Graves returning from the noon-hour dinner break. Her smile, the unreserved smile of this pretty teacher, had him reaching into his pocket and offering her his jack-knife, wickedly sharp. Then he simplified matters by taking over the apple. He sat on the step beside her and proceeded to display an exactitude, a hatred of waste, a remarkable aptitude with his hands. One thin, continuous peel slid off his blade and curled into his lap. His hands were sunburnt and dry and nicked, familiar with gopher holes and fox diggings and snake squirmings.

The same feeling of fascination came over her that used to set-tle on her as a child watching her mother bandage a cut knee, or roll a lemon under her palm, or scrape batter off her fingers with a bone-handled knife, or peel potatoes with such infinite regard for the flesh that her peelings, too, were skin-thin and elegant. How it lulls a person, the sight of work done easily and well and without conscious thought.

A shadow fell over them. Parley moved through the school like mustard gas in subtle form. You were aware afterward that you'd been poisoned.

From behind them, "So, there's *something* he can do."

Michael's nut-brown face went scarlet and he was gone.

"Fifteen years old and thick as a plank."

An unpleasant voice. It had an unending complaint in it, a tone of resentment, a sourness.

"Fourteen," she said.

She fixed her eyes on the naked apple Michael had shoved into her hands. Parley went back inside and she ate it; she swallowed it down. Then she stood up, wiped her hands on her handkerchief and watched all the brave children come back to school.

At home (she boarded with the Kowalchuks, who had the barber-shop), she prepared her lessons, the old speller her favorite diver-sion, the early lessons as opposed to the advanced. Who had written this speller? Anonymous, like the makers of medieval churches. In the early sample sentences, everything was an action, a picture, and how absorbing and comforting the sentences were.

1. Warm rain aids the growing grain.
2. Bail the water out of the sailboat. Do you see a fairy? No, but I hear hail on the roof.
3. The squaw dried her hair in the sun. I spied a squaw near the church. A robin chirps on the rail fence.
4. Mules drag loads over soft roads. Toads live away from water.
5. A warm scarf covers my throat.

From there she flipped ahead to advanced grade seven, where sentences lost their loveliness, their physical charge, and became riddles spoken with too many teeth. "The peevish patient suffers keenly from swollen tonsils." "The shrewd sentinel visited a Turkish bazaar." "It is quite probable that he will entrust his mettlesome horse to the reliable hostler."

In the same fashion, child advanced to adult, to inscrutable Parley Burns. "The auditor found traces of tactful swindling." "His ill-humored demeanor resulted from a trivial dispute with his employer."

"Neither dyspepsia nor neuralgia is conducive to vivacity."

This was the future, these advanced thickets for later grades, these complicated burning bushes so tangled and uncongenial. The writers must have enjoyed their cleverness as they laid on alliteration and fancy vocabulary, but peace of mind was the price you paid—pleasure. Loss of pleasure. Loss of a clear view. Why didn't they realize that a sentence, like a person, can take only so much? But this was school. Lessons carried you from simple to complex, from the everyday to the abstract, as if this were progress.

Connie had her own ideas about that. For years her father had promised her mother that one day they would leave their eastern Ontario farm and move to Toronto, where she would be able to attend concerts and be close to her sister, who also played piano and had a fine voice. Instead, one winter's night there came a knock on the door and a man wrapped in furs stepped into their lives, her mother's youngest brother (my great-uncle Jimmy, who died a long, slow death from Parkinson's disease), full of stories about the West so enchanting that in the spring her father went with him out to Saskatchewan. At the age of sixty, her susceptible dad fell in love with the prairie and persuaded her mother, twenty years younger, to leave the Ottawa Valley and take up a wide expanse of grassy land near Weyburn. Her mother lasted ten months. Inflammation of the bowel. Dead at forty-one. As she lay dying, she had Connie spread bolts of corduroy and denim on the floor beside her bed, and from her pillow she instructed her on how to cut out pants for her father and two young brothers.

What gnawed at Connie most was her role in her mother's fate, the chronic asthma and bronchitis her father had used as bait. "Connie will be cured in no time. The air out there is clear as a bell." That's what happened, too. All her breathing troubles vanished as soon as they got to the prairies. So nothing was simple. But did that mean everything had to be willfully complicated? She flipped back to:

7. At night homemade candles gave a poor light.
8. Our mother fried some eggs for supper. She dried her damp cloak near the stove.
9. Beech trees and lilacs grew by the school.
10. My apron is too loose.
11. Snowflakes do not harm green wheat.
12. Place a bowl of prunes on the table. Are you able to reach that plain saucer?
13. In France they waste little.

Her grades were four, five and six. Five rows of seven desks. And what a difference there was between sitting behind a small, hard desk and being at the front, chalk at the ready, on view. Various freckled faces and the big boys at the back. To her mild astonishment, she liked seeing each member of her small audience—Molly of the chapped and bitten lips, olive-skinned Tula, black-eyed Stefan, Michael who didn't take his eyes off her face.

She wanted to dress well for them, since they had to look at her all day, and so she alternated her three necklaces, the silver locket from her mother, the entwined gold chain from her great-aunt Charlotte in Aberdeen, and the long strand of coral beads from her mother's sister in Ontario. These last had a gold clasp on which initials were engraved in an old and flourishing script. *A.K.D.* Her mother's mother. Agnes Kerr Douglas.

A generous gift, the coral beads, as Aunt Evelyn had so little. She, too, had been a schoolteacher before marrying a struggling would-be farmer who had given her an engagement ring with the smallest diamond in the world. The story was a legend in our family. How one summer, after picking strawberries all afternoon, Evelyn was doing the supper dishes and noticed with a sick jolt the tiny void in her ring: the diamond had fallen into the strawberry field. They went back outside, she and her husband, and she tried to remember exactly where she had picked, and they patted the ground under the same leaves and between the same rows, searching until it was dark, but they could not find the diamond. Nothing to be done. Evelyn canned the fruit and stored the jars on shelves; she wore her ring without the diamond. In the winter they began to eat their way through the preserves. One day toward Christmas, her husband was eating the usual dish of berries for dessert when he bit down on something hard. A filling come loose, for Pete's sake; what next? He fished it out of his mouth. It was the diamond.

Restoration is even more miraculous than discovery. The Bible was right about that. A prodigal diamond outweighs a fat ruby.

Connie first heard the story from her mother, then coaxed it out of her aunt when Evelyn came by train to see her ailing sister and arrived in time for the funeral. The day after the funeral, Evelyn gave the coral beads to fifteen-year-old Connie, who would give them to me years later on the day I was married.

Evelyn stayed for a month, helping to finish the clothes for the men, as she called the widower and his pair of small sons. They sewed and talked, plump aunt and skinny niece, and Evelyn confessed that the loneliest two years of her life were the first two years of marriage. The farm was isolated, the work was hard, and her husband refused to have a child until they were on their feet.

Connie said, "What happened after two years?"

"I began a correspondence course. And that gave me something else to think about."

What a sad, soft, passive woman her aunt was. What a sweet and boneless woman.

"How did the two of you meet, anyway?"

In a boarding house in Toronto, when she was going to normal school to become a teacher and he was working as a clerk at Eaton's—this was before a bachelor uncle did him the dubious favor of leaving him the small farm southwest of Toronto. Their rooms were side by side, separated by the bathroom they shared, and he heard her throwing up every morning before another day of practice teaching. "He asked me to marry him because he was lonely."

"Not sympathetic?" Connie said. She was holding out for a little romance.

"No." Her aunt did not back away from the implications that rippled over her marriage. "Just lonely."

Late Friday afternoon. A flurry of movement behind her as she wrote on the blackboard. She wheeled around.

Unaccountably, Michael had darted away from his desk. In the scramble, Parley reached the boy before the boy reached his goal. He grabbed him and cuffed him back into his seat, then took the long wooden pointer from the sill below the blackboard and stood poised.

A girl let out a gasp as the snake slid past her feet on the varnished wooden floor, and Parley stepped forward and brought the pointer down.

His dark, grisly excitement, high cheekbones, contorted mouth, *arousal*—Connie had seen it before, at an Orange Day parade in Toronto when the drum and fife band came around the corner in full regalia to find their way blocked by a car: the drum major upped with his orb and smashed it through the windshield.

Parley bared his cold teeth. "Dispose of your viper," he told Michael. "Then find me in my office."

Afterward, when school was over, Connie erased the blackboard from top to bottom. Bits and nubs of chalk lay beside the pointer on the grooved wooden sill, fitted grooves for laying the varying lengths down. The dusky light on the blackboard, the felt eraser in her hand. How drying it was, though Parley's fingers never looked dry, his perfect hands, if you liked that kind of hand, square and shapely with soft black hair on the backs and fingers, hands that had the life of the body in them—he seemed of one violent piece— and they weren't the hands of a man who had ever worked outside, despite his claims, the nails too long and carefully trimmed.

She stood at the board, feeling revolted, and in that moment he came through the door.

To be caught like that is to be caught forever, tied to the person in a new and endless way, for you've worn your hatred on your face. After that, he began his extra, inexplicable attentions to her.

We let these people into our lives. They enter, and because we let them stay to work on our minds and hearts and imaginations, it's as if we have invited them in.

4

CORAL

"It was a garter snake," she said to Michael the following Monday, shortly after four o'clock. She had asked him to stay behind.

He nodded. He had found it curled up on a rock, soaking up the last dregs of autumn sun. Harmless.

She wrote on the blackboard: *He walked straight past the wolf and picked up the dead garter snake.* Common sense told her to have movement toward something he cared about.

Michael copied the words slowly and accurately. She erased them from the board, had him place a ruler over what he had written, then write the words from memory. *He wakt past the fol and pickt up the ded grtre snake.*

She already knew that some children can't help making things hard. They expect to be stumped, expect to be confounded. They see assignments, tests, examinations not as neutral entities with obvious and expected answers, but as hedges in which their untidy brains get lost, and inwardly they seize up and panic. "Don't make it hard for yourself," she would tell her youngest brother (my father, for whom she had sewed pants). "All the teacher wants to see is that you understand what you've been taught." But something additional and mysterious was going on with Michael. He couldn't remember the same word from one line to the next. He couldn't even recognize it.

There were things he would never forget. Her strong hand was one. How she leaned all her weight on the knuckles, a red pencil sticking out from between her chalky fingers. And the effect on him of her long, warm body right there beside him. How incredibly alive that was.

She asked him to describe how a snake sheds its skin. He felt his hot forehead get hotter. On the edge of his vision was the stack of black workbooks on her desk. Close to the bottom was his, full of red circles around his misspelled words. And everybody knew. He spelled everything wrong.

"What happens to the skin?" Her voice was patient, her perfume nice-smelling, warm, close.

"It splits."

"All the way down?"

"Around the corners of its mouth."

"Its *mouth*?"

He had her interest and he leaned forward. "The eyes get milky and hazy and the skin peels at the corners of its mouth. I see them around woodpiles. They curve themselves left and right and left and right, looking for something to hook onto, a stone or a forked stick. Then it tugs and leaves its skin behind," and he paused, choosing his words for accuracy and effect, "like a woman's stocking."

He knew things, not things that were of any value at school. But he knew a lot, enough to impress someone if he wanted to impress her.

He watches his pretty mother, she thought. And what a feeling it must be to shed your skin and be nude in the open air.

"What does the new skin look like?"

"Nude," he said, and her face yielded a smile. "Fresh," he said. "Flexible."

"Not wet?"

"Not wet. Haven't you seen them?"

"I've seen them. I've seen old snakeskins too. I'm getting you to give me the words."

She wrote them on the board and he copied them. They were going to lick this, she said, they were going to have him reading and writing well by Christmas.

Her face was like a sudden silver dollar in a dark corner. Wanting to give her more, everything she wanted, he said, "The snake hooks on and pulls itself through its mouth and then the skin drops in a ring on the floor."

"On the ground."

"I'll bring you one if you like." And now his voice was the confident, outdoorsy voice she knew at recess.

"All right." She smiled and gave him one of her winks. She could wink either eye with equal ease, a rare and enviable talent.

He said, "You'll be able to see the pattern the scales make on the skin."

And again she wrote his words on the blackboard, impressed by his turn of phrase, which brought to mind a passage in one of the *Royal Readers* about lowly earthworms—Darwin's last book was about his future companions of the grave. She located the passage for Michael (flipping past another favorite part, the destruction of Pompeii with its haunting picture of the casts of bodies discovered in the ruins—a girl of fifteen lying on her side, legs drawn up convulsively, her hand clenched around the torn fabric of her dress, embroidered sandals on her feet, dressed exactly as she was on August 24, A.D. 79, when the sky went dark and the sea rolled back, and ash poured down and buried her for seventeen hundred years). The great naturalist, she explained to Michael, had kept his worms in earth-filled pots in his study with the intention of seeing how much mental power they displayed. He concluded that although worms are deaf, have no sense of smell, and can just distinguish between light and darkness, their sense of touch is a form of intelligence in itself, for they line their burrows with their castings, or excrement, and with leaves, seizing the stalks either by their pointed ends or by their broader ends, depending on which will do the best job of plugging the mouths of their burrows.

"'It is a marvelous reflection,'" she read aloud, "'that the whole of the superficial mold over any wide, turf-covered expanse has passed, and will again pass, every few years through the bodies of worms.'"

Michael was as intrigued as she was. They were intrigued by the worms, and the snake, and each other.

"Worms," she added, skimming the last few lines, "are surpassed only by the even lowlier corals—also animals—that have constructed innumerable reefs and islands in great tropical oceans."

She touched the orange-red beads at her throat. A coral necklace recently startled into nervous life by Parley Burns.

On Friday they had left the school together—this was after he murdered the snake. They walked to the road and she realized he was walking her home; her lodgings were on the same street as his. They didn't speak as they moved from road to wooden sidewalk. Lilac bushes grew beside several front doors, hedges of caragana separated one wide lot from another. Nine hundred and twenty people lived in Jewel. Off the main street ran side streets of smallish houses built from cement blocks and wood, most with chickens, or pigs, or horses, with crab apple trees and box elder trees and currant bushes and patches of grass.

She held herself away from him, but rigidity gets you no further than disgust. Her discomfort seemed to please him; to be familiar, perhaps.

When she turned to go up the beaten path to the Kowalchuks' unpainted frame house, she finally looked him in the face, and his eyes went to her necklace. He said, "'Of his bones are coral made, Those are pearls that were his eyes.'"

Poetry and punishment. In the 1920s children knew the difference between Shakespeare and Tennyson and Keats just as they knew the difference between a thump on the head, a pointer across the knuckles, a strap on the open palm, a belt on the backside.

From that day forward, Parley Burns escorted her home more often than not.

5

TUTORED

She had learned to read when she was four. Great-aunt Charlotte was with them that year and it was her way of helping out, to take Connie in hand while her mother dealt with the new baby. They were still on their farm in eastern Ontario then, on the flat and fertile plain between Argyle and the Ottawa River. Connie sat on an overturned washtub in the kitchen and Charlotte's big knuckles full of arthritis moved along the lines, helping her sound out words. Connie was working on *mouse* when an actual mouse ran over her bare toes and she climbed her aunt like a tree.

Old Charlotte, full of admiration for the creature so smart it knew its own name, called after it, "'O, what a panic's in thy breastie!'"

Parley would be the second Burns in Connie's experience, a name bundled up in childish, lasting, skin-tingling drama.

Charlotte was her mother's rich aunt, one of her few relatives: Charlotte Constance Douglas, married to Charles Hayes, a dissipated Aberdeen banker. Connie's own name was Agnes Constance Flood, but her mother was Agnes and so she was Connie. Since Aunt Charlotte took no prisoners when it came to reading, her small niece ingested early a sense of evil lurking in the fog and scratching its bad pen. Tulkinghorn grubbed about in her dreams, and *Bleak House* was the rustly black of Charlotte's lap. Later on, in the period of her asthma, when she wasn't well enough to go to school, Connie went through every book in the house, including a big, heavy copy of *The Canterbury Tales*. Michael's spellings would remind her of Chaucer's, and it occurred to her during that teaching fall of 1929 that commas hadn't always ruled the waves. The ancient, original spellings and punctuations were changeable, restless, like the boy himself. *To finilise my dicion on wether I should where my scarf or not I lookt outside and I noticed that the street was scilent. All I heard was the thundering wind of the bleek midwinter.*

At his desk he twisted his legs, sighed, bit his tongue, chewed his fingers, muttered to himself. "Oh, no, that's not right." "Uh-oh, I failed on this one last time." "How do you expect me to do this?" And once he said to Connie, "My sister has all the brains."

His sister was a natural student, but Michael was the beauty. Susan missed by a fraction of an inch his stunning face.

"Don't grumble," Connie said, convinced he was a boy with deep ability. "You have one kind of brains, your sister has another."

But already he was prey to the thought that would plague him for the rest of his days: what would my life have been like if I had been good at school?

"Anyway," she added, "maybe it's not you. Maybe it's your teachers."

They digested this radical notion. To Connie it was less radical than obvious, since she was a teacher with exactly three months of training.

Nearly every day she worked with him after school, never pretending he was anything but a hard case, which relieved her feelings and his, too. "This is a desecration," she said, seeing *haws* for *house*. And they both laughed.

Teaching ran in her family on her mother's side. Her brothers would become teachers, too, and so would I. But most of Connie's methods came from a beloved and irascible man who had taught her in the upper grades. "Don't be afraid to ask a stupid question," Syd Goodwin would say, and to himself he would mutter, "Ask a stupid question, and the answer goes on and on." Snakebite, he had taken to calling her, and it had the same soothing–exciting effect as snow stuffed down the back of her neck, or her hat snatched off at recess: she knew she was liked and it made her happy.

She began to call Michael Slim. "Slim, my unteachable pupil," she would say, her face full of energy and amusement, and he responded with his remarkable smile. It seemed never to occur to her to give up on him or on anyone else in her classroom. There wasn't a single child who didn't wish to please her. Michael was her biggest challenge, and they had an understanding, a rapport.

She had a name for me, too. She called me Curly after my mother lamented my bone-straight hair. She believed her role as a teacher was to lead children through an anxious passage into a mental clearing, and her role as an aunt was to send me books and recordings and on her rare visits to soothe me by loving me and loving my parents. It is the most relaxing thing in the world for the child of reliable, solitary parents to see them befriended. And the most surprising, the most eye-opening, to discover that they have lives and interests and loves of their own.

I remember the utter change in atmosphere whenever Connie came to visit. She was full of stories and laughs, she was risqué, unzipped, fun. My parents were liberated for a moment, reconnected to their lives before they had children. They relaxed and came out of themselves, allowing me a glimpse of a past as promising as my own future seemed to be whenever I was in my aunt's company.

* * *

What for Connie was slipping outside on a summer's day was endless winter for Michael—he had to don a mountain of clothing and
struggle through the drifts.

"Put down your pencil for a minute, shake out your hands. Relax
your jaw. Get up and touch your toes."

Movement always helps. A world of thoughts occurred to her
whenever she rode a train, and a lesser world whenever she went
for a walk. She began to compile a working vocabulary for a junior
naturalist. *Earth, lair, burrow, den, stream, brook, mountain, cloud,
thunder, lightning.* Influenced by Parley, she looked up derivations
and learned that almost none of these words, so close to life, came
from French. The exception was *mountain,* from the Old French
montaigne. The simple, earthy words were Old English. And so she
found herself taking sides as she read the dictionary, arguing with
Parley about the merits of English versus French as she used to
argue with her father about the merits of Robert Service. "A campfire poet isn't a real poet? You might as well say a campfire isn't a
real fire." And she had stomped upstairs and slammed her door,
even though she knew perfectly well what her father meant, and
agreed.

Michael liked to be in her wake as she strode around the schoolyard. He liked her tallness and her moods.

A teacher's sudden shift in temper—that's what children watched
out for. The snarl and snap. The crazy whirlwind of Attila bearing
down in her mustard suit and thick legs and penciled scalp. Hairs
in her snorting nostrils.

Miss Fluelling, moist and over-warm in her suit, suffered erratic
surges in temperature, each one preceded by an oncoming train of
dread that rocked through her and left her drenched. If a child happened to be standing on the tracks, the train overwhelmed them
both, mutton and lamb.

A few years earlier she had gone too far. It happens to every
teacher. She had brought her pointer down on Michael Graves's
arm, raising a blood weal the length of half a ruler. The next day

she received a visit from Harold Graves of Graves Hardware, a man known to have a fiery temper of his own, and soon after that she slipped on the school steps and came down so hard on her wrist, it broke. In her place arrived the wispy, ineffectual wife of a local farmer, and the children learned what heaven was. It was immense relief, then boredom.

They studied their teachers for changes in temper, vagaries of mood, variations in wardrobe, indications of having shaved or bathed or washed their hair. Every release was temporary. Recess, dinner break, recess, the end of the day—all were followed by more school. The maiming of Miss Fluelling was temporary, too. She returned in September, a splotch of unmistakable color in the doorway of the school.

Children cannot believe that adults have forgotten what it's like to be a child. What a sad chasm that is. The dumbfounded child on one side, the forgetful adult on the other—the perfect pink taste buds of youth, and the scalded, swollen, scummy-white tongues of age. Every so often there's a truce, like the performance of *Tess* in that prairie school, when all the teachers and all the students were conscripted to play one role or another.

6

TESS

Parley wrote his own version of *Tess,* based on the play he had seen three years earlier in London. Yes, he announced, he had seen this very play performed at the Barnes Theater on a rainy April afternoon with Thomas Hardy himself in the audience, looking very small and old.

Parley Burns reminded Connie of a rarity her father had spoken about, the single white pine that stood in a patch of aspens near the confluence of the Saskatchewan and Bow Rivers. One Pine, it was called, for no other pines grew within sixty miles of it. Parley, too, stood alone and inspired superstitious respect and awe.

She watched him turn the school into a theater and it started on his blackboard. He brought everyone into his classroom on the second floor and there they stood knee-deep, all grades crowded together, while he wrote *D'Urberville* at the top of one column and *Durbeyfield* at the top of another, then listed below the former numerous French words and place names, and below the latter, English bastardizations. He spoke this last word, *bastardization,* with the precise enunciation of a trained actor, and stared down the sniggerers. A lesson in language and history, the drama of both, and how they played into the drama at hand of Tess, the beautiful maid who murders the rogue who seduced her; "who deflowered her," he said deliberately, and again he stared them down. The only sound was the gurgle of Miss Miller's stomach followed by the noisy hush of her crimson face.

"Our version will be short and basic," he went on, "and consist of nine scenes with narration in between." He listed them on the board: *Knighthood, Strawberries, Dance, Lost Letter, Wedding, Separation, Eviction, Murder, Stonehenge.* "We will need to manufacture blood," he added, a glint in his eye.

Connie's classroom had the school's battle-scarred piano, scorched around the edges of its varnished top by hundreds of cigarette butts balanced there over the years. Loose keys, but a lively sound familiar to anyone who attended school concerts and dances. Hers was the biggest classroom, the one normally used for school productions of any kind. Parley, measuring tape in hand, scouted out the space as she was having Michael do extra work after school.

"Is he making any progress?" he said.

"He is. He has an excellent memory."

Parley folded his arms and leaned against her desk, unhurried, implacable. "He knows how to memorize. That's his crutch. He needs to know how to read. Take away his crutch," he said.

He reappeared as she closed her classroom door, and they headed outside and walked to the road.

"You like the boy," he said.

She lifted her hand. Of course.

"But you don't like men, if observation serves."

She stopped. Her workbooks were folded into her chest. It had been a long day.

"What kind of thing is that to say to me?"

She felt the bones in her head being reknit—unknit and reknit—by these sly questions that weren't even questions. She resumed walking.

"You are so dedicated," he said to her next.

"I'm not so dedicated."

"You're much too modest."

But she wasn't that either.

They passed Graves Hardware, a deep and narrow store with dark corners and high shelves. In the summer men sat on a bench outside the door. In the winter, around the stove inside.

He said, "There's a concert on the radio tonight. You might care to join us. Mrs. Wilson's radio. You're someone who would appreciate Brahms."

Her mother had loved Brahms.

That evening she would sit in his landlady's wallpapered living room, listening to the many-knobbed radio that sat on a table next to a window full of geraniums. Why is it, she wondered, that for every slow movement you get two fast movements, instead of the other way around, when the slow movements are a thousand times better? Who made these rules, anyway?

By the end Parley's eyes were wet, and she felt torn in half.

Blushing Mary Miller said, "He likes you." They were in the schoolyard together at recess. Mary held the handbell in the crook of her arm. "He walks you home."

"I don't like it, that's why."

"You don't?"

"I hate it, Mary."

Mary, who had a wide face and eyes of no particular color, gave her a startled look and a small "oh." After a moment, she said, "But he's such a gentleman."

"He's a sadist. A gentleman sadist." And Connie laughed.

She came on hard to Mary's soft; sharp to Mary's mild. "A gentleman sadist," she repeated, feeling that she had stumbled upon the truth, a pearl of truth produced by the irritating sand of Mary Miller.

"Mother thinks we're lucky to have him. He's doing so much for the school. All his experience."

"Then what is he doing *here*? If he's so experienced?"

"Well, I never thought of that."

Mary was not a stupid woman, but she had stupid eyes. They looked blank or they looked surprised. She was like soft mud. She would teach until the end of her days. She would live with her mother, who had been a schoolteacher herself. She would plod in her sensible shoes through one day after another, not a good teacher, but adequate, and her mother was adequate company, and everything was adequate and only adequate.

The weather was colder by now. They were in their coats and woolen tams, standing with their arms folded for warmth near the back door of the school.

"You never wanted," and Connie waved her hand toward the horizon, "to just take off?"

"I can't. Everybody else did. It would break my mother's heart if I left."

Parley Burns strode back and forth at the foot of the schoolyard, smoking one of his cigarettes.

"He makes me feel despicable," Connie said, yielding to meet Mary's sad honesty halfway. "I can't explain it."

Mary regarded her. "You must encourage him."

"But I don't."

"Or he wouldn't walk you home."

She raised the handbell and rang it. Recess was over.

Connie stood there, registering the forcible prick of Mary's assessment. The needle in the haystack of Mary.

Parley assigned the work and play of *Tess*, handing out parts, choosing certain students to write the in-between narration, others to gather costumes and props, others to make copies of the text. He assigned Michael to build the columns of Stonehenge, telling him they needed to be tall but portable, impressive but light. "You're in charge," he said, giving the job to the son of the man who owned the hardware store.

Connie's classroom became the hub of the enterprise. Immediately to the inside-left of the door was the cloakroom from which the fledgling actors, dancers, musicians made their entrances and exits. The scene of Tess's home was played with chairs and a small square table, tablecloth, teacups. When the chairs and table were removed, a bench and milk pails formed a dairy. Later, the corner of the schoolroom became Stonehenge.

TIME: evening. SEASON: summer.

Parley Burns printed the words on Connie's blackboard, and they quickened her heart. At fourteen, swept up in her father's plans to move West, she had asked herself what she would do with her own life, and the answer had come with the urgency of youth: I will go onstage. But nothing had happened the way she planned. At fifteen, she saw her mother die. At seventeen, she was training to be a teacher. At eighteen, she was teaching school. At nineteen, she would turn her back on teaching and take up newspaper reporting. At thirty, she would remake her life yet again.

But the biggest change, she told me more than once, was her mother's death. In historical accounts you find reports of deep and early snowfalls that continued day and night for weeks, after which nothing was ever the same. Fruit trees died, never to reestablish themselves, and it wasn't just the quantity of snow that was to blame, but the unprepared earth, not yet frozen, and the leafy innocence of the branches now groaning under a double weight. You see the same thing with bereaved children. Connie and my father, for example.

And why the early desire to be an actress? I pressed her on this, because I'd had the same impulse. In her case, when she was twelve, she had played the first witch and the second assassin in *Macbeth*, coached to enunciate each word with demonic relish by storming, funny, unforgettable Mr. Goodwin. One lucky girl was assigned to be the Manager of Blood: Ada Lempke took Mr. Goodwin's recipe and cooked up a syrup of water and sugar doctored with red food coloring and a smidgen of green. He trained them all in the best way to slit a throat onstage: knee the victim from behind, then haul back the head to expose the doomed throat. *Macbeth murthers sleep, innocent sleep.* "It's a play about insomnia," he taught, "moral insomnia, about not being able to close your eyes to the dark within. Notice how Macbeth's language becomes more and more like the witches' as the play unfolds." *Approach thou like the rugged Russian bear, The arm'd rhinoceros, or th' Hyrcan tiger; Take any shape but that, and my firm nerves shall never tremble.*

Syd Goodwin was another rarity, venting his spleen on property rather than on children. He banged the wall with the pointer, booted the side of his desk, once took a running kick at an empty bushel basket in the schoolyard and broke his toe on the rock inside. The kids laughed themselves sick over that, and he laughed too, eventually. Outside of Shakespeare, he had the fullest range of insults Connie had ever heard. *Numbskull, knucklehead, nitwit, chowderhead, lamebrain, meathead, dim bulb, dough head, bonehead, fathead, lunkhead, blockhead, hole in the head, mongoose, muttonhead, hambone.* He was a mighty walker, too, taking them on extensive and impulsive field trips, his rousing battle cry being "It's too beautiful to stay inside!"

Enter John Durbeyfield *carrying a basket. He is met by old* Mr. Tringham, *an antiquarian.*

Most of the parts had been handed out. Jake Aarp, a blustery boy in grade ten, was drunken "Sir" John, Tess's father. Small Henry Rhodes was Mr. Tringham, the antiquarian. Red Peter (for his red hair and as a shortened form of Alfred) played Tess's brother Abraham. Susan Graves was Tess, of course. Her friend Hildy Kowalchuk played Joan Durbeyfield, the mother.

Parley said, "It takes almost nothing to make you feel the role. A shawl—and you're Tess. A hat set at a certain angle—and you're her useless father." He set a brimmed cap on his own head. "Deep disguise," he deadpanned. "It works for the actor and it works for the audience. We all want to believe."

He had not settled on the boy who would play the seducer, bad Alec. In the meantime, he played the rogue himself.

Alec D'Urberville *enters with a cigarette and a little basket of strawberries.*

The strawberries had been constructed by the children in Miss Fluelling's class from papier mâché painted red, stems painted green.

Alec *takes a strawberry from the basket* and Parley cannot resist: he holds it aloft.

"*Papier mâché*, from the French. *Papier*, for paper. *Mâché*, past participle of *mâcher*, to chew."

He *holds it by the stem to her mouth*. Tess *covers her mouth*. He *persists*; she *retreats till she is against the wall; laughs distressfully, and takes it with her lips as offered.*

Alec: There's a darling.

Connie watched him rehearse the rickety bones of the play and at night she reread the novel to remind herself of its agonizing beauty and depth. The terrible death of the horse. The seduction and fall of Tess. The milk meadows, and the blessed world of Tess's one happy summer.

She said to Parley as he walked her home, "I think you should have the scene with Prince. There are boys who would love to play a horse, for one thing. For another, you can't understand Tess unless you know she blames herself for his death."

She knew how to stage it, too. Tess and her brother would rock side to side on the bench, the make-believe wagon, pulled by ancient, decrepit Prince (two boys under a blanket) on their pre-dawn way to market. From the cloakroom would come the snores of the drunken father. Now Tess and her brother drift asleep. The light on the wagon goes out. The fast-moving Royal Mail whips around the corner, collides with the wagon, and poor Prince is killed in the smashup. This was the book's striking symmetry: an unintentional murder opens the book, an intentional murder closes it.

Parley said, "Then we'll need more blood."

The fog of disturbed creation filled the school—excitement, wariness, alarm, envy. Everyone entered Parley's mood. On the sidelines Mary Miller stood ablushing and in charge of props. Propsy, he called her, which pleased and titillated her. Miss Fluelling offered to play the piano between scenes, musical interludes to keep things moving; she played as she taught, rolling her hard and agile fingers across the keys with aggressive panache, and watching her, children felt their heads hurt. Susan Graves was a perfect Tess, having a certain refinement and being malleable, yet impulsive.

During rehearsals Connie formed her abiding impression of the gentleman sadist. She saw his face redden with animated pleasure, a kind of happy horror, when he accused Susan of being wooden, incapable of the large, relaxed gesture, the brave self-exposure he wanted.

"Tess is a physical being," he said. "'A sunned cat.' You need to act with your body as well as your head."

The confused girl ran the back of her hand across her forehead, unconsciously repeating her mother's gesture at the end of washday.

Parley said, "When a woman is attracted to a man, she plays with her hair. Lift your hair off the back of your neck. Not like that. Fluff it up."

He stepped behind her and lifted her hair high, exposing in the process the back of her neck. "Well," he said. "No wonder."

Susan tried to turn, but he caught her by the shoulder.

"No wonder you're Tess. Look at that." Then, "Look at this," he said to Connie.

She had been fetching workbooks from her desk. She put them down and went over to look. A red birthmark, wide and irregular, splashed its way across the back of Susan's neck.

Parley said, "You, my girl, were strangled in a previous life."

He let her go and she faced them, alarmed, alert to her fortune being told.

"I knew you were special," Parley said.

"Then so am I." Connie smiled to dispel his effect on the girl. "I've got the same kind of mark. Not as big. But it's common."

Only to have her ponytail swept aside and the back of her neck examined. "You weren't strangled," Parley said. "You were clubbed."

There are children who remember past lives. Parley's youngest sister had been such a one. Peggy Rose, who was remarkable for the low, mature voice that came out of her four-year-old mouth and the livid birthmark that circled her neck. Parley told Connie on the way home that his sister was named after the grandmother who had committed suicide, hanging herself in the barn.

"My sister was born old," he said. "You know the look some children have?" He paused and ground his cigarette under the toe of his shoe. "She wouldn't go near the barn. We none of us ever mentioned Granny's suicide, but she knew."

They walked on and he said, "In my family we see ghosts."

"I've never seen a ghost." Her envy was considerable.

"A yellow dog appeared early in the morning to announce deaths."

"So before your grandmother hung herself—"

"—hanged herself. You saw the dog."

"Out by the water pump."

He didn't wear gloves or a hat or overshoes, but his scarf was tightly coiled around his neck.

"Granny Rose made a job of it," he said. "She got up on the hayloft and tied one end of the rope around the beam and the other end around her neck, and then she jumped. I thought it was a wild turkey hanging down. A dead body is *heavy*. They cut the rope and they needed two men to hold her as she came down."

He lit another cigarette with his bluish-white fingers, the black hairs smoothly attractive between the knuckles. "A year later my sister was born with a strangle mark around her neck. Girls are lucky. They can hide things under their long hair."

That queasy fall of 1929 was like being at sea on an anchored boat. The school rocked in the unfathomable waves of Parley. His way of looking at Connie, at Susan, at girls in general. His way of looking at Michael. He wasn't aware he wasn't alone, or didn't care. They weren't a director's eyes, assessing talent. Or bedroom eyes. They were more like the eyes of a night prowler standing outside your bedroom window.

There was the day he rounded on Connie for heaving a theatrical sigh of exasperation just for the pleasure of it. "Having an artistic temperament," he snapped, "does not make you an artist."

It was obvious he was talking about his savage disappointment in himself and it was childish of him to be so transparent in his self-pity. She folded her arms and asked him why, with his love of theater, he wasn't *in* theater, why was he here in the middle of nowhere with a bunch of nobodies.

Her forthright temper quieted him, just as it settled down a class. An honest answer came sheepishly out of his mouth. He had tried to be an actor. He didn't have the talent.

"I wasn't good enough. That's the truth."

A trim, tall, disdainful man. He pursed his lips, picked up a pencil and sharpened it to a fine point in the pencil sharpener screwed to the edge of her scuffed and darkly varnished desk. But he was more real to her now, more human.

Word filtered from his landlady, Mrs. Wilson, to Mrs. Kowalchuk, and from Mrs. Kowalchuk to Connie, that he was a perfectly ordered man who liked a bowl of porridge for breakfast and a bowl of porridge before bed. Porridge-breath, thought Connie, for whatever sorry woman might share his bed.

Over the years she would read widely and catch glimpses of Parley Burns in figures like Odin, the Norse god, solemn, aloof, and so abstemious that he gave any food set before him to the two wolves at his feet. All she had to do was pull an egg sandwich out of her lunch pail, and he fled.

One day he called Jake Aarp a Sassenach for not remembering his lines as Sir John Durbeyfield, then wrote *Sassenach* on the blackboard. "To the dictionary," he said. Jake found the word and reported back that a Sassenach was what the Celts called an Englishman.

"An invading, unwelcome Englishman," Parley said.

He illuminated the insult by pulling down the roller map of Europe and using a pointer to show where the Angles and Saxons and Jutes sailed across the North Sea and invaded England in 449. "They slaughtered the native Celts, who either fled or, like King Arthur, resisted. But gradually the old Celts were driven westward," he said, "and in their place the Anglo-Saxons set up seven kingdoms, including Hardy's Wessex, *here*. The beaten Celts called the Anglo-Saxon invaders Sassenachs, from which we get *Saxon*. Then a few hundred years later, the Norsemen swept down, murdering, plundering, pillaging, until Alfred the Great, King of Wessex, fought back. In 878 he had his great victory at the Battle of Ethandune, right about *here*. The Danes retreated, and Alfred rebuilt the monasteries and schools and saved the English language from disappearing. Hence, 'Great.' Two hundred years later came the Norman Conquest of 1066, and French entered the picture, enriching primitive English with thousands of beautiful words like 'enter' and 'enrich.' *Entrer. Enrichir.*"

He called them the "Hardy Players *du nouveau monde.*" They were all assembled now. The boy who would play Alec was a fourteen-year-old with a head of thick dark hair named John Jacobs, older brother of brown-eyed Tula. "Goodbye, my four months' cousin," he rolled off his tongue, "I was born bad, and lived bad, and should die bad."

Parley had also settled on who would play the parson's son, the great love of Tess's life, "educated, reserved, subtle, sad, differing" Angel Clare.

"You're the type," he said to Michael, interrupting his reading lesson with Connie. Having fled the invading thespians, she was now using Miss Fluelling's classroom for after-school tutoring. "You'll have no trouble learning the lines, not with that memory of yours. Here." He put a gray fedora on Michael's head.

"You can't have the brother playing the husband," Connie said.

"Come now. It's just acting."

"They *aren't* actors."

She stood up and Michael took off the fedora, and Stefan Fuchs got saddled with the weak and unconvincing character of Angel Clare.

It really wasn't hard, she discovered, to hold her own against Parley, even if she felt shaken afterward, more soiled than triumphant. She thought she had his measure: he was harmless so long as you didn't let yourself be pushed around. Such miscalculations abound. News drifted in about millionaires throwing themselves out of windows, but no one in 1929 had any idea that the world was entering the Great Depression. It took two years, Connie told me, for the truth to settle in.

To give the effect of oncoming disaster, Parley covered oil lamps with red tissue paper. "Make them a little uncomfortable," he said of the future audience. "If they have to strain to see, they'll pay more attention."

He wooed the same way, if wooing it was. With extra energy he leaned forward and said to Connie, "Flirt comes from *fleur*. To give flowers."

She had to smile as she looked away. He wasn't like anyone else.

If Connie failed to understand him, what was a thirteen-year-old girl to make of this complicated man?

"Susan," he said in his lordly way, "*Miss Graves*. Do me the kindness of remembering that Tess calls the letter 'my life.' You must handle it as if it is precious."

He was referring to Tess's written confession about her sinful past (the seduction by Alec; the infant who died) to Angel Clare, the pastor's son she dotes on and hopes to marry.

"Susan, what is the most important thing in the world to you?"

Her lips moved.

"I can't hear you."

Her eyes sought the window and the window provided an answer, as it often does. "My dog."

"Your dog. What's the dog's name?"

"Mabel."

"Pretend the letter is Mabel."

A stepladder served as the stairs leading up to Angel's attic room. A carpeted board nailed to the top of the ladder was the threshold of the pretend doorway. Susan climbed the steps and slid the folded letter halfway under the threshold, then gave it a gentle caress before pushing it very slowly the rest of the way.

Connie watched, fascinated by the terrible moment when Tess's life slides not across the floor into Angel's view, but out of sight under the carpet. Susan had an extraordinarily sensitive face.

Parley kept lines to a minimum. The play was more like the reenactment of a crime scene, a pantomimed version of an old, sad story. To convey the plot and the passage of time, he wrote big inter-titles on the blackboard, like the written frames in silent pictures.

TESS THINKS ANGEL HAS FORGIVEN HER.

THE WEDDING GOES FORWARD.

"Before the wedding," he said to Susan, "you'll brush your hair. Then after the murder, you'll brush your hair again, and the contrast will speak volumes."

Pre-wedding Susan ran her hands up through the hair on the back of her head, then brushed her hair slowly and thoughtfully. She put on a pair of white gloves. The stepladder on its side became the altar where she and Angel knelt and were married.

TESS TELLS ANGEL HER PAST.

HE ABANDONS HER AND GOES TO BRAZIL.

A YEAR PASSES.

SCENE: *THE TOWN WHERE ANGEL'S PARENTS LIVE.*

Now the stepladder on its side becomes the hedge into which Tess shoves her boots before putting on shoes to enter Angel's town and seek help from his parents.

The stage consisted of six boxes, four feet by six feet wide and eighteen inches high, pushed together, and built by the boys under Michael's supervision. Parley's landlady had sewn the curtain from scraps of sheets and counterpanes dyed black. Parley hung them on a long pole suspended from the ceiling, and two boys opened and closed them.

Connie, curious about Hardy (who had died the year before) and even more curious about Parley the bachelor, said to him, "When you saw Thomas Hardy, was he with his wife? Did he *have* a wife?"

"She was sitting right beside him. I didn't get a good look, I was too far away. That would have been his second wife. His first wife died, and he married someone much younger."

"Were there children?"

"None he admitted to."

Interesting.

Like school, *Tess* was bursting with sex, yet leached of it. School oozed prepuberty, puberty, post-puberty, premenopause, menopause. Connie never tired of watching Mary blush. Never stopped looking to see if Parley returned her interest. She felt his eyes follow her instead, a glance she one day returned with a level stare until he clicked his teeth and looked away.

Tess underlay all other subjects, like lace brought from the old country. Dorset on the Canadian plains, and the plains worked their way into the story.

"Propsy," Parley cried, "find me a big mirror."

One of the children, Tula, offered up the fact that her grandfather had a standing mirror in a mahogany frame. Tula took Miss Miller, who enlisted Connie for moral support, to see the old man known as the Scholar of Jewel, thanks to his glass-fronted bookcase full of books. Oscar Jacobs.

He was small, nimble, leathery, a reformed alcoholic from Montreal whose farming son had come West to own land and cultivate it scientifically. (This was Tula's father.) The old man himself had been a peddler of fabrics and threads until his wife opened a dry goods shop in Montreal, which they ran together until she died. He welcomed the two teachers and his granddaughter into his snug house that smelled of peppermint and woodsmoke, and introduced them to the pet crow that came and went through a half-open window in the summer kitchen. "Esau, meet Miss Flood, meet Miss Miller." Then he found a dust cloth and polished the handsome mirror, which happened to be perfect for their needs.

Proudly, Tula opened the glass doors of her grandfather's bookcase, and Connie smelled the smell she would spend the rest of her life walking into. (I remember being with her once in a used bookstore on Queen Street in Toronto when it began to rain. While we waited, we fell into conversation with the owner, a man from Medicine Hat, who told us that the dry summers and winters in the prairies were benevolent toward books, whereas the humid east ruined them with mildew. Connie was looking for illustrated books about birds for a friend of hers who carved wood. At the time I didn't know who the friend was, but now I know it was Michael.)

Oscar Jacobs drew from his bookcase a copy of *Hurlbut's Story of the Bible*. "Travelers leave books behind," he said to Connie and Mary as he opened it. He read out the name in the front. "'Mrs. Harry Stumpf, Wiarton, Ontario.'"

"I've heard of Wiarton," Connie said. "But not Mrs. Stumpf!"

He put the book away and pulled out another. *Madame Bovary*. "I remember particularly," he said, "how she changes color after she poisons herself. Such a beautiful woman."

And the woman in Mary who wanted to be beautiful said, "What made her beautiful?"

"Her great dark eyes and dark hair. Full lips, small teeth. She was outstandingly beautiful. Mrs. Graves reminds me of Emma Bovary. Wilda."

"Is that Mrs. Graves's name?" Connie said. "Wilda?"

"La brunette."

"You speak French."

"Bad French. Very bad."

"You could teach me."

He raised his eyebrows, and she explained what it had been like trying to teach French without being able to speak a word, and he allowed that he would be honored to teach her whatever he knew.

After a second's hesitation, she ventured, "And how much would the lessons be?"

That drew a smile. "I don't have any material in French, you know, except for the Eaton's catalog."

And so Connie would learn the French words for various hats and dresses and fabrics and shoes. *Toile* and *chiffon* and *tweed importé* and *flanelle* and *crêpe de chine* and *chambray* or cambric, the smooth cotton that took its name, he told her, from Cambrai, the town in northern France that manufactured it. She learned a peddler's poetic and utilitarian French, and it suited her. *Un chic ornement de métal embellit le collet. Une valeur remarquable. Le dernier cri du chic.* Galosh, it turned out, came from the French *galoche*. Every child's pleasure, sloshing along in the spring in unbuckled galoshes, long underwear folded just right to keep young legs from being rubbed sore, was steeped in an old French word.

Oscar had true European charm. He offered her nuts and candies. His hands were olive-skinned and shiny, large hands for such a small man. Against his protests, she paid him twenty-five cents a lesson.

Her gift was the ability to step back. She saw not a principal with a specialty in French, but a thwarted man mounting a little production to give his theatrical bent an outlet, and to give himself time with Susan, who displeased him as much as she pleased him, that's what Connie saw. Females displeased him as much as they pleased him.

Girls were never strapped, it was an unwritten rule, but one girl Parley picked on more than once. A big, well-formed farm girl with a wide, damp face, Sarah Wilkeson, the oldest of a large brood, who often arrived late to school. Parley wielded the strap on her large open palms and she lost control of her bladder. Her humiliation seemed to relax him. He told her to find a cloth and get down on her hands and knees and wipe it up. The whole time he watched her.

Connie heard about it at recess and took Sarah downstairs into the basement to the box that contained a few mismatched mittens and unclaimed items of clothing. She helped the girl change out of her soggy drawers and felt herself become an island of sanity in the girl's grateful eyes. It was a lesson in emotional geography. Parley was the volcano that rearranged land and air, and she was the outlying island born as a result.

The next day, teaching synonyms, she asked her class for all the words they knew for "punish." They took turns going to the blackboard and soon they were standing in a cluster, adding more and more words until they filled the board from top to bottom. *Spank, belt, thump, smack, whack, swat, slap, strap, hit, strike, kick, whip, lash, cane, burn, twist, punch, break, knock, rap, bend, shake, poke, pound, thrash, slam, crack, crush, beat, choke.* When Parley came into her classroom at the end of school to work on the play, he stopped short and scanned the words she had chosen not to erase.

"English," he said, "has a monosyllabic soul."

Even with the standing mirror, he could not make the murder scene work. Susan, in dressing gown and slippers, her long hair tied back with a ribbon, sat at a bountiful breakfast table. By now Tess's father had died, and with the family facing eviction, and no one else to turn to, Tess had allowed bad Alec to come to the rescue, meaning she had become his mistress.

A knocking at the door and Tess *goes to answer it.* Angel Clare *enters, hatless, weary, ill, back from Brazil. He puts his arms around her and she steps back.*

Tess: It's too late. *(Pointing to the breakfast table for two, her dressing gown, etc.)*

Angel *absorbs the scene and leaves.*

Tess *closes the door and leans against it sobbing.*

Alec *from the cloakroom-bedroom yawns, then calls out:* Tess, bring yourself and my tea in here.

Tess *goes to the table and picks up the cup and saucer. Then she puts them down and picks up a knife.*

Parley had coached John Jacobs to thump his chest with both fists to produce the gruesome, gulping intake that would be his last breath on earth. It was the boy's moment of glory and he gave it his all, doing it in the schoolyard on command.

Tess *emerges from the bedroom with her cloak half-dragging from one shoulder and carrying her gloves. She tries to put them on, but they slip off her bloody hands.*

Parley instructed Susan, "Understand that she doesn't know what she's doing. She doesn't even know they're a pair of gloves."

She takes her brush in her half-gloved hands and tries to brush her hair, but the brush bangs against her head.

Angel *reenters. He loosens the brush from her rigid fingers, one finger at a time. Puts her cloak over both shoulders.* Come. *They leave together.*

Moments later the Landlady *rushes in.*

And this was the sticking point. No matter how effective Susan was with her gloves and her hair, everything was ruined by Klara Munz bursting in and yelling, "Mrs. D'Urberville! Mrs. D'Urberville! There's a red stain on the ceilin' and blood's drippin' down."

Then one day it occurred to Parley to have Klara say the words in German, followed by broken English, and the effect worked. It sounded like the end of the world.

He paced the schoolyard as he smoked, and she heard him talking to himself sometimes. Not as Michael did, saying, "I'm no good at this," but in the third person. "Burns was losing his mind." Or, "Burns was about to lose his temper." Or, "They decided to torture Burns again." He said these things looking at his feet, or sometimes looking straight at you, his eyes furious.

One day he had Susan bring Mabel to school, the dog that was a nervous cross between a collie and a spaniel. They were working on the scene when Angel Clare comes back, but much too late, and Tess sobs after she sends him away. Susan was at the front of the room and the dog lay by the door. Without warning, Parley lunged at the pet as if about to deliver a swift kick. The dog squealed, and Susan cried out and sprang toward her.

"That's what I want," Parley said to her. "That look on your face. Remember it and duplicate it."

Cowering under a desk, the dog vomited, and would not come out when the girl reached for her.

They were to put on two performances of *Tess* late in November in that prairie schoolhouse. They did it a third time, owing to popular demand. Susan Graves made people cry. She was unthreatening and very powerful.

There were some who went to all three performances. Susan was known in Jewel. More than just recognized, she was known. She blossomed in the role. It was one of those transformations we all long for. She became sensuous and warm and human; her body actually looked riper and fuller. You could see what sort of woman she would be at thirty. She even had a consistent accent, rustic English, and some who didn't know her thought she came from Dorset. After each show she was applauded heartily and praised. Parley was heard to say, "She has talent. She has a gift."

Only Mary Miller found something to criticize. She went up to Susan with a smile and fingered her blouse, which was open at the throat. "That's so unlike you," she said. "Did he *make* you undo all these buttons?"

"No one made me." And she removed herself from Miss Miller's jealousy.

At the first performance, Michael had looked away when his sister came onstage, terrified that she would forget the lines he had heard her rehearsing endlessly behind her closed bedroom door, not in whispers but at full volume, flinging the words about the room. She was *somebody*, he realized, somebody with a purpose. He watched his mother in the audience and that was almost as gratifying, her astonished pride. Even his father seemed impressed.

The second performance was a Saturday matinee and another success. The final performance was to be Saturday night. Susan didn't come home for supper, she stayed at the school to have extra rehearsal time with Mr. Burns. Michael saw her at 6:30, when he went over an hour before the show began. She was too keyed up to speak to him, too flushed with glory and alarm. But again, everything went perfectly. She established the pace—that was most striking—she did not rush a single gesture or word.

Oscar Jacobs would say later to Connie during their French lesson that he fell in love with that talented girl.

At the end, during the bows, Parley presented Susan with a bouquet, and Mary Miller tripped over a bench. She landed hard. Connie went to her aid, and when she next looked at the stage, she saw that Parley had put his arm around Susan. They were taking a bow together. For the first time, Susan seemed stiff, self-conscious. That had been the wonder of her, how at home she had been on the little stage, but now she looked ready to flee.

Monday morning, Mary turned up leaning on her mother's cane.

"I have weak ankles," she told Connie at recess, "which is surprising given how thick they are."

Parley was pacing on the far side of the schoolyard. They watched him, and Connie said, "Why do you suppose he smiles like that?"

"Like what?"

Connie imitated the clamp of his bared teeth.

"I would never ask. That's his business," Mary said.

Connie turned away from the prim dead end beside her to watch the children milling about. The schoolyard was threaded with stories. There was Susan Graves not far from a cluster of girls, but not exactly one of them, admired rather than embraced. There was Elsa, whose pale reading face only occasionally looked up from a book; her brother had been killed by lightning while riding on a load of hay in 1927. There was Tula, talented with a crayon, whose persistent headaches were worrisome in a child of nine. Like all the girls, she wore long underwear under her dress and overshoes buckled up with three buckles. Michael was tussling with Red Peter, whose father broke horses and had competed in the Imperial Rodeo in Wembley, England, in 1924. There was Miss Fluelling, her scalp be-penciled with the noodlings of a four-year-old. And here was Parley turning up the collar of his coat and coming toward her.

Now that the play was over, he began to walk her home again, and to Connie it felt like subtle persecution. It felt like that, she didn't know if it was. It felt as if he saw through her, read her mind, and at the same time she was obscure to him, and he was indifferent to her. After a few days of this, she said she preferred to walk home alone, having things on her mind she wanted to think about. "Oh," he said. "Pardon me for ruining your day." And he fell back and maintained a twenty-five-foot gap between them. In the end, it seemed simpler to endure his company.

The days were much shorter now. They walked home in the dark—Parley to Mrs. Wilson's porridge, Connie to more potatoes. Recently, Mrs. Kowalchuk had taken to tossing them hot and thickly sliced into a bowl with thinly sliced onions, which cooked a little in their heat, then a splash of vinegar, and salt and pepper; they were delicious.

Toward Christmas she began to read *A Christmas Carol* to her class, and one afternoon she had them write up the story in scenes (they knew all about scenes from staging the play), and Michael wrote, *Scrooge woke up at 12 o'clock he lisend to the big booms of the clock the big booms the loud full sounds of the big clok.*

Connie corrected his spelling and punctuated his rolling repetition. *Scrooge woke up at 12 o'clock. He listened to the big booms of the clock, the big booms, the loud, full sounds of the big clock.*

He had gone on to write about *aproching as sighlently as humanly possible* and *weighting in the black scielence of the savadgely wether beten trees.*

His way with words was like a small child's way with color—an aptitude that generally fades into eight-year-old mist. And his good vocabulary came from where? "Do your parents like to read?"

"My father says my mother reads every day and most of the night."

Connie went to see her, the brunette, who welcomed her and told her that Michael had been the quickest child, walking at nine months, talking before he was one, remembering the words to the songs she sang, loving to cook with her in the kitchen. "I would read him things and suddenly discover that he knew them. 'The moon on the breast of the new-fallen snow, / Gave the luster of midday to objects below.' But when I tried to teach him to read, we got nowhere. Nothing was wrong with his eyes, either. He could see a ladybug at a hundred feet. In grade one he tore out two-thirds of his hair, he was so frustrated. I found tufts of it behind his bed and under the chair. But he talks and thinks *well*."

Her son reminded her, she said, of an older brother who had also been backward in reading, though sharp as a tack in other ways.

Connie asked what had become of him, this older brother.

Well, that was a sad story. He got in with the wrong sort, and died young and badly. She had named Michael after him. "My sister spent hours teaching my brother. She would do the same for Michael, but we're so far away. Pontiac County. I don't suppose you've heard of it."

Connie knew it well enough. It was in Quebec, across the river from where she was born, a wooded and rolling part of the world with some good farmland.

The next day, on one of those awkward walks home with Parley, Connie found herself talking about her visit to Mrs. Graves. "I wish I knew what to do. I wish I *knew* more."

"Not every child is a scholar," he said. "You can't gift-wrap a toad."

She pushed her hands deeper into her pockets.

"You think I'm harsh. But either you have it or you don't."

He wore an aftershave scent and she smelled it in her room sometimes when she turned her head quickly. There he was, perched on her shoulder and floating around her head.

7

THE INSPECTOR

Connie didn't tell Parley that she was taking French lessons, but he knew. He began to speak to her in French, and she would have to ask him to repeat himself and still not understand. It was a little game he played. You should have come to *me* for French lessons.

In December, the school geared up for the customary Christmas concert of recitations, songs, drills, plays, a mighty endeavor that involved every child and turned Connie's classroom back into a theater. The children stayed in at recess writing out copies of the songs and skits, they stayed after school and helped each other memorize their parts, and soon whole Friday afternoons were given over to practicing. Tula drew Christmas scenes freehand on the blackboard with colored chalk, and it was her idea to string across the ceiling blue crepe paper of various lengths in a great X-shaped fringe that moved prettily in the air currents.

At noon on the Friday of the evening concert, the children went home and the school trustees came in and set up a Christmas tree in the hallway and adorned it with glass and paper ornaments. Everyone came back in the evening dressed in their best to see the splendid tree and underneath it, for each child, a bag of candies, nuts and oranges. As with *Tess*, the school filled up until there was standing room only.

Parley didn't don the Santa beard or the comic wig. He was the director, never the ham. Connie loved to wear a costume. Mrs. Kowalchuk had provided her with an old taffeta ballgown her mother had worn, and she sashayed about calling herself Madame Pompadour. It was afterward—after the children had sung their final chorus and the bags of treats were handed out, after the mothers had served the evening lunch of coffee, sandwiches and cake and the room was cleared for dancing, after the caller had announced the first of many dances and everyone, even Parley, danced until two in the morning, after "Home, Sweet Home" had been played and everyone gathered up their things to leave—it was after this that Parley put his hand on Connie's shoulder and asked her to stay behind. They would tidy up a bit. He took the broom to the scattered orange peels, nutshells and cigarette butts on the floor, while she brushed crumbs and wrappings off the lunch table into a wastebasket. Then he put aside the broom and came over to her and stood so close that she felt her knees give way a little. He put a small wrapped box into her hands.

She had been aware of him all night—of his dapper head and shoulders moving slightly above the crowd. Sometimes she lost sight of him, whenever the dancing spilled out into the hallway. But more often than not, he was near Susan or Susan was near him, and her young face was back to its keyed-up look of being Tess, but pinker, wilder.

Connie herself was an inspired gift-giver. When my father was twelve, he became the envy of every boy he knew, thanks to Connie, who had given him a full archery set, a real bow and real arrows. "I had a very good older sister," he would say many years later.

She opened Parley's gift and found herself holding something from Paris in the palm of her hand. A souvenir he had picked up during his time in France, a miniature Eiffel Tower four inches tall. She didn't know if she was more thrilled or alarmed.

The drama club continued. It met every Wednesday at four. Wednesdays, then, were the one weekday when Connie was sure to be free of Parley's company after school. On a Wednesday in January, to her surprise, Susan materialized beside her as she headed down the school steps.

"No drama club today?"

"My father needs me at the store."

Instead of slipping ahead, however, Susan stayed close. Once before, she had sought out Connie's company. While rehearsing *Tess*, she had approached after school with a quiet question. "When Tess comes home pregnant, would her back have ached?"

The girl struck Connie as inspired, over-aware of herself, and alone.

"What play are you working on now, Susan?"

"It's not a play. It's a story by Tolstoy."

"Ah, which one?"

Susan pushed her knitted hat back off her forehead. Her face was tight, tense, reddened by the wind and the cold. "'Master and the Man.'"

Looking across stubbled fields covered in thin snow, Connie said, "Do you like the drama club?"

"Not anymore."

"Not anymore?"

"No."

"Then you don't have to go."

Susan raised her eyes to Connie's.

"It's just a club, Susan. You can go or not. If you've lost interest, that's allowed."

"But what would I say?"

"Maybe your father needs you every Wednesday at the store?"

She shook her head. That would mean talking to her father. She had never talked to her father in her life. She did as she was told, that's all.

They kept walking, the wind at their backs, snow underfoot.

"He's not God," Connie said. "You're the one with something special."

Susan dipped her head, unconvinced on both counts. And when is it ever convincing, the belief others have in your abilities? You know perfectly well they can't see the mess inside you.

They came to Graves Hardware, and before they parted Connie said, "*Why* don't you like it anymore?"

"I can't do anything right. I don't know why."

The next day, Parley buttonholed her as soon as she entered the school. "Susan."

"I'm sorry."

"We waited for you. I sent everyone home. Next week we'll have to work extra hard to make up for lost time."

Then she knew she couldn't miss it, any more than she could miss church.

In early February, Parley warned his staff that the school inspector would be coming one day soon. Have your attendance registers in order, have your classes prepared.

But the days went by and the inspector didn't come. On the last day of February, not one but two storms were building up in the sky. They were in for it, Parley said to Connie as they walked home. "*La nuit de l'âme*," he said.

She wouldn't ask. She refused to indulge him.

"The night of the soul," he said finally.

He was one of those English people who wished he wasn't, and it stirred her sympathy that he didn't like himself any more than she liked him. He was a troubled man who wanted to be *un homme troublé.*

"What happened to the inspector?" she said.

"He'll come when you least expect it."

But then he soothed her fears. She was doing a good job, she needn't worry. He would give him a favorable report. "You have potential," he said.

"Susan is the one with potential."

"Susan."

For a moment she thought he was going to disagree, but no.

"She could be famous one day. She could be great," he said. "She would make an excellent Miss Havisham, an excellent Ophelia. In a year or so, when she's sixteen, she should leave this godforsaken hole and move to a city. New York or Toronto or Boston."

Connie looked at him curiously. In a year Susan would be fourteen.

"You should think of doing the same," he said.

"Miss Havisham," she said thoughtfully, struck by the image of Susan as the jilted, desiccated bride; she had the right sort of intensity, the right sort of precarious sense of herself. "I love *Great Expectations.*"

"Dickens." He gave the name weight. "Hardy pales in comparison."

"I love Hardy."

"Of course, neither of them is equal to Melville at his best."

"And who is better than Melville?" What a ranking, comparing, depressing mind he had. "I know the answer. Shakespeare."

"I was going to say Tolstoy."

"Tolstoy. Does Susan still come to your drama club?"

"Why wouldn't she?"

"I hope you *tell* her how good she is."

He misunderstood. He thought she wanted praise for herself, and once again he told her she was doing an admirable job.

The blizzard arrived and lasted three days, after which the weather cleared. In general, the winter of 1930 was mild, with little snow. Connie was at the back of the classroom, in a pool of sunshine, when there came a knock on the door. Parley never knocked. She made her way to the front of the room as the door opened and a compact, energetic man stepped through.

"Snakebite," he said.

That short, quick step of his and he was shaking her hand and all the children saw Miss Flood's face glow with happiness. He turned to address them—they were standing beside their desks—and told them their teacher was a former pupil of his.

And to Connie, "I wondered what became of you."

Syd Goodwin was one of those men who at first glance looks ugly, then increasingly and amazingly attractive thereafter. He had a squarish forehead and deep-set eyes, a thick neck and a wide smile.

He moved around the room, running his eyes over the parsing and math on the blackboard that stretched across the front and down one side of the class, nodding his approval, and then he leaned against Connie's desk and proceeded to talk. He told them about seeing a wolf devour a doe, a big wolf, bigger than your average German shepherd and musty brown, the same color as old goldenrod. This was north of Saskatoon. He had been about a hundred feet away, partly concealed by a tree, watching the wolf yank and pull and look up periodically. Then an eagle arrived, a mature bald eagle. "My gracious. Now that was a sight. And the ravens. Ten of them like pairs of gloves, bobbing and swaying in the branches, scolding away."

A conversation ensued in which he wanted to know what they had seen of note recently, and Michael talked more than anyone else about birds, burrows, tracks in the snow, oncoming storms, huge moons. After that, Syd shifted the topic to current events. "We're in the midst of an economic collapse," he told them. "Let's see how long it lasts. Let's pay attention." And he quoted H. G. Wells to the effect that history was a race between education and catastrophe.

Connie said from the side of the room, "What if education is the catastrophe?"

He took in her thoughtful face. He would tell her later that he remembered where she had sat in his classroom, second row, two desks back. The slope of her shoulders, the part in her hair. She was always curious, sometimes vehement, an attentive presence, taller than her schoolmates, a good runner, her hair in a ponytail then, too. He remembered the change when her mother died, the protracted absence from school and his visit to the farmhouse a few miles out of town to make sure she wasn't giving up her education. The father had been at a loss and there were two small brothers. At fifteen, she was running the household. But then the father quickly remarried, and Connie returned to school. A year later, he himself left for Regina.

She said, "I don't mean learning the wrong things, but the wrong way."

He saw her face aching for answers, and the children were all eyes, all ears. "That's schooling," he said, "not education. There's a real difference."

Of course. She nodded, appreciating his point. "Yes."

She was a better student than a teacher, she would confess to him when they shared their sandwiches in the empty classroom at noon. "The boy who knew about birds," she said. "When he feels capable, you saw, he's entirely single-minded."

"A bright boy."

"Michael." Gladdened and reassured to hear him say it. "But it's such a struggle for him. I wish I knew more about teaching."

"I remember you were a great reader."

"I believe in reading."

Her claim to fame, the thing that earned her a reputation for eccentricity, was her policy that she would not disturb her pupils to do lessons so long as they were immersed in a book. The girl with the reading face, Elsa Franks, spent entire days, excluding lunch and recess, absorbed in page after page of Dickens until the light failed in the afternoon, and then she raised her head and turned her mind to the lessons at hand.

Connie had set up large projects next to the western windows, one of them a contour map made of salt and flour and water, and colored appropriately, of the town and the area around it, the Cypress Hills to the west and wheat fields to the east, Frenchman River running through. It was like a fairy tale, their personal king-dom. The school windows were without screens, and in the fall bees and butterflies and grasshoppers found their way inside, where they remained in jars. They joined rocks, bones, plants, and ongoing efforts at identification. Connie liked to tell them about summer nights in eastern Ontario, the incredible moths, pale green luna and huge, decorative cecropia, that beat against the screen door and got grabbed and eaten by vivid birds, indigo buntings, orioles, blue jays the size of yachts. And about one night in March when the snow was deep and someone tapped on the front door, but no one was there, and another tap came, but no one was at the back door either. It turned out the sounds were coming from the kitchen—from the big jar on top of the icebox in which the massive caterpillar she had found in September had spun its brown cocoon and hung suspended like a mouse from a cherry twig, month after month, until now it was piercing and tapping its way out of its dull self into a splendid cecropia moth, six inches across, wings speckled gray-brown and rusty, with eyespots on the lilac tips.

Her old teacher stayed for another forty-five minutes after the children came back from dinner (shortchanging Miss Fluelling's class, but Miss Fluelling was an old hand). He stood at the front and talked about thrilling books: *Tom Sawyer, Huck Finn, Treasure Island.* "'Keep your weather eye open for a seafaring man with one leg.'" He recited the lines about illiterate Jo in *Bleak House.* "'It must be a strange state to be like Jo! To shuffle through the streets, unfamiliar with the shapes and in utter darkness as to the meaning, of those mysterious symbols, so abundant over the shops, and the corner of streets, and on the doors, and in the windows! To see people read, and to see people write, and to see the postman deliver letters, and not to have the least idea of all that language—to be, to every scrap of it, stone blind and dumb! It must be very puzzling.'"

How impressive he was, reciting from memory. The air in the room became charged and still. He went on to recite the graveyard scene so skillfully, putting the proper emotion in the proper place, that you understood how clueless Lady Dedlock was about being poor and how admirably matter-of-fact Little Jo was about life and death "and the berryin ground. I wants to go there and be berried."

Connie said, "Where I grew up they pronounced berries 'burries.' 'We're going burrying,' they say in the Ottawa Valley."

And the farmers said *swally*. Don't swally that water.

Later, when they were alone, he told her that her principal thought highly of her, and saw her face cloud over and shut down. "I gather you can't say the same."

She weighed her answer. "I can't get used to him."

"No."

"I don't like the way he looks at people."

"You mean, at you."

"Not just me."

"Girls."

"Not just girls."

She stared at the floor, then raised her eyes to take in his concerned, professional face. "His qualifications are excellent, I know." Then she said, "Michael isn't the only boy who's behind in reading and spelling. What should I be doing for them? That's what I want to know."

He liked her question. "Have patience," he said. "Keep them at it. Give them words they haven't seen before, but not too many at a time."

"How many?"

"Five? Five new words and five old words every Monday. Spend the week getting them to use them over and over."

"Repetition."

"Mastery. Bring what they know forward every time you add something new."

"Will you be coming back, do you think?"

"I might manage one more visit before June. *Deo volente* and weather permitting."

Which induced her to say with a smile, "I can't wait."

"Listen to yourself. The poor English language. You *have* to wait. *I* can't wait, so I'm leaving tomorrow."

"I don't *wish* to wait."

"You're *looking forward* to seeing me."

"I know," she said.

The next day she glanced up from deciphering a paragraph in Michael's workbook to see his attention trained on her face. "What is it, Michael?" His eyes made a wounded swerve to the left and down.

"Tell me in writing then."

He wrote, *You have a diskusting look on your face you don't blev in me do you.*

How hard it was being Michael Graves. He could not keep his place on the page. He skipped lines, missed words, got shanghaied by the letters he recognized: no matter where *f* appeared in a word, he seemed to think the word started with *f*. Yet he knew everyone's lines in *Tess* and hurled them as jokes in the schoolyard. And so she found herself preoccupied with him to the point of fascination.

"I wish you believed in yourself," she said. He looked at her, waiting. "But that will come. I believe in you."

His untidy grace was that of a growing thing in a field, or a loose and wild garden. So was his spelling. *Dide* for died, *crake* for crack, *padded* for paid, *wille* for while, *lockt* for locked, *loct* for looked, *wute* for what. How was it possible to read a word aloud three times, write it out three times, shoving it into your skull, then two lines later fail to recognize it?

She gave up on his ever remembering the difference between *this* and *that* and *then,* and in exasperation she wrote *concentration* on the board. It offered no difficulty. *Conservation, renovation, communion.* He got them all, spelled them all. It turned out he had far less trouble with words that were so long he went through them at a reasonable speed. The smaller ones he guessed at, trying desperately not to be slow. "Don't try to be fast," she said. "Take your time with every single word."

Michael wasn't the only child she tutored. Two others stayed afterward for extra help. Red Peter and Ivan Munz, also hardy, muscular, energetic boys. She pulled the desks into a semicircle and got them to help each other, and they were like a wagon train drawn up against the dangers of the night.

What Michael loved most about her, I know, was that she spared him the shame of reading aloud. She never singled anyone out, either for public ridicule or overpraise. One afternoon he pocketed a piece of blackboard chalk and returned it days later, setting on her desk a minute bird carved like the tiniest of lilies. She had to use a magnifying glass to really see the chalk feathers and careful beak.

The next time they were alone she called him a genius, and he felt the novelty of being a teacher's pet. That awkward glory. He asked her when her birthday was. After that, April 20 wasn't like any other day in the year.

In March the light advanced at such a pace that restlessness overtook them all. Connie considered taking the train to Swift Current to buy herself a spring hat. A new boy had entered the class. Small, neat Herbert in his diamond-patterned cardigan of red, blue and green. His forehead was wide, his brown eyes were steady, he learned at lightning speed. After several weeks of her devoted attention, and knowing he would surprise his classmates, she asked him to read aloud. He stood beside his desk and read a page from the *Reader* almost perfectly. Then, to make him feel less conspicuous, she said he could pick someone else to take a turn. Surveying the class, he pointed at Michael. Connie did not save him. He read not nearly so well as Herbert Unger with his month of English.

Outside, the sunlight was lean and long and leading up to something. Red Peter set up a scuffle in the back of the room—noise and movement, and he was at the center of it. She called him forward and he took his time. He, too, had been neglected in favor of Herbert. She meant to exile him to the hall for twenty minutes, but his slowness provoked her into saying his name more sharply than she intended, and the class went quiet. She folded her arms. They thought she was angrier than she was, and suddenly she was even angrier than they thought. It happens to every teacher. Red, a tough little bruiser of a boy, pretended to trip and earned himself admiring titters. Then he turned his head and mouthed something, and the class broke into laughter. What did it matter? Send him outside, isolate him. Instead, she opened the deep bottom drawer on the right side of her desk and took out the strap.

She discovered that she knew exactly how to use it, as if a long line of teacher-ancestors had passed on the knowledge. The length of black rubber with heavy fiber worked into it had the texture of a thin tire. It was a foot and a half long, three-eighths of an inch thick, and a little over two inches wide. Corporal punishment. The hand turns pink, orangey red, brick red, engorged—the colors come fast. Her face was hot, furious, and that too came from a place so old she wouldn't have known it existed in the ordinary course of things. Do we take on anger the way we take on our names? She saw a tear roll down the boy's cheek and her hand began to shake and she put down the strap.

They stared at her. Not a stranger, but not the teacher they had thought she was. And they gave her no more grief that day.

After school she walked home by herself. At the sound of Parley's steps behind her, she turned around and told him no. She felt the heat in her face. Not today, she said. He backed up, then stepped to the side and went around her. She watched him until he was well along and then she resumed walking. The blood was still pumping through her. She thought it had drained away in shock, but it was still on the warpath.

We are frail at this time of year, she would say to me years later. February, March. More vulnerable than at any other time. Oppressed by the leaden sky outside, and winds of doubt inside. It's a big job not to turn everything into a test, an opportunity to deride one's intelligence. My bad memory, my brains such as they are, my soul such as it is. She saw it every year among her students. She recognized it in herself. We are vulnerable and exposed and given to sudden ferocities.

Something terrible had happened to her when she strapped that boy. The pleasure she had felt, whamming his powerless, insubordinate hand, shamed her. The savage satisfaction. No wonder punishment ruled the world. She recalled in the same breath Parley's arousal when he beat the snake to a pulp, and felt revolted by herself.

The wind was cold. New snow skiffed across the crusty surface of old snow and she watched it for a while. There was the immediate question of tomorrow and how she was going to carry on. She could not apologize. She was the teacher. How she felt wasn't their problem. She would have to look them in the face and find a tone and a manner that were not contrite and not defensive and not unaware: yesterday was yesterday, today is another day.

Tomorrow came. She put on her coral necklace for luck and because it had been admired by small Tula, among others. She put on a freshly ironed blouse and skirt. She went to school early and was standing next to the windows when the children filed in, her arms folded, and her expression as neutral as she could make it. But what awkwardness, skittishness, avoidance of eyes. They seated themselves. She went to her desk to open the attendance book and discovered another piece of carved chalk sitting on the book, and looked up to see Michael staring down at his hands. She picked up the chalk and saw the spout and handle of a teapot, so ingenious, and she smiled and opened the wide shallow drawer of her desk and put it beside the carved bird. His thoughtfulness and skill.

Her voice was husky when she called out their names and ticked them off.

Michael saw the effect of his gift on her face and posture. Later that morning, their eyes met and she gave him a small, acknowledging wink, and the bond between them was stronger and deeper.

It would seem that she had gained ground. All day the children worked hard to please her.

Something else every child present remembered was the day a week later when Miss Mary Miller unraveled in front of them. She was doing cursive on the blackboard, writing the word *tramp* in sweeping letters. She stopped on the *p* and stood motionless. The children, quiet to begin with, went silent. They saw the back of her neck below her bobbed hair go pinkish red—a new eraser, the pink of the British Empire. She put down the chalk and walked out the door, and she didn't come back.

Parley found her in his office after the four o'clock bell. Her face was damp with half-dried tears. "Go home," he said. "Rest. We'll manage."

He and Miss Fluelling shared Mary's workload. They spread themselves out as the mud of spring appeared and exposed skin turned even more chapped and raw. The earth, formerly locked and secure, became unstable, and grasses shot up from below and parted the firm ground.

Into this wound-up setting came Syd Goodwin one more time.

Connie was the first to arrive that morning, drawn outside by the April warmth. She saw the automobile parked beside the school, a blue Whippet, a two-door sedan with an emblem on the back, a red triangle indicating the novelty of four-wheel brakes. Syd was behind the wheel, hat over his eyes, asleep. On the seat beside him lay a Thermos inside its leather sleeve and a folded newspaper. In the back, a battered suitcase and some rolled-up maps and several books. "Good morning," she said close to his ear.

He gave a stir, pushed back his hat, and they were laughing together. She told him he looked more like a traveling salesman than a school inspector, and he said he happened to come from a long line of noble peddlers.

That day he took the entire school on a field trip south to the swollen creek and the weir, leading the way in his gray flannels and white shirt and heavy shoes. What was paradise? It was Syd Goodwin saying, "Find five things that move."

The gush and gurgle of ice water cooled the air. Michael, also in a white shirt, pointed out migrating ducks, muskrats, a hawk skimming low over the ground, spreading terror.

"A harrier," Mr. Goodwin said. "You can see how it got its name."

The children were more intelligent as soon as they stepped outside, except for a few, like reading Elsa, who stumbled about as if she were lost. Parley Burns was the last to arrive and the first to leave, not an outdoorsman, fastidious about his shoes. But there was a moment when Michael asked in his carrying voice what was the inspector's opinion of snakes. Mr. Goodwin replied that they were among the most useful of beings. Small snakes, he said, were the jewelry of the earth. And Michael's look lorded it over Parley.

Connie was touched by the boy's hero-worship of her old teacher. The two of them belonged together. Mr. Goodwin enthused about a dancing-ground for sage grouse near his uncle's ranch. He said the young birds were very tame and confiding. They dust-bathed in his uncle's yard and invaded the vegetable garden and plucked out the hearts of the lettuce. Michael was the first to spot the bunch of crocuses coming out of the grass, bell-shaped, and on the backs of the bluish petals, silky-white hairs.

Mr. Goodwin squatted and touched the open flowers with his fingertips. "Prairie anemones or windflowers. *Anemone* is the Greek for wind. Such fragile, precious things."

She gazed down at the flowers, too, and Michael moved to her side and startled her by wishing her happy birthday. It was April 20. She was nineteen.

A child lies like a gray pebble on the shore until a certain teacher picks him up and dips him in water, and suddenly you see all the colors and patterns in the dull stone, and it's marvelous for the stone and marvelous for the teacher.

Connie had no chance to speak to Syd Goodwin alone until they were back at school. He poked his head into her room after everyone had been dismissed. "You're still here," he said.

"You never used the strap. But you lost your temper all the time. I never minded." She answered herself, "You never directed it at us, though. You never took out your frustrations on us."

"Weak teachers rely on the strap."

"I didn't feel weak when I used it. I felt the urge to hurt."

He thought she was sorry and concerned. She was both, but that wasn't the whole story.

"The thing is, the boy's been good as gold ever since."

"Which boy?"

"Red Peter. Alfred."

"You're lucky he doesn't hate your guts. There are schools that forbid it."

"I didn't know that."

"A private school outside Toronto for one."

His voice was serious, and she felt herself slip in his estimation.

"I learned something," she said, rubbing the back of her neck, and then she was staring around herself at the floor and on her desk and around her desk, looking for the coral beads she had put on that morning.

He couldn't help her search for them either. He was expected at a trustee's for supper. Unlike Aunt Evelyn and her diamond, she would have to look alone.

She tried to recollect the feel of them sliding off her neck as she retraced her steps and strained to catch a glimpse of coral red. Mary's house flickered on the edge of her vision—poor Mary, lost in fatigue and unable to rouse herself. She had gone to see her two weeks ago and found her in her nightgown, propped up in bed, encircled by pillows.

"These ankles of mine," Mary had said.

"And your back."

"There's nothing the matter with my back."

"Sorry."

"It's my feet. I can't stand all day."

"No."

"I can't stand all day, you know."

Connie sat on the bed and almost slid off, what with the pillows and the legs and the unidentifiable lumps.

"I can't figure it out," Mary said. "Where does a man get flowers in November?"

It took a moment. Then it came. The bouquet Parley had given Susan when she played Tess.

"Mrs. Wilson has geraniums and African violets. It was just a posy, Mary."

"He likes Susan more than he likes you. She's a bit of a tramp, really."

Connie shifted on the bed. It was quiet, except for the radio downstairs and the sound of Mary's mother moving about. "It's hard to know who he likes. Or if he likes anybody."

"You're not afraid of him. He doesn't like that."

"Oh, I'm a little afraid," Connie said.

"Susan's scared to death of him, but she pretends she's not."

Susan had changed. She was thinner, paler, the same creamy Irish coloring, but as if snatched from Ireland too soon, before the sea air had worked its roses into her cheeks. Connie heard her laughing at recess sometimes and she sounded artificially gay, fake. She understood that Susan couldn't extricate herself from the drama club, and perhaps didn't want to, but whenever she tried to speak to her, Susan seemed both grateful for the attention and eager to get away.

"Susan's a faker," Mary said.

Connie winced. "I don't think she's a faker. Or a tramp. Not at all."

"I know so."

Mary's insinuations had worked their way under her skin, as Mary's insinuations tended to do. Connie had not been back to see her.

Upon reaching the riverbank, she began to search in earnest. Rain was on its way and her necklace would be muddied, buried, berried, burried. But the necklace was nowhere to be found, and it didn't rain.

She rose early the next day to resume her search, going outside with only a light jacket for warmth. She had the world to herself, the boundless prairie rolling south across the border into the Great Plains and north toward poplar country and black spruce. At the foot of the street she heard something that made her pause. The sound of typing came from Mrs. Wilson's house, an open window on the second floor. It came in fits and starts, a train of private thought making its way onto a page. How secretive it sounded as it called attention to itself. It couldn't be anyone but Parley.

She continued on toward the creek and here was Syd Goodwin on his way back. His shirt open at the neck, awaiting his tie, and looped through his fingers her dusty necklace. Now she remembers pulling her sweater over her head. She must have taken the beads with it and not realized.

"Where was it?" Accepting it gratefully from his outstretched hand and acutely aware of him standing so close. He was her height, no taller.

"Under a willow bush. Here." He took the necklace back and stepped behind her. She bent her head while he opened the clasp and she felt his breath on the back of her neck and his cool, fumbling fingers.

"You just happened upon it?"

"I conducted a scientific search. A bloodhound couldn't have been more thorough."

Her smiling face studied the ground.

"Mr. Kowalchuk told me you hadn't managed to find it. There," he said. And she reached behind her neck and felt it to be secure, then turned around and looked into his face.

"You were going to tell me what you learned," he said.

"What I learned."

"Yesterday. You said you learned something."

Her glance fell on his hands. He wore a wedding band; he always had.

"I learned that children want to forgive us. They're eager to forgive."

"If you're pretty," he said.

"I don't think that matters." She looked into his playful, deep-set eyes. He was minimizing her point, missing her point. "*You're* not pretty. No one would ever accuse you of being pretty. But we forgave you."

He laughed, and they started back toward town. She knew that his people were Jewish and that they had been bookbinders in Glasgow before moving to Winnipeg. He had talked about it in geography class. How they came out of Galicia, which was now a part of Poland. How maps may look stationary, but boundaries shift, worlds open up, other worlds and civilizations pass away. And none of us is stuck or alone, because coursing through us is everything that brought us to where we are.

She told him she was learning French from an old gentleman who kept peppermints in a bowl and schnapps hidden behind his books, and as she talked she was thinking that being an inspector meant not being at home for long stretches of time. You wouldn't see your wife all that much; you might not even like her.

"Do you have children?" she ventured.

He shook his head. They slowed their pace. In another month it would be hot and the absence of trees would hurt, but now the light itself was like gold leaf. She took off her jacket and folded it over her arm.

"Plants are so grateful," he said, looking around him. "You give them water and they say thank you. You can hear them." He spread his hands wide. "The earth is offering us its beauty."

She was wearing a dress and she was wearing it for him—a dark-blue dress with a pale-blue collar, and a very deep waist.

Michael's eyes were on her all day. He loved to watch her at her desk—how fast she wrote, how determined and intent and slightly comical she looked when she concentrated hard. He took her anger in his stride. It was her lack of attention that caused him anguish.

"Michael?" She was at the blackboard now, her back to the class, her mind full of Syd's departure. "Have you finished your work?"

She could read him from a distance and with her eyes closed.

*   *   *

That afternoon, Parley Burns walked her home. His eyes were dark and his face was white from lack of sleep. He looked more like a prisoner than a principal.

"I heard you typing," she said, curious to see his reaction. But his eyes were on the ground. "This morning."

"Then you were up early."

"I could hazard a guess about what you're writing."

"You won't guess."

"You're writing a play."

He gave her a surprised and bitter look.

She said, "I'd write one too, if I knew how."

Her gift for difficult men came from being able to see around their belligerent corners to the mud puddle behind. I've seen her with my father and I know. Rudeness that would reduce anyone else to blistered agony seemed to smooth her skin like some all-knowing cream.

He said, "You got on well with the inspector."

She had noticed his own efforts to please. He was more than ingratiating, he was groveling—smiling, smiling, and pretending to be interested in birds.

"Since you're so good at guessing," he said, "guess what I'm writing the play about."

"Wait, let me think." She considered for a moment. "Ghosts."

"Wrong."

"School?"

"Wrong again."

"Thomas Hardy. Thomas Hardy and his wives."

"You," he said.

And her mind swung to all those occasions when he had sat at the back observing her.

"It's not about me. Why would it be about me?"

He clicked his teeth; he had her. They walked on without speaking until he said, "There's a book you should read. If you'll allow me."

So she continued on with him past her own lodgings to Mrs. Wilson's and they entered the geranium-filled house. She waited while he went upstairs and came back with his copy of *Jude the Obscure*, which he put into her hands.

"Thank you," she said.

She carried the book home and set it on her small desk, aware that Parley's fingerprints were on every page. She had already plowed her way through *Jude the Obscure*. But instead of saying so, she had accepted his copy, caught in an act of insincerity spawned by the desire to keep things simple, when things were anything but simple. All around her was the curdled essence of this clever man, who found ways to bind you to him, to get you into his pot, where you simmered.

8

May 11

She remembered the leafy Ontario light on her mother's face, the perfumed air in the one-hundred-tree orchard of McIntosh Reds, Snows, Wealthys, Tallman Sweets and Pippins, and she wished very much that her classroom windows faced east instead of west. He weighed on her heart, this strange man who hadn't learned how to tell the time until he was eleven, a recent confession that had paved the way to a larger boast, that he mastered Latin in a year. She saw the artfully humble braggart he had become. She also saw the eleven-year-old boy, outfoxed by a clock.

Michael pulled her back to the present. "You look sad when you're not talking."

She turned from the window and went back to her desk where he was waiting, touched that he would notice such a thing, and impressed that he was so bound and determined to improve. It was after four o'clock. He was here for extra help. And here for her, of course. She was aware of that.

He would never be a speller. His sister was the one who could spell.

But the next day Susan got caught cheating on a French test. Several words inked on her palm. Her cupped hand was a dead giveaway. Any teacher, let alone Parley, would have spotted it.

He took hold of the long wooden pointer and indicated the carved plaque high on the wall above the maps. "What does it say, Susan?"

She stood beside her desk and read the words aloud. *Honesty is the best policy.*

Unless honesty is impossible. And then you try other means.

"I'm surprised at you." His voice was icy.

He kept her at her desk after everyone else had left. The days were long now, adolescent, bursting their buttons with light. She heard children calling to each other outside and Mabel barking across the road. Her father must have come home.

Mr. Burns worked at his desk and she sat with folded hands, waiting.

Michael was pouring himself a glass of water from the enamel pitcher on the table when his sister came sobbing through the kitchen door. It was about five o'clock. His mother was at the table, serving coffee to a neighbor, Mrs. Peter. His father—he's not sure where his father was. He seemed to loom and fill the whole kitchen, but he was probably sitting at the table with his smallest child, his pet, on his knee. Susan's face was wild, and so was her hair, so was her dress. She swayed and her voice when it came out was choked and cracked. "Mr. Burns," she got out. "Mr. Burns." Then hiccups took over.

His mother went to put her arms around her, but his father blocked the way. He laid his hand on Susan's shoulder and marched her up to her room, away from the shocked eyes of Mrs. Peter, who left them then to sort out their sorrows.

They waited a long time for his father to come back down, and when he came, he came alone. He told Michael to take his little sister outside. They would call him when they were ready for him to bring her back in.

The air was hot and dry and windy. Michael took Evie over to the pump and they filled a bucket and played at pitching stones into the water. And all the while he was thinking of Susan. What had she done?

Half an hour went by before they got called in for supper. It was dead quiet in the kitchen. His parents said nothing. His mother was serving out the food, her face blotched and strained.

"Where's Susan?" he said.

His father replied without looking at him. "She's going to stay in her room."

After supper Michael slipped upstairs, but the door to her room was locked. He tapped on the door and called to her softly. She didn't answer. He pressed his ear to the door and heard nothing.

The next morning she wasn't at the breakfast table. He watched his father put a bowl of porridge and a glass of milk on a tray and take it upstairs. He listened, and when his father was at the top of the stairs, he followed, and so he saw him take a key out of his pocket and unlock Susan's door.

In town, there was silence bled into by whispered talk. Connie heard the rumor in the schoolyard that Parley Burns did something to Susan Graves on the cloakroom floor, and didn't believe it.

"Michael? I haven't seen Susan for a couple of days."

He looked away. "She has the mumps."

A sultry wind blew day after day. It chafed the air and made it pinkish, coarse. From her classroom window, Connie could see the house across the road and sometimes she thought she saw Susan standing in an upstairs window. Something half-buried came back, a memory of Parley Burns fairly smacking his lips on the word *deflowered* when speaking about Tess. Yet he behaved as if nothing had happened. He seemed no different.

She asked Michael a second time how Susan was and he snapped at her. "How am I supposed to know?"

He stopped coming for extra help.

On Thursday of this long, strange week, after school was over she walked across the road to the big white house and knocked on the side door, the kitchen door. Probably Mr. Graves had seen her coming. Anyway, it was he who answered the door and he did not invite her in. She knew his reputation for being taciturn and headstrong, one of those overdecisive men who acts hastily, closing off options and possibilities, and then guards the bit of manly ground he has backed himself onto. The children took after their mother.

She said she had come to inquire after Susan.

"You're her teacher, are you?"

It was just an aggressive way of saying no to her. He knew who her teacher was.

"I'm concerned about her. She's missing quite a bit of school."

"No reason to be concerned. She's well enough." The door was being closed. "Good night," he said.

The next day Mary came back to school, puffier about the face, but otherwise the same: wispy eyes, soft skin, short brown hair. She resumed her teaching duties and at recess she told Connie that Susan had been spreading lies.

The story had flaked out, like skin off an old man's pate, drifting through town: how the Kowalchuk girl had seen Susan stumble out of the school, seen her blazing, sobbing face and roughed-up dress—and so had Mrs. Peter. How there were marks on her arms where he had laid the pointer across them to prevent a struggle. How her father was so ashamed that he had locked her in her bedroom and would not let her out. How he was selling the house and business and moving the family away.

"Something happened," Connie said to Mary. "He did something awful."

"You don't understand him. You don't like him and you don't understand him."

"Then explain him to me, Mary."

"I think he's a lonely man."

She had a loyal face. And her eyes weren't colorless after all: they were hazel.

"A lonely man," she went on, "with dreams and lots of bottled-up emotions. Maybe they got the better of him. But he wouldn't mean to hurt her."

"What about the bruises?" The rumored bruises.

"As I say, his emotions might have got the better of him. But he's a good man."

"He likes to use the strap. He likes to use it on girls," Connie said.

At the end of school that day, Friday, she went to her classroom windows and once again she thought she saw shape and movement in the upstairs window across the way. She stood there for a few minutes, pondering.

Then she went out into the hallway and climbed the stairs, up past the landing with the two sets of bookshelves and down the hall to Parley's office.

The door was open and he was behind his desk, writing with his fountain pen. He raised his eyes as she entered and watched as she lowered herself onto the straight-backed chair facing his desk, a chair warmed by many nervous bottoms.

His face struck her as a combination of movie star and Blind Pew in *Treasure Island.* Darkness not just under his eyes, but all around them.

"I'm not a monster," he said quietly, and she realized she was staring, and looked away.

His office was immaculate. He had told her he had been a field hand, a farm boy. He must have hated it. Nothing of the field was here. A dustless, airless room, hostile to children.

He lifted his hand and rubbed the side of his forehead with his fingertips, then ran his fingers out across his face, a delicate, fanlike, elderly movement.

"You're tired," she said.

"I'm always tired."

Once again she could not take her eyes off him. His left eyelid fluttered. He touched it with one finger to arrest it.

"Susan," she forced herself to say.

He looked at her, but said nothing.

She leaned forward. "She's only thirteen."

"Fifteen."

"You really should learn how to count, Mr. Burns."

"I understand," he said, to forestall her, it seemed, and he began to move papers around his desk. Miss Fluelling had analyzed his handwriting, a hobby of hers, and she said it showed he had huge, unsatisfied ambitions and gout.

He cleared his throat. "You're the only person in this place I've been able to converse with on anything like my level. There are three, maybe four readers in this town. I tried to get Susan to read books, but she misunderstood my intentions. I frightened her."

"I think you did more than frighten her."

"Well now, it would be her word against mine, wouldn't it." He leaned back and studied her. "You don't know anything," he said.

His eyes spilled contempt. He pushed his chair farther back. He crossed his legs. "How many years of university do you have? How much teacher training?"

The schoolteacher in him had reasserted itself. He was asking questions to which he knew the answers. Because he was afraid, she realized. He was afraid.

"I don't want to spoil your fun," he was saying, "but the Graves boy deliberately makes mistakes to have more of your time. He monopolizes you."

There was some truth to that. She was silent.

"A good teacher would never let that happen," he said.

"Let's get back to Susan."

He cleared his throat and cleared it again. "The trustees have my resignation. You're the first to know."

Then he *had* done something very wrong.

"I haven't made up my mind about my next step," he said.

She watched him dig his knuckles into his eyes, reaming them out like little glass jars. "Come with me," he said, with his knuckles in his eyes.

"*With you?*"

"Yes." And his eyes sprang at her. "We could start a school. My experience. Your personality." His eyes were burning holes in her. "A good private school with theater as the focus. Shakespeare. Oscar Wilde. Euripides."

"You need help," she managed.

"*Your* help."

"What happened with Susan?"

He glared at her. And then in front of her eyes his face had a little breakdown. He gripped the edge of his desk with both hands, fighting tears.

Her own eyes were suddenly wet with those sympathetic tears we get against our will. She watched him grip the edge of his desk harder. Then he banged the desk with his fist and she jumped.

"Sorry," she said. She stood up.

"Wait."

She sat down again. She watched him get control of himself, but he was still all mussed with emotion.

He said, "You could take the lower grades, I could take the upper."

"I don't think so."

"Why not?"

"You need a doctor. You have no business teaching children. You're unfit."

That was the word she had been searching for. *Unfit.*

Having said it, she stood up again. This time she kept herself out of the punishment chair and got through the door and downstairs and outside, to the wind blowing about, and to her abiding conviction that he was mad and she was out of her depth.

Two days later, Wilda Graves was outside with the dog and her youngest child. It was Sunday evening. Her head was aching from argument and despair. Even here, in the part of the yard that was most out of the wind, breezes pulled at the pins in her hair. She pushed a strand behind her ear and resecured the pin. The big garden called out for attention, but why start when Harold said they had no future here anymore. There was no future at all that she could see. She raised her eyes to the dark, fast-moving clouds on the horizon and for some reason she swiveled her head and looked back at the house. She stood transfixed, disbelieving. Smoke was pouring out of the eaves.

And then the roof burst into flames.

Now slow motion takes over and softly hobbles her. She is aware of her clumsiness reaching out to pick up Evie, her fumbling hands as she hoists the child and carries her to the water pump on its low platform thirty feet from the house, wraps those chubby arms around the pump and tells her not to let go, not to move an inch. Then half runs, half falls toward Susan, who is screaming in the upstairs window.

Others come running, among them Michael and his father, the one from a friend's house, the other from his desk at the store. Connie at home hears the general pulse, the boots in the street, and she goes out and sees dark smoke billowing into the sky. Then she is running, too—she thinks the school is on fire—everyone is carrying buckets, or grabbing them—a town without a fire department.

Buckets—hand over hand—and the heat is astounding. It sends things wheeling through the air, boards, pieces of metal, a black stocking, a shoe. The glare is unearthly and the roar of the flames and the groaning of wooden beams toppling, exploding.

Some have rushed into the burning house to grab what they can. They've come out with a clock, a chair, plates, a tray with six loaves of rising bread. But no one can get to the second floor. A few try, the mother, the father, Michael. They try more than once, but the wall of flames and smoke beats them back. Smoke has replaced Susan in the window. Her screams have stopped.

Parley has joined the brigade. Connie sees the fire play on his face, and his hands are shaking.

Everyone knows Susan has perished. The girl with such talent and presence and imagination. Why wouldn't she smash the window and jump? We would have caught her—we would have caught her in a blanket. And others give the same answers. Her hair was in flames. She was on fire. She succumbed to the smoke. She choked on the smoke. It was too late. Voices jostle each other, different accents, male and female.

And the stunned family stands a little apart. The mother has her arms around her son and daughter, hugging them close, watching the end of everything. The father is with them, but alone.

The loaves of bread, forgotten at the side of the house, baked to perfection. Connie picked up the tray, using burned rags as oven mitts, and stood, uncertain what to do. Across the road, the school was bathed in light as if a miracle were taking place. The miracle was the direction of the wind, out toward the prairie and away from town. She saw the line of men making the fire trench that kept the flames from jumping and spreading. She turned in the other direction and took the tray of bread to Mrs. Peter's house, two hundred yards down the road and the nearest house; it had become a base of operations of sorts. Then she returned to the scene of the fire. She had caught glimpses of Michael, but then lost track of him.

The wind dropped, rain began to fall, and now the smoke really stank. She saw Parley standing by himself in his shirtsleeves. He raised his blackened hands and rubbed his forehead, then rolled his sleeves down and spent the longest time trying to put his cufflinks back in. No one went near him or spoke to him.

She felt a hand on her shoulder, Oscar Jacobs telling her it was time to go home, there was nothing left for them to do.

"Have you seen Michael?" she said.

He put his arm through hers and led the way to the Peters' house, where Mrs. Peter was bandaging the boy's hands. It wasn't so very late, about ten o'clock, almost a normal bedtime. Michael was sitting on the top step with Mrs. Peter. He lifted his head as Connie approached and stopped on the lower step. She put out her hand and touched his singed hair, pushed it back off his forehead, stroked the side of his smeared face. Her touch went right into him and his shoulders began to shake. He brought his arm up to his eyes and twisted away.

She wanted to sit beside him and put her arm around him, but that would have undone him completely. And so she left him to kind and neutral Mrs. Peter and her bandages.

The next day they were gone. They had family north of Jewel, it was said, in Saskatoon. They had gone to be with family.

Parley stayed on, despite the talk. He taught his classes and no one interfered. A grim, bad, shattered man with a blood weal on his lower lip, still faultlessly dressed. It took Connie a while to understand that he believed he was being responsible by finishing out the last three weeks of the school year.

Mary Miller said to Connie, "You can tell he's hurting inside."

"How can you tell, Mary?"

"His eyes."

Those pale-brown unreadable eyes.

"The life's gone out of them," Mary said. "He's devastated."

"I wonder if she set it herself," Mrs. Kowalchuk said.

It was the middle of the night and she and Connie were in the kitchen, since neither of them could sleep. Connie in her nightgown gripped a glass of water. Mrs. Kowalchuk in housecoat and slippers sat down with a heavy sigh. The smell of smoke permeated everything. Connie smelled it on her nightgown. The following winter she would put on her winter coat and smell smoke on the fur collar.

"But her door was locked," Connie said. "That's what they say."

"He didn't keep her in the dark."

"No."

Oil lamps, matches. Wooden houses, woodstoves, winds, proximity. Nearly everything went up in flames at one time or another.

"Burns is a peculiar man," Mrs. Kowalchuk said. "An educated man. But we don't know his past."

"I know a little."

"How he ended up here?"

"I don't know that."

"And we don't really know what happened."

"But what do you think?"

"I think he must have meddled with her."

"Raped her, you mean."

"I don't know. All I really know is that Harold Graves couldn't look people in the face he was so ashamed."

"Poor Susan."

They eased their feelings by condemning the father and pitying the mother, by calling the father a tyrant and then by pitying him, too.

The drag of the story was like a child pulling on her arm until it ached. The day after it happened, she had walked around the edges of the charred and toppled house, the air still oppressive, headachy, and the stench indescribable. Then she had caught a whiff of sweet plums, overcooked preserves. The pantry, it must have been, or the root cellar.

One evening that week Connie walked over to Oscar Jacobs's for a French lesson that seemed not just beside the point but a gross impossibility. She would not be able to concentrate on French for one second. But she wanted his company.

She knocked and entered. He came toward her and led her into the room with the standing mirror.

"I can think of only one thing," Connie said. "I'm sorry."

"*Le feu*," he said. "*L'incendie*."

Connie repeated the words and searched for others. The house burned to the ground, *la jeune fille dedans*.

"*A l'intérieur*."

They sat at the round table, which was covered with patterned fabric, not your usual tablecloth but a length of pale-yellow cotton with a delicate blue design that was actually dress material, he told her when she admired it and rested her eyes on it. The exercise of saying in French what had happened, no matter how stilted and halting and mixed with English, lifted the horror a little. They were back on the night in question, the house was burning, the girl inside. And afterward, Connie said, the next day, *la prochaine journée,* it was so odd. I caught a whiff of something pleasant, not burned to a crisp, but hot juices from preserves and melted paraffin. I don't suppose a man would have experienced the smell as I did; only women make preserves. *La confiture, les conserves.* The glass had melted, *le verre fondu,* and I picked up a piece. It was still warm. It, too, had that agreeable smell. *L'odeur agréable et sucré.*

Finding new words for things drew her into another world. Oscar Jacobs put a beret on her head.

Even when everything had fallen apart, how lovely it was to learn.

Parley was never investigated, arrested, charged, impugned, or punished. He dressed with even more care; dishevelment, shabbiness did not set in; he never lost his appearance of authority. But Connie noticed a tremor in his right hand. He reached for a glass of water and had to retrieve his shaking hand. Arrogance rescued him. He spilled something? He pretended he hadn't. Someone else would clean it up. Mary Miller would clean it up.

He had his shoes resoled and the shoemaker did the work without a word. The new soles were so slippery that Parley walked on ice thereafter, in danger of spreading his length on the floor.

Life went on around the burned house. Black as ink, or prunes, or the blood weal on Parley's lip. Connie would find herself staring at the ruins from her classroom windows. ("Come in from the window, Michael," she remembered saying to him whenever his attention drifted.) Eventually, she would give her head a shake and try, without much success, to concentrate. She still stayed late to help any pupils who needed it. And then she walked home alone. Parley avoided her now and she returned the favor.

The only official change was that on the last day of May, which was the last day of school, they had no end-of-the-year picnic, no old-shoe races, egg-and-spoon races, three-legged races.

Parley disappeared the next day.

It would be a hot, dry summer, one in a long string of such summers. The following year, dust would begin to stir in April, and by the middle of May, full-blown dust storms would be whipping across the prairies.

Connie told me she never had any difficulty understanding what was soon to happen—a world in which selected victims, mainly Jews, were put into ovens and people did nothing.

9

ARGYLE

Chokecherries don't get picked anymore, not really. In the past, those who did the picking were Depression children who loved Fred Astaire and grew up when movies were utterly fabulous. Children knew all about the effort that conceals effort. They also aspired to the casual and tossed-off and natural. Fewer pickers and fewer chokecherries, too. An edge plant, drawn to disturbed or abandoned ground, especially where two habitats meet, like field and bush. This last being the kind of place where you're most likely to see a fox, and where a lone girl is such easy prey it makes you shiver.

Children used to pick as the sound of crickets rose up around them. They stripped the trusses of mahogany-red and almost-black cherries off the twigs and into the pails at their feet, and whatever fell by the wayside lay soft and rotting on the ground.

A murder opens up the landscape. It becomes known in every one of its intimate parts, trod upon, inspected, combed over, revisited.

A bad surgeon has been operating and afterward the anesthetic lifts, and you discover you will be gasping in pain for the rest of your life.

When I visited the hill, seventy years later, five deer wandered into the sunlight from the thicket of brambles and haws and undergrowth that sloped down to the creek. The water was very low, a narrow and slow-moving stream. The chokecherries along its edge with their black and bitter fruit were unpicked. The tall grasses had gone blond. It was October, the month of memory, when the earth gives up its colors and every bruised leaf and bent grass and autumn flower turns into a sunset in the evening of the year. A town I had seen in passing only once or twice before felt very familiar, my mother's hometown in the valley.

The older you get, the closer your loves are to the surface, my mother said, a year and a half ago. She was thinking then about the paintings she wanted to finish. Nothing else really mattered to her, except my father. Her children were doing well; they didn't need her. Other preoccupations and worries no longer had much hold on her. *The older you get, the closer your loves are to the surface.* She was breathing rarefied air, the ether you come upon at high altitudes. I understood finally how long-held grievances and petty smallnesses might get burned off, and pure creativity and humor remain.

I learned to understand the word *realpolitik* from Connie. Salman Rushdie, she said, was getting a lesson in *realpolitik*.

"That's why I went to Europe," she said. "I wanted to understand the real world. Anyway, that's what I told myself."

She was the adored and distant relative, living in the States, visiting seldom. The commanding aunt who dressed in black, the fine teacher, the elegant woman who arrived one day holding a silver onion as a gift.

I remember a heated disagreement she had with my father, heated on his side, not hers, about human nature. Connie said it polluted the finest and elevated the lowest; it was the vast, deep well from which we all drew. My father rejected the very notion, saying there was no such thing as human nature. Never sure of himself, he came across as too sure, but that doesn't mean he was wrong. He meant there was no one human nature, each of us is different.

Connie held the more catholic view that we carry the past forward, not as original sin, though she understood the concept well enough, but as personal history. She took great interest in my birthmarks—the saucer-sized one on my left knee, brown and raised, and other, smaller ones on my arms and chest, some brown, some red, so many I could be a speckled trout. It was her theory that I received them as burns in a former life. How else to account for my memories of a place I had never seen, a love of grasses and wind, a nostalgia for the prairie, unless some hidden and very old connection were doing its work. Certainly moments of déjà vu peppered my childhood to the extent that Connie once took out her notebook and began to jot them down.

I liked being picked out in this way, by her, by the past. I recalled a set of back stairs that led to a bedroom, and the sensation of waiting there and my despair as footsteps climbed toward me. I had an inordinate fear of fire as a child and couldn't be left alone near a campfire or a fireplace. But I have a lot of my father in me, too, and never entirely fell for what Connie implied, that a girl who died in a fire in Jewel, Saskatchewan, might have come back as me. I didn't care to share myself in quite that way. I took my father's vigorous view and turned it: there is so much *more* than human nature. In December, I look out of the upstairs window and see reddish berries on the sprawling vine on the garden fence, and respond from head to toe. Simple berries on a bare branch in late fall, early winter. Why do they move me so?

A few days after Parley disappeared from Jewel, Connie went home to her father's farm outside Weyburn on the other side of Saskatchewan. My father has told me what her visits were like, the anticipation beforehand and the pleasure during. She was eight years older than he was and he worshipped her; my dad would always have a great appreciation for capable women. Connie took over the kitchen and made recipes passed on by her mother's aunt Charlotte, clootie pudding and berry-and-apple crumble among them. At the kitchen table she and her brothers ate the results, after which my father laid his head against her shoulder in contentment.

She didn't get on with her stepmother, however, not a bit. Zoe's cold and baleful look—like something out of Grimm—followed by the gush of insincere praise. Connie escaped the fickleness of jealousy by moving to Regina. She enrolled in a business course, not having the heart for teaching anymore, then got a job as a secretary for the *Leader Post,* and soon, Connie being Connie, she was doing reporting and writing a column. Like all reporters, she haunted the train station to interview travelers passing through. Syd Goodwin was never among them, and neither was the Graves family. As the drought intensified and dust storms thickened, she wrote about cars passing each other in the road unawares and travelers so coated with dust they were unrecognizable, except by the gold in their teeth.

Connie's pay at the *Leader Post* was ninety dollars a month in 1931, increased after a year to a hundred dollars, then cut back in 1933 to ninety dollars, and cut back again in 1934 to eighty dollars a month. She saved her money, amassing five hundred dollars by 1935. Then she made an arrangement with the Sifton newspaper chain to receive a stipend of ten dollars a week for freelance articles from overseas. In early August of 1935, she took the train north to Fort Churchill, and in return for writing about shipping grain to Europe via the new route of Hudson Bay, she got free passage to England on a cargo ship and saw icebergs the size of mountains.

In England she spent several months writing about unemployment and unrest, then traveled to Paris to get warm and to feel less grim, and stayed near the Seine, climbing six floors to her room with its little woodstove and sofa bed and table, and its window in the roof that opened on hinges, allowing her to see, if she stood on a chair, all the rooftops of Paris. She learned to smoke and to speak French, to dress with style and economy, to recognize prejudice, and never to minimize a gathering menace. She stayed almost two years and would have stayed longer had she married the young doctor who proposed to her. But in the spring of 1937, having broken up with him, she left a Europe more and more at war and came back to Canada. On a windy day in late March, she entered the offices of the *Ottawa Journal* and talked herself into a job.

Several months later, she heard about the murder of a schoolgirl up the valley in Argyle. Moved by more than natural curiosity, she persuaded her editor to let her handle the story. After all, she said, she came from the area, knew the town, knew its history, and could pick up stories and recipes for the women's page while she was at it.

The town of Argyle lay in the heart of a long valley formed by the waters of the Ottawa River, a very old valley and therefore so broad that you didn't perceive it as one unless you were close to the river. Parts of the valley were pastoral and parts were deep woods. The towns were small and filled with Scots (if you were a Scot— otherwise, Scots, Irish, French, Poles, Germans). To be from a town that identified itself with a valley, and from a valley that resembled a plain, and a plain that felt like an island—this was being from Argyle. My mother said to me recently, "No place seemed farther away."

After Connie came upon Parley Burns in the cemetery, she inquired about him. But she did not go to see him until there was a good reason to do so. The reason came when twenty-year-old John Coyle was arrested for the murder. The next afternoon, Connie went to Parley's high school. It was a large collegiate, three stories tall, red brick, a block from Argyle Street. Inside, down a wide corridor, past a drinking fountain and several cabinets of trophies and photographs, was the large outer office run by a secretary, who was efficient, unmarried and in love with the principal, so everyone thought. Miss Wood had Connie wait at the counter while she checked with Mr. Burns in his small inner office—PRINCIPAL IAN BURNS, M.A. on a metal plate below the frosted glass—and then she waved Connie over.

He half rose as she entered, older than he had seemed in the cemetery, his hair completely gray. He wore glasses now, horn-rimmed with round lenses. He had lost or mastered his tic. Now he had a mustache exactly like Hitler's.

She took the first of two empty chairs, remembering all too well the last time she had been in an office of his. He sat down and leaned forward on his elbows. He pressed his fingertips together and regarded her over them with no pretense of pleasure. It was late August, about three weeks after Ethel's murder. A timetabling sheet was spread in front of him. He had been toiling away with pencil and eraser. His hands trembled noticeably, both hands.

Connie did not refer to the one thing they were thinking about, but it was everywhere, that horror of seven years ago, in every particle of air. She asked him if he had taught John Coyle. The answer was yes. He had taught him French, for which he showed the aptitude of a flea. "Not like yourself," he said. "If you remember."

The windows were open. A breeze came in and ruffled his papers. It was uncanny, creepy to be facing him again across a principal's desk, he in control and she asking him questions he didn't care for. She persisted and began to get more out of him. He said that Johnny had been a member of his drama club, but too inhibited to perform. "Until we did *King Lear*, that is."

"He didn't play Lear." She was trying to get a fix on the young man as well as on Parley.

"He played Gloucester after he was blinded. He could do it because he could close his eyes."

It was a detail she would always remember for what it said about getting through life, the tricks we use to persuade ourselves not to be afraid. It was typical of Parley that he would immediately understand what was going on with the boy.

"And you like him?"

"He's a normal, decent lad."

"The hair in the girl's hand," she said.

"Yes."

"The hair she grabbed in the struggle. It's the same color as his hair."

"Blond."

"Yes." Had it been gray—but it wasn't gray. The instant she had seen Parley in the cemetery, she had suspected him; but the hair was blond, which would seem to rule him out. "And pointed," she said. Which indicated something altogether strange. "What's your understanding of 'pointed'?"

"What's yours?"

"Hair that's never been cut, never barbered."

"Johnny's almost a fixture in the barbershop. I often see him there when I walk by."

"Then how." She spread her hands, looking for an explanation.

"It might be pubic hair," he said.

They regarded each other. She had had the same thought. "But wouldn't they know that? Wouldn't it be identified as such?"

"They don't know much. They're pinning the murder on a boy who couldn't possibly have done it."

He didn't go on. He was waiting to be asked. Making her work, she thought.

But then he said what he meant. "He's a cripple."

"Well, he uses a cane. He can walk."

"The girl was running away. They found spilled cherries along the path. You don't need to run away from a cripple."

The moment lengthened. In the years since Susan's death, she had once or twice found herself telling the story. How a principal kept a thirteen-year-old girl after school, how she had stumbled home sobbing and in disarray, how her father was so ashamed, so worried about appearances that he locked her in her room. How a week later, their house caught fire, and because there was no fire department everyone formed a brigade and fought the burning house with buckets of water. They could see the girl screaming in the upstairs window. But no one could get to her.

And what anyone who heard the story wanted to know was what had become of the principal.

"You told me in the cemetery that you taught the dead girl's sisters."

"Strong students. Isabel, particularly. She played Cordelia."

"I don't know how you have the heart for it," she said, saying what she had been thinking. "Heading up another drama club."

She saw the tic jump at the corner of his eye. She was baiting him. It was beneath her. Again, he pressed his fingertips together, then leaned his chin against the scaffolding of his fingers and studied her. He was behind his desk and his face was behind the desk he had made with his hands. His exhausted eyes looked almost drugged from lack of sleep and overwork. He was waiting for her to leave, that was obvious.

She said, "I always wondered if I'd see the Graves family again, too."

Her mouth was dry. She wasn't afraid of him, but her mouth was dry.

She said, "I think about them."

He held her gaze, but his expression changed. "So do I," he said.

In the outer office, she stopped and spoke for a moment to Miss Wood. "Soon you'll be very busy. The start of school. A busy time."

"We will. But he has everything under control. He works so hard."

"Then so do you, I imagine."

"He's not a vigorous man either. I wouldn't let him give blood last year. He was working so hard he had nothing to spare."

"I met his wife in the library."

Miss Wood made no response, a studied neutrality.

"I didn't learn if they have children."

"*She* does. From her first marriage. We expect great things of Doris. She's the top scholar in the school."

"Doris Burns?"

"Mr. Burns is adopting her officially, so yes, soon she'll be Doris Burns."

Ethel's body had been discovered in a sort of alcove, bordered by a fence and heavy shrubbery, a hundred yards from the road and three-quarters of a mile southwest of the center of town but within town limits. She was lying flat on her back, her head turned sideways and her left arm raised over part of her face. The entire left side of her head was crushed and her jaw was broken. An abrasion on her left arm near her shoulder was thought to have come from trying to shield herself from blows. Her dress and slip were raised around her waist, and her panties were missing.

The body was removed to the undertaking parlors of M. M. Macswain. Macswain had become the town's undertaker after my grandfather, undertaker and furniture-maker, died when my mother was a child.

The search party had been led by Chief of Police Moses Reed, on whose doorstep a baby in a basket had been laid seventeen years before with a note saying that since the baby was his, he could raise it; and Mrs. Reed did. The baby grew up to be Olive Reed, a fast friend of my mother's for a time, a fast friend and a fast girl, what in those days was called "easy," "an open door"; eventually, my mother told me, she ran off with the circus.

After the murder, Argyle shifted into a darker register not entirely out of keeping with a town where it wasn't uncommon for so-called nieces to live with so-called aunts (who were really daughters and mothers, or grandmothers) and with male relatives, what kind of relative never being clear. My mother's friendship with Olive relied on two things: their mutual fascination with movies, which they discussed endlessly, and my mother's singular fascination with Olive's boils. Olive always notified her when one of her boils was ready to pop, since the look of pus worming its way out of a hole in the skin was something my mother never tired of watching. She was not squeamish, and neither am I.

During the inquest, and again during the trial, Connie roomed with my grandmother. The big brick house with its front veranda is still there. Some of the furniture eventually got passed on to me—a matching oversized rocker and armchair, reupholstered in light-green velvet by my mother, and the most uncomfortable furniture imaginable, the seats so deep your spine has to go on a journey and arrives sorry it ever got there.

*   *   *

Ethel had left her home in the apartment block on Argyle Street around 9:30 in the morning. She followed Opeongo Street (within town limits Opeongo Road was a street) as it turned and ran southerly down to a bridge across Smith's Creek, beyond which rose the gentle hill owned by the Iveys but almost communal in nature, where pickers helped themselves not just to chokecherries but to wild apples and plums. This part of town, blending as it did into countryside, was an open world with pathways, wagon lanes, creek and bush, even a well from which strangers helped themselves.

After the murder, Ethel's movements and Johnny's became everyone else's, routes as well-worn as the one in Seamus Heaney's poem about the trail of tears an old friend followed on his way to boarding school, the streams he passed being the same streams an earlier traveler had passed and described in 1608 as he pondered the travels of Aeneas; and so the boy was accompanied, more than he knew, on the lonely road to school at the end of summer.

Old histories and geographies accompanied Ethel, too. She was walking on a settlement road that overlay a lumbermen's tote-road that followed an Indian trail ninety-nine miles long. It commenced at the Ottawa River and crossed the Bonnechere River at Argyle, and then took a northwesterly course between the Bonnechere and the Madawaska Rivers, both tributaries of the Ottawa, on to Lake Opeongo in Algonquin Park. The road penetrated vast timberlands and opened them up to small farmers whose land was not under water but "under rock," as one blunt speaker put it. Scruffy, rugged, a pleasure for the eyes, this scenic variety of hillside, bush and swamp. The road's glory days, when it bustled with horses, wagons, hotels and mills, went from 1860 to 1890. Then the lumber tycoon J. R. Booth put through his private railway. Everything went by rail after that, and the Opeongo died. Settlements became ghost towns. Blueberries grew in the crevices of rocks, and straggly chokecherries sprang up along split-rail fences, where they attracted birds in quantity.

The chokecherry, like Ethel, never grows very tall. Dangling white fingers of flowers make it conspicuous in the spring. Then in early August the cherries ripen in clusters, like grapes. An early traveler to the New World wrote that "if they be not very ripe, they so furre the mouth that the tongue will cleave to the roofe, and the throate wax horse with swallowing those red Bullies (as I may call them) being little better in taste."

Ethel entered the field through a farm gate. She knew where she was going, for only the day before, a civic holiday, she and her parents and sisters had walked this very road, something they often did, and spoken to a young man on a cane who was coming down the hill with a heavy pail of chokecherries. Her father had asked him where the best picking was and he had mentioned Ivey's bush farther up the road, the fence on its far side straddled with chokecherry trees.

From the farm gate a beaten path led across the field to the fairly open bush, then continued along the edge of the bush, inside the rail fence. On the other side of the fence lay a field of oats. It's not impossible that Ethel, being a reader, was privy to Hardy's startling thought in *Tess* about the countless times we pass back and forth over the day we will die without having the slightest premonition. Just ahead, the chokecherry trees were twittering with birds.

Before his arrest, and after, John Coyle maintained his innocence. He did so publicly and at some length at the long-delayed inquest that took place two weeks after he was jailed and five weeks after the murder, in early September. By then school was already under way.

"You would come in from the lake, having had a coolish August," my mother said to me a year ago, her voice relaxing into clarity as she remembered those times. "The east wind would come down over the lake and blow in over us at the cabin, and the weather would just then change. It would reverse itself and you would have days of warm, sunny weather. It wasn't high summer. It was September."

"The beginning of school," I said. "Without fail, the weather is perfect."

She laughed with me as the first days of school flooded our minds, uneasiness and perfect weather going hand in hand, as all schoolchildren know.

The coroner and his jury assembled in the old Temperance Hall on Raglan Street, and over the course of the afternoon they heard a series of witnesses, expert and otherwise, lay out the story.

Johnny recounted that on the day of the murder he got up around nine o'clock and did some work for his mother, then he left the house at 10:45 a.m. (the coroner had put the time of the murder at somewhere between ten and eleven in the morning) and went to the Russell drugstore, where he bought the *Ottawa Journal* (Connie's paper being the most popular one in rural eastern Ontario). He went on to the Odd Fellows Hall and read the paper. From there he went to Peever's butcher shop and bought meat for dinner and took it home. At 11:25 a.m., he said, precise to the minute, he took a small tomato tin and went over the bridge on Opeongo Street, saw children picking cherries on his left, stopped and spoke to them, then turned to his right over a sag in the fence and, heading northwesterly across Ivey's fields, picked a few cherries, then continued more directly north to the right-of-way of the National Railway, ascended to the high trestle bridge across Smith's Creek, and returned home over the bridge, a distance of just under a mile. He arrived home at five minutes after twelve, when his people were sitting down to dinner.

In the evening, he went to a softball match in the grounds of the Argyle Electric Company, across from the C.N.R. train station, and there he first heard of the disappearance and search for the girl, whom he didn't know, he said, making a claim that was later shown to be untrue. With three men that he met at the game, section men who worked for the railway, he went up the hill to the Ivey farm and saw a woman walking in the fairly open bush, calling out, "Ethel, Ethel!" It was Miss Rosamond Ivey, who knew him, and would testify in turn that he joined her in the search, sharing her opinion that terrible things were happening in the world and expressing his own fear that they were going to find something. They separated, she said, at the big stump a few hundred feet in from the northern edge of the bush. She went to the right, he went to the left. About two minutes later, he called out, "I have found her, and she is dead!" He would tell Police Chief Reed (when he arrived twenty minutes later) that he had stumbled over something, likely the large round stone that proved to be the murder weapon, and then fallen over the girl, getting her blood on his hands.

The evidence was largely against him. The police chief said that daylight still remained when he got to the scene; it was unlikely anyone would have "stumbled" over a body. The railwaymen who had accompanied Johnny said he told them he had seen the girl on the bridge at ten that morning and warned her against going out alone after cherries, contradicting his statements that he was nowhere near the hill until after 11:30 and that he didn't know the girl. The railwaymen agreed that it was coming on dusk when Johnny found the body, but quite clear. A neighbor, a housewife, said she saw him at 7:30 the next morning hanging out a pair of pants and a shirt that had just been washed; never before had she seen him thus engaged. Another neighbor, a schoolteacher, was reading on her veranda the morning of the murder and saw Ethel pass by on the other side of the hedge, heading toward Ivey Hill. A little later, she saw "somebody carrying a cane" go by in the same direction, walking hurriedly, and it had to be Johnny—for everyone knew he relied on a cane, having been injured three years earlier (by a baseball driven into his leg, curiously enough) and having been operated on more than once by the very doctor who recently had died on the operating table. Then a medical expert from Toronto, Dr. Hugh Norman, sealed the young man's fate by saying that the hairs in the dead child's clenched right hand corresponded with hair from John Coyle's head. They were similar. He could not swear they were the same.

Connie was at the side of the room taking copious notes. It was a warm and cloudless day. At six o'clock the coroner's jury withdrew, and at seven they returned and delivered their opinion that the evidence pointed toward John Coyle.

Connie stood up and saw Parley Burns in the far corner of the packed hall, the glint of his glasses, the cloth of his good suit. She made her way over to him and it was a malicious question, but she asked if he believed the guilty person would ever be punished.

"I feel sorry for the boy," he said.

A young man who was lame and had no history of misbehavior, who had listened intently and without apparent shame throughout the inquest. But how do you read anyone, how can you possibly know? She had asked almost everyone she talked to what they thought of Mr. Burns, and he seemed to be held in universal respect: he ran a good school, he was articulate and well spoken in public, he was a regular churchgoer and supporter of community life. Among the schoolboys she asked, there was fear mingled with fondness. Among the schoolgirls, uneasiness and alarm. My mother told her that Parley Burns gave her the creeps. My grandmother, on the other hand, called him a great gentleman; she was impressed by his manner, appearance, education, success. But my grandmother and Parley Burns were similar, perhaps, in their antisocial self-esteem. My grandmother was a most fastidious woman, yet my mother had once come upon her in the bathroom using the family-shared facecloth to wipe her bottom.

"John's a good, respectable boy," Parley said. He fingered his tie and smoothed it.

Parley would make himself very unpopular by defending Johnny Coyle. Only a few people in Argyle spoke out for the young man. Another was his minister, who happened to be Parley's minister as well. People hated them for it, these two outsiders: Reverend Dunning from Toronto, whose sleek car moved silently down the street, and who lectured his congregation on their shortcomings; and Parley Burns, who taught French and gave the derivation of *tolerance* when he urged it upon the school assembly as a virtue to be prized. Neither man was silenced by the immense sympathy for Ethel's family.

All her life Connie would veer between wanting to understand Parley and believing that no explanation would ever suffice. But then, explaining and understanding are different things. The former requires beady eyes, and the latter, the kind of long look that gazes out the window and sees the troubled sky extending over the troubled world.

10

TRIAL

At the trial in November, a summer story unfolded as winter took hold and snow fell on the woods and fields and pathways in question. Johnny pleaded not guilty, but never took the stand in his own defense. The jury consisted of farmers and barbers and storekeepers from the surrounding area. Spectators filled all available space in the courtroom for the ten long days of the trial.

Everything already learned at the inquest came out again, but more exhaustively. Ethel's small, proud mother remembered exactly what her daughter had worn. A light-blue dress with pockets and a little white tie at the neck and a little belt at the waist. A green slip, a pair of white panties, white broadcloth cotton panties with elastic at the top. No socks. Brown sandals. Ethel had risen about nine o'clock, her mother said, and for breakfast she had eaten a bowl of cornflakes and drunk a glass of milk.

"Did she by any chance eat any potatoes that morning?" the Crown prosecutor asked.

"No, she did not."

"Was she not rather dressed up to go berry picking?"

"That was a favorite dress, handed down from her older sister. And she planned to go afterward to Mrs. Handford and Mrs. Davis and sell them whatever cherries she had picked."

"I am awfully sorry to have to question you, Mrs. Weir, but might she have gone outside without her panties on?"

"No, absolutely not."

"And were you with her all the time she was dressing?"

"I was not in the bedroom, but she had on part of her garments as she came out of the bedroom, and she was in the act of slipping her little dress over her slip just as we were alone in the house."

The potatoes remained a mystery, too: the semi-digested potatoes found in her stomach, along with cereal and a few chokecherries. Had hoboes shared a potato with her before following her into the bush? Certainly at some point she had tried to run away. Over a hundred and fifty spilled cherries were found on the path about forty feet from where her body lay. Her two pails—preserving kettles with handles—were upright on the ground four feet from her right shoulder.

How late children slept during the Argyle summer. None seemed to rise before nine. You get the sense of a long, timeless season when children were left entirely to their own devices. And so it was when I was a child. Days were green pastures of imaginative plenty when we amused and fulfilled ourselves in the wide world of a small town. Distances were as nothing, since they led not to school but to water. The taste of it suddenly sloshing up your nose, a gulping, sputtering, half-drowning pleasure that was part of being afloat and over your head.

An eleven-year-old girl giving unsworn testimony (she was deemed to be too young to understand the full import of taking an oath) said that on August 3 she had left home at ten o'clock to pick apples in Ivey's field. Pointing out her route on the enlarged map of the town, she said, "I crossed this here railway track, and there was a field here and a field there, and you had to go over more, and there was the apple tree." At about twenty-five minutes to eleven, she said, she heard a scream coming from Ivey's bush.

"What was the scream you heard?"

"'Help' without the *p*," she said clearly.

"Could you tell whether it was a big person's voice or a little person's voice?"

"No—it was a child's voice. I told the girls I was with, 'Are you coming home? Because I heard someone in the bush.'"

Guided by the judge, who was a former local politician, the jury would disregard the girl's bright testimony because it was uncorroborated, unlike the similarly unsworn testimony of three even younger children who were picking chokecherries on the left-hand side of Opeongo Street and claimed to have seen John Coyle go up the hill and come back down, and then go up the hill again and come back down again. They told their story after the police inspector took them on a candy-buying expedition. But since it tallied, partly, with the next testimony, it was given weight.

The bread-delivery man was next. He said he had seen John Coyle from his horse-drawn wagon at 10:40 a.m. heading home from the direction of the bridge in "a blue shirt, kind of a faded blue and I am not sure, but I think he had a pair of grayish pants on."

Johnny had said at the inquest that he didn't leave his home until 10:45, when he went out the back door and downtown. So he shouldn't have been anywhere near the bridge.

Connie didn't believe the bread man actually remembered what John Coyle was wearing on August 3. Even she, who loved clothes, couldn't say what someone in passing had had on days after the fact. Far more to the point was the delivery man's testimony that Johnny looked normal and was walking "at an ordinary pace." He didn't see Macbeth walking by, and yet the body in the woods would have been lying in a pool of blood, the left side of her head pounded in by a big stone, her shoulders bloodstained, her hands bloody. There wasn't an inch of her that wasn't scratched or bruised. Upper lip, left arm, hips, buttocks, legs, groin—an abrasion of the skin above her clitoris, an abrasion on the left side of the vagina, and a slight one at the bottom of the fold. Bruises the size of a bean on the outer surface of her right arm two inches above the wrist. A bruise on the right ring-finger in front of the knuckle, a bruise on the left thumb just above the thumbnail—where she had been grabbed and held, one assumed. The upper lip bruised where her mouth had been pressed shut.

In her left hand, some debris of grass and dirt. And in her right hand, some grass and clover leaves and bits of fiber and more than a dozen hairs.

Connie would write that there were any number of angles and levels to see things from. Through a thin hedge as you sat reading on your veranda; from the side door as you threw coffee grounds on your flower bed at 7:30 in the morning; from a horse-drawn bread wagon on a hot and sticky summer's day; from the side of the road as you picked the chokecherries you hoped to sell to rich housewives; through the undergrowth at dusk.

Much was made of the available light when John Coyle, having joined the search, stumbled over Ethel's body a little before eight. Since he had come through the woods, there would have been less light than if he had come by way of the oat field. And those who came after him, once he set up the cry, had the advantage of seeing him standing there and soon surrounded by others. Naturally, Ethel's body was apparent to them right away. These were details raised by Johnny's lawyer, who made the more general point about the obscuring effect of dusk, known to anyone, he said, who has driven an automobile. He used the French expression, *entre chien et loup*. The hour that blurs dog and wolf.

Yet all the witnesses were steadfast in saying that it was still quite clear outside, especially since that part of the bush faced west and received as much light from the setting sun as the open field itself.

Among the few testifying on Johnny's behalf was the high school principal, Ian Burns, who said he knew the accused well and that he was a very good boy who provided him with a Christmas tree every year. (The one occasion when the tree wasn't up to snuff, Parley had paid Johnny seventy-five cents instead of the usual dollar, after which the boy was very careful to search out the perfect tree.) Another was a neighbor who swore that she had often seen Johnny Coyle hang laundry on the line, it was not the unheard-of event that an earlier witness had claimed it to be. Yet another was an employee at the train station, who said that on the afternoon of the murder, John Coyle had shipped eighteen pounds of chokecherries to his brother in Northern Ontario, and he had acted quite normally, and yes, he did know the accused well enough to know what normal was. The last was the pharmacist in whose drugstore Johnny bought his daily newspaper. Mr. Russell didn't remember if Johnny had been in that particular morning, but he agreed that it was his customary practice to read the paper in the store, talking all the while about the latest baseball scores, a young man who was unfailingly pleasant and polite. (The butcher from whom Johnny claimed to have bought meat for the midday meal had maintained an unhelpful silence about the boy; he couldn't say, he had told the police, one way or the other.)

Examination of Johnny's clothing, some of it recently washed, had failed to reveal any traces of blood, and none of the fibers from Ethel's hand matched any of his clothes. In the end, the burden of evidence fell upon the hairs in her hand.

They were hairs of two kinds, according to the experts, some similar to the hair on the girl's head, others to hairs procured from the head of the accused. These last Johnny had given willingly upon being accosted in the street by the police chief, pulling eight hairs out of the top of his head and dropping them into the proffered envelope. They were then sent to the same lab in Toronto where a professor, an expert in textiles, a "wool man," had examined under his microscope the fibers in Ethel's hand and compared them with the fabric of the pants and shirts taken from Johnny's bedroom.

Connie, and everyone else, was waiting for the professor to say whether the eight blond hairs from Coyle's head matched, or failed to match, any of the twenty hairs found in Ethel's hand.

In the courtroom a big clock on the wall above the judge showed the hours in Roman numerals. The judge himself had a pocket watch he was in the habit of consulting instead. He rolled it in his fingers and periodically opened the lid, sometimes to check the time, sometimes to inspect a spot of tenderness just above his left eye in the polished interior of the watch case.

The expert professor took the stand, a man of medium height with a profound crease in his forehead and an unfathomable way of expressing himself. He said, "I found a similarity in eight of those with the hair contained in the envelope, whereas the other twelve were dissimilar in that they were of a blond type of hair, while the other eight, and those in the envelope, were of the brunette or darker type of hair."

The judge seemed unfazed, but a restless movement went through the courtroom. How was anyone to follow such testimony? The professor was saying, if you went over it carefully, that the twelve hairs that corresponded to the girl's dark hair were blond, and those in the envelope, namely blond-haired Coyle's, were dark.

The Crown glossed over the startling confusion that would never be clarified and asked if the blond hair in the girl's hand could have come from the head of the accused. The answer was, "I would say they could."

The defense was quick. "But you will not swear they did?"

"No, I cannot do so."

During the break, Connie stood in the raw November wind on the courtroom steps and tried to think about everything she knew, and it seemed very little. A courtroom wasn't the place to find truth. Neither was a newspaper. How could you ever find the truth when there were so many witnesses to everything except the crime, all of them with meandering memories and half-visions guided by lawyers casting doubt and spreading quibbles. She breathed in the cold air and looked out at the iciness on the curb and the patches of snow. Her childhood home was twenty miles from here, close to the Ottawa River and still blessed with a big orchard, the brick house unchanged; she had driven by in her beloved Plymouth last summer.

Parley came out behind her and lit a cigarette. Her hair blew into her eyes. (She hated her hair. She had gone to a hairdresser two weeks ago and she hated the results.) She turned a little more into the wind.

"You visit him in jail," she said. She had checked with the jail keeper and learned that Johnny's parents had gone once, a brother had gone twice, but his regular visitors were his minister and Ian Burns.

"I bring him books. That's all. It's very little."

"What books?"

"*Call of the Wild. White Fang.* Adventures. A jail cell is pretty small."

Parley returned her gaze with his underslept eyes. His formerly manicured nails were bitten, his teeth stained brown.

"You should be teaching," he said to her. "You were a very good teacher."

"That's not what you said at the time."

She had to remind him. "You said a good teacher would never allow herself to be monopolized by a demanding student."

"You were excellent," he said.

She felt her heart soften toward him. Not just the compliment, but the teeth stained by too much coffee, the sorry nails. She asked him what he thought of the professor, and he shook his head. "Gibberish," he said. She asked what about the judge, and he said, "My father had shingles and they started with a pain right there." He touched his eye. "That man is about to learn the meaning of misery. He thinks Johnny did it, of course."

"But you still think he's innocent."

"I do."

"I veer back and forth. I make up my mind and then I change my mind. Why doesn't he take the stand? Why are there so many holes in his story?"

Parley looked out at the street. "I think he got excited on the day of the murder. He overstated things to impress the railway-men. And then he got caught in contradictions. The real culprits are long gone."

"Culprits," she said. "More than one?"

Slowly, he ground his cigarette butt under his foot. He had toe rubbers on his shoes. He still didn't wear gloves. "The hairs in her hand. Blond and dark. Why would she be pulling out her own hair?"

It was a good point.

He turned to go back inside and she said, "Wait."

He stopped, he waited.

"Every time I see you I think of Jewel. I think of Susan." She kept her eyes on his face. "What really happened?"

He looked straight ahead and didn't answer. She kept quiet, she gave him time.

"I handled her roughly," he said. "I don't excuse myself."

"Roughly?"

"I went too far."

"How far?"

"Not as far as you think."

She understood him, she even believed him.

"Of course, you don't believe me," he said.

The knowledge of Parley going unpunished made her doubly fas-cinated when the Crown made its case against a young man with a blameless history. There is always a first time, the Crown lawyer said in his summation; a first time that doesn't necessarily lead to a second time.

"Men who are not moral perverts, subject to passions, do things which they could not do otherwise. There may come a time when a good man, a saintly man, breaks down. History is full of such cases."

The prosecution gave no example, and she couldn't think of a single one.

He went on. "It was impossible for John Coyle to have been at home, gone to the drugstore, Odd Fellows Hall, butcher store, and back home, unless the children and the bread driver were lying or utterly mistaken. And I know the jury will not disbelieve the children.

"Regarding the stone, and regarding the stumble. The accused could not possibly have stumbled over that particular stone, since a larger one was in the way, and he could not possibly have stumbled at all, since it was still daylight.

"But we wish to be fair in this case," he said. "We produced a fiber found in the clenched hand of the little girl, but we could not link it to John Coyle, though Professor Tippett said the hair could have come from his head."

Johnny's lawyer was also effective. He criticized the police for improperly influencing the children, who came forward with evidence two weeks after the murder, and only when a reward was offered, by giving them candy and suggesting to them what they might have seen. He reminded the jury of the spilled cherries forty feet from the body, which indicated that the girl was running away. "It could not have been from John Coyle, because he cannot run." He reminded them that on the evening the dead girl was discovered, the accused helped to carry her body from the bush to the road, then drove back to town with the police chief. "I suggest to you he was acting in a perfectly normal manner. Is it possible for a good, respectable boy to commit a crime like this, the crime of a fiend, at a quarter to eleven in the morning, and walk into the home of a neighbor two hours later, perfectly normal?" He ended by stressing, "Why should you be asked to say the hairs came from Coyle's head when no one else can?"

Today happens to be another August 3. It is hot, bright, in blossom with white sweet clover, daisies, goldenrod, the flowers of the field, and all the old-fashioned flowers in the garden: hollyhocks, dahlias, coneflowers, phlox. Amid the blooms and all the fruit coming on like dusk (blueberries, tomatoes, apples, plums), I watch the evening light. At a quarter to eight it is bright. At fifteen minutes after eight, very clear. At twenty-five after eight the sun sets, and ten minutes later it is still quite clear. The whole expanse of time has gone by, from Johnny's stumbling over the body to the coroner's examination of the body and the crime scene, and the light has moved from bright to quite clear.

The prosecution maintained Johnny knew exactly what he was looking for. Certainly he headed directly for it. From the stump, where he parted company with Miss Rosamond Ivey, it took two minutes, she said, for him to reach the dead girl. Later, when the police timed themselves going in a straight line over the same route, it took them the same two minutes.

He knew exactly what he was looking for. It's an assumption people are quick to make as they replace someone else's doubt with their own certitude. Arguably, he went to where he knew the chokecherries were.

The jury retired at 3:59 p.m. The foreman returned to the courtroom at 7:43 p.m. to ask a question about the hairs. It was obvious that he was deeply troubled and hopelessly confused. The two experts were recalled and in a measure identified the hairs, and the juror seemed satisfied: the blond hairs in the envelope were similar to the blond hairs in the girl's hand. Defense counsel then tried to cross-examine the experts, but the judge would not allow it. The foreman went back to advise the other jurors, and after that it took a mere thirteen minutes for them to return with their verdict.

John Coyle stood erect when His Lordship addressed him. His lawyer sat at his desk with his face almost buried in his hands. The judge consulted a calendar and sentenced Johnny to hang in two months' time, on February 10, 1938.

11

RESCUE

The following autumn, Connie was on her way to the *Journal* offices in downtown Ottawa, Queen Street, when she saw her old teacher walking ahead of her, his squarish head and short neck and broad back, and she called out his name and caught up with him; but it wasn't him. She felt moved even so, and the impression lasted. To find Syd Goodwin one moment and lose him the next doubled, rather than halved, the little shock of recognition.

She was a great walker in those days. Long strolls in Beechwood Cemetery, longer walks on the country trail through the woods in Manor Park, and a considerable trek one weekend to Wakefield on the other side of the river, in Quebec. Inspired by the city editor who had hiked the twenty miles there and back over the course of two days, Connie rose early one Saturday morning, packed a knapsack with sandwiches, apples, a Thermos of coffee and nightclothes, and set out. She crossed the Ottawa

River on Mr. Seguin's ferryboat and continued by foot from Gatineau Point, intending to stay the night in the Wakefield Hotel and walk back the next day. It was late September of 1938, six months after Johnny Coyle's acquittal.

She had only just written up a retrospective on the case in which she allowed herself to speculate about the people involved and the mood of the town. She dwelled on Johnny, a visible yet isolated young man, who had managed to place himself at the center of the drama, first by boasting that he had warned Ethel against picking berries alone, and then by joining the search for her and discovering her body. In playing the hero, he had drawn himself into a tissue of contradictory statements, and the town, with some few exceptions, had believed the worst of him. Reading the piece, I can't tell if Connie's sympathies lay at all with Johnny, but it's obvious they lay with Ethel, with the young girl who had a quiet, independent spirit, "a bright child familiar with that part of the country. She had walked up and down that road so often with her father and mother." The Ontario Court of Appeal, wrote Connie, had found so many irregularities in the trial and such "shockingly confused" testimony about the hairs in the dead girl's hand that, rather than call for a new trial, they acquitted Johnny altogether; in their view, the evidence pointed as much to his innocence as to his guilt. A few months later, the Supreme Court of Canada upheld their verdict, and in June of 1938 Johnny became a free and exonerated man, she wrote, while the guilty party roamed free, possibly in the town itself.

Connie told me later something she didn't include in the article, that Johnny then moved to Niagara Falls, having in hand a character reference given by Parley Burns, and took up his life again under an assumed name.

On her walk to Wakefield, the leaves were more advanced than she had expected and than everyone said they ought to be. The first remarkable ripeness of color, shimmering and intense. Sometimes a flash of pink set back in the woods amid the other colors, actual pink. Deep oranges, burgundies. And at one point a grotesquerie of black: six turkey vultures feasting on a dead deer.

She carried the map the editor had sketched for her, but no flash-light, and the weather, promising at dawn, became troublesome by late afternoon, with a cool wind bringing rain. She was following a route a few countrywomen walked when they brought butter from their farms to the market in Ottawa. Under a winter moon, she would have found her way in the candlelight of snowshine and moonshine, but in the rain it became very dark. She lost the trail. The rain picked up and she took refuge in a thicket of trees, where soft thumps recalled the strange thuds that mystified Tess. In the book it was pheasants (scattered onto far branches by a shooting party and weakened by loss of blood), falling with a sound that revealed its source only in daylight. Then Tess, still months away from her own hangman, went out and wrung their twitching necks. Connie would discover apples falling, and there was someone she knew gathering the bruised fruit.

"You're soaked to the skin," he said.

He took her hand and led her across the field to his farmhouse, hidden by trees. A young man with little education would carve out security in other ways—any work that offered itself, and mostly it was land work, field work, bush work. He was frugal, and intent upon making a solid perch for himself in a quiet place with room enough for a workshop and a vegetable garden and a woodlot.

He led her into his kitchen, and it was large and perfect. A wood-stove crackled out heat, the air quivered with light and warmth. Oil lamps made yellow pools of light. On the table, a spray of black twigs and scarlet leaves poked out of a glass jar. Next to two low windows was a sofa, and over the back of the sofa a hand-knitted child's sweater, and in the far corner of the sofa, his mother.

"Mrs. Graves," Connie said.

His mother stretched out her hand and Connie took it. "I'm Connie Flood. I taught in Jewel."

"Jewel." The sad, thinned face drew back as if slapped.

Connie turned awkwardly toward the coat rack. Among all the surprises was another. His brown leather school bag hung from a hook.

"You didn't get rid of it," she said to him.

Michael took her sopping coat and gave her a big sweater to put on and drew her to a chair next to the woodstove. Her hand still tingled from the warm pressure of his fingers. She sat there dazed by the long hours outside and the sudden turn of events and the marvelous warmth. She was remembering that Mrs. Graves had a sister, or was it a brother, in this part of the world. Was it the brother who had been backward in school? Some relative, some connection. Michael was twenty-three, she calculated. Solid, muscular, handsome, eager, intent.

"I'm so lucky," she said, turning to look at him.

"I couldn't believe it was you."

He held her gaze and she saw that his eyes had grown up, too.

"Pardon me," his mother said to her finally. "You're the first person I've seen from that place since we left it."

The table was set for supper. Michael added another plate and more utensils. She noticed that his hands were black on the knuckles from attending to the stove. He had large palms and smallish fingers, scratched and worked over. Not a reader's hands, or an office worker's hands, or a teacher's hands. He gave her a glass of gin, and she sipped it, glancing around at the large wall calendar of luscious fruits and berries, at the birds' nests on the windowsill, the wood stacked neatly behind the stove. Rain beat on the roof and poured down the windows. She told him about the dead deer on the side of the road, the haunch torn open and feasted upon by turkey vultures. He would have butchered it, he said, taken the haunches for steak. "The rump down to the back of the knee. If the roadkill is fresh, and it would have been."

They sat together for the meal, his mother weak and without appetite. Nevertheless, she said in a proud, proprietary voice, "These are our carrots and our beets."

"Miss Flood was my best teacher. She had it over the others like snow."

"Connie," Connie said.

It was the most delicious meal of her life. After the long, wet, lost walk, to be rescued by Michael, of all people, and taken into this welcoming farm kitchen and fed cheesed eggs (cooked in a frying pan, slices of cheddar melted on top) and gin.

That night she lay in the bed he had made up for her on the kitchen sofa, clean sheets tucked carefully around the cushions, blankets folded and carefully tucked. She stayed awake for a long time, dazzled and bemused, then slept a little, woke up, slept a little more. In the morning she dressed in her dry clothes, still slightly warm from the stove, and went outside. She found the path to the privy. Then she walked around for a while, looking at the house in the early-morning mist, its side veranda and deep windowsills, this place where Michael Graves lived with his mother.

They were three miles from Wakefield, he had told her, so she had almost made it. He knew the route she had taken. In the early days, he said, geese were walked through tar and then sand to toughen their feet in preparation for the same long walk to market.

She headed back to the side kitchen door, and down the far path he came. She waited for him, taking in his small, knowing smile and easy-moving body. He came right up to her and took hold of her elbow with a firm, relaxed grip. Was she ready for breakfast?

She turned toward the house, aware of him right behind her, every inch of him inches away.

The far path down which he had come led to a log workshop a hundred yards from the house. After breakfast he took her into its dusty, aromatic interior of workbench, tables, woodstove, three north-facing windows. From one of the tables he picked up a drawing, a map of early Canada illustrated in the margins with flora and fauna.

"I'm going to be in a book," he said, cocky, self-mocking.

He was boyish, still, through and through. He will be a boyish old man, she thought, if, despite everything that's happened to him, he is boyish now. She had a sudden vision of the old man he would become, and it was very much what I saw myself the night he came to talk about her fifty years later. That evening, in the fading summer light on my back porch, his face grew more and more youthful and handsome. Then the shadows lengthened, they hollowed out his features and he was old. It took fifteen minutes.

Connie looked up at the sound of the car that drew Michael to the open doorway. He waved to a man he called Ralph. A talkative customer, who wanted snowshoes and looked at paddles and admired them, but he had several already, he said, including one made from a single piece of cedar by a native Indian. Michael took the man outside to inspect a half-finished canoe on sawhorses, and Connie sank into an ancient armchair in the corner of the shop. What is it, she wondered, that unlocks the mind and frees it to go deeper, unfreezes the mind and allows it to learn? In Michael's case, the out-of-doors and doing things by hand and being left alone.

He found her asleep in the chair. He said her name. Then he leaned over her, his hands on the arms of the chair, and she opened her eyes. His face was right above hers.

She went up in a flame of shyness and laughter.

"I have to go," she said.

"Already?"

"It's getting on. It's eleven o'clock."

"Is it really? Time flew." His genuine surprise flattered, pleased her. "You haven't seen the woodlot or the pond."

He took her across the mowed field and they entered a large woodlot, and no, he didn't own the farm, not at all, he paid rent and looked after it, a caretaker, if you like. They were here through his aunt, his mother's older sister, who lived not far away and knew the owner. Connie nodded. That was the connection.

The woodlot had a good deal of ash, he pointed out, which was the correct wood for snowshoes, as it was for paddles; a cedar paddle might look nice, but it couldn't take the punishment a paddle had to take; ash was hard as a hammer. She was wearing a blouse patterned white and blue. An open collar. The thick gray cardigan he had lent her the night before. They heard a bird deep in the woods, a blue jay's stabbing cry, and he startled her by saying that almost every day he heard or saw something so beautiful it was like tapping into all the sorrows of the world. It struck her that he felt things more deeply than she did, and expressed them better.

The pond, usually muddied by horses, he explained, was like clear spring water, and the field mowed to the edge of it. A summer so rainy the horses had drunk out of the trough instead of going down to the pond, and the turbulent skies were dramatic and fresh as they were out West. He told her that otters followed the streams this time of year; they followed the water channels to the beaver ponds and scooted along the bottom and went after the frogs curled up in the mud. He wouldn't mind coming back as an otter, he said. "What about you? You'd want to be something svelte. A mink. Or a marten. Minks can be nasty, though. Martens are gentler. Or an otter, too, why not?"

"What are otters like?" she said, smiling back at him.

"Vain and snazzy."

Her smile widened. "You're not a wolf?"

"I'm not a predator, Connie."

"But you're vain."

"Predators play it close to the vest. Sneaky, cunning, weighing things out, panting. Hiding away, but being in charge."

And she almost told him then about having seen Parley Burns.

They sat on his veranda in summer chairs and he continued to speak in that communing way, not wanting her to go. A huge clutch of rose mallow, tied to the railing to keep it from falling over, took his eye. "Look how the pink floats without stress," he said.

"You should have gone on to study science."

"In school?"

"Yes."

"*Sound it out, Michael!*" And he was on the verge of tears, they came that quickly. "You would not believe what recalling that brings back." The immensity of the memory had turned his face red.

She touched his arm and he recovered himself. A moment passed.

"You said you were going to be in a book."

"*Text*book." He wrinkled his nose. "Remember Syd Goodwin?"

"I thought I saw him on Queen Street."

"You probably did. His office is near there. Gilmour and O'Connor."

"No, it wasn't him."

"He works for the public school board. He writes books, too. That's what I'm illustrating, one of his books. And he wants me to teach woodworking classes in the schools."

"That's amazing," she said.

"He came out here to buy a canoe. I knew him right away."

"He was my favorite teacher." She smiled. "He had it over the others like snow."

Then something she had been too hesitant to broach came out quite naturally. She asked if the child's sweater on the sofa belonged to his sister, the little girl who held on to the pump as the house burned down. It did. And without prompting, he told her that Evie was living with his father. His father had family in Toronto. As far as he knew, they were in Toronto.

He looked off into the distance as he said these things, at the fields that rolled toward wooded hills in the north.

"I saw Parley Burns again," she said. His eyes swung back and fixed her with such a savage look that she had to glance away. "He's the principal in Argyle. Up the valley."

"Hasn't he been horsewhipped yet?"

In the afternoon he drove her back to Ottawa, and the next morning she had a dream just before waking. A letter from him, and in the dream she scanned it, then gave it to her mother to read. Her mother got to the end and handed it back, discomfited. Connie looked and saw that his final word was *anatomy*, suggestively, what she might do to his. Then she turned to the beginning, and the letter was full of smudges, grammatical errors, lines that went up and down.

She lay in bed for a few more minutes, thinking about his country kitchen, the sofa against the wall, Evie's sweater displayed across the back. A homespun composition of color, light, comforting objects. All the childhood pleasures and griefs. Moments of sunshine as the day wore on. Gray sky giving way to blue.

She would write him a letter.

They will recede, she wrote of school and its miseries. *If you don't dwell on them, they will recede.*

Two days later, he took the letter out of the mailbox at the end of his lane, thrilled to see her strong, familiar hand. He read it standing right there and misread *recede.*

They will succeed, is what he read. His old torments would succeed.

12

PROPOSAL

For several days during that fall of 1938, the front and back gardens near Connie's apartment on Cooper Street were full of migrating warblers. They balanced on tall coneflowers and picked out the seeds. All the talk was of Hitler's intentions, the yielding of England and France, the "peace with honor." Ottawa's mayor wanted to name a part of Confederation Square "Chamberlain Way" for the statesman of the century, but Connie's editor advised extreme caution in naming any thoroughfare after Neville Chamberlain, who looked, he said, like his own umbrella.

That fall the outlying fields and woods penetrated the city with their cooler climate, river-fed, lake-fed. The temperature dropped, only to rise again. No answer came to her letter, no telephone call either. His mother took messages for him while he worked in his shop, and knowing this held her back from calling, yet her fingers itched to call. It was the age-old pattern of urges suppressed, peace purchased, only to have a resurgence more violent than ever of first intentions.

Around this time Syd Goodwin walked into the offices of the *Journal*. He was forty-one years old, in a marriage that was a prolonged disaster. He would tell Connie that the thought of seeing her again had resurrected his old zest for life. He had intended to surprise her by walking up to her desk unannounced, but she saw him first with one of the quick upward glances that helped her gather her thoughts before attacking the next paragraph, and she leapt to her feet and called his name and embraced him.

He seemed delighted to the core of his being. "Michael Graves told me you were here."

"Michael."

"He's doing some work for me."

"I know. I saw one of the drawings. How is he?"

"Top-notch."

They took the elevator, run by a tired old man who clanged the heavy gate shut with a great crash of metal, down to the lobby and went next door to a sad, dark-looking café. Syd Goodwin was smaller than she remembered, and worn down, but still solid and almost instantly attractive, and nervous, perhaps. When he talked he scratched parts of himself in rotation, back of his head, side of his neck, his wrists, the back of his hands.

He wanted to know how she had come to the *Journal,* and she described returning from France and going for a job interview on a terrifically windy day, when because of her haste there had been no time to comb her hair. "So my hair was like this." Wispy and a little out of hand and long enough, once again, to pull into a simple knot at the nape of her neck.

"Your hair was as it should be."

A pause, a smile as he looked into her eyes, and then he wanted to know what she had worn for the interview. She could not think of another man who would have troubled to ask. She described the brown suede pumps with peephole toes and the linen jacket and skirt, and was he asking because he could see that clothes mattered to her, or because he wanted to imagine in detail what she had looked like, or because he knew that she would enjoy the telling? In any case, women's clothes were not beneath him.

He had been drawn to Ottawa, he told her, the way so many were, drawn by work and not intending to stay, then staying. The public schools were the most progressive in the country, thanks to an unconventional chief inspector of schools who opposed the strap and favored what he himself believed in: school gardens, nature study, art, woodworking, music, good literature, making things with one's hands. Syd had come to help him with his reforms, about five years ago.

Then he didn't know what more to say about himself, and in the silence his emotions almost got the better of him. He muscled his way through his discomposure by looking down and gripping his mug with both hands, by coughing and clearing his throat and taking his ear and twisting it. "Sorry." And he changed the subject back to work. It was one of the few words he said with a Scottish accent. *Weark.* And he said it with the passion Scots reserve for that word alone. Michael had handled his discomposure differently, giving in to it and passing it on to her.

He was writing a textbook, he said, that would present history as a series of disasters and moments of grace. War and peace. The idea had come to him after talking to Michael, who told him he always got stuck on the pointy bits. Will I remember this? The lists of settlements, names of capitals, chronology of leaders. I'll never remember this. "What do you remember?" Weaponry, rubble, disasters, mainly disasters.

He was paying Michael to make graphic, modern-looking illustrations of events for which there were no photographs, replacing the copperplate renditions and pen-and-ink drawings that make history look so arid.

"That's a mistake," she said. "The modern look."

She turned her coffee mug in her large hands. Draped over her shoulders was a black woolen cape made in France with braided frog fastenings, and made to last, to withstand countless winters. She was still wearing it when I was a girl.

"You have to let the past be old," she said. "You can't yank it into the present and tart it up with fancy drawings."

"Imagine you saying a dirty word like that."

He eyed her, and she smiled faintly and looked away. She hadn't expected that, and would have preferred more finesse, yet it did the trick. Sex was in the open now, right between them.

"I'm enjoying this," he said.

"Women make that mistake when they dress too young for their years and look even older."

The truth drew appreciative laughter from across the table.

"I like your idea of disasters," she said. "I'm just saying that we're in the present when the past touches us. If you could teach history as a series of shocks. The shock when something happens, and the shock when we stumble upon it a second time."

"I'm going to enlist you in my enterprise," he said.

She couldn't help herself. She drove to the curve of land beyond the curving road, which seemed to narrow and form an inviting angle there, his house quite visible now that all the leaves were down. It was unseasonably warm, a sunny November morning.

"I thought of coming to see you," she had said to him on the phone.

"Come."

She turned in at the mailbox and followed the lane into the wide-open clearing where house and outbuildings stood, and there she saw a mud-spattered automobile she didn't recognize. She parked and got out of her car. The door of the house opened and Michael came out.

What she had missed in Europe was what she had missed out West, a landscape full of swimming lakes and pine needles baking in the sun and rock you could walk across like banquet tables. Jacob's pillow wasn't so hard to imagine here, how he might have rested his head on a stone and dreamt of a ladder rising up to heaven, and then years later met up with the brother he had wronged only to find himself forgiven. Like Esau, this part of the world was a wild and generous place.

Michael walked across the grass toward her, relaxed-looking, almost sleepy. She had a long time, or it seemed like a long time, to watch him.

Inside, Mrs. Graves lay with her eyes closed on the kitchen sofa. The doctor sat in his shirtsleeves at the table. Michael had been giving him something to eat, a sandwich, a bowl of soup.

"That's a well-traveled Ford," she said to the doctor.

"I learned how to swear driving that Ford."

His sharp, humorous eyes were even brighter when he took off his glasses to polish them with his handkerchief. Michael told him that Miss Flood had been his teacher, and the doctor confessed that geometry had nearly finished him off. "But my father begged me to keep going, to make more of myself than he had." He put his glasses back on and took the cup of coffee Michael handed him. "He came to my room in the dark and tried to persuade me, but I told him I wasn't going back. Then he said I could drop geometry for the rest of the year. You make up your mind you're *not* going to do something and that's when the floodgates open."

And so it is with love. You say no. You turn your back on it. And the next day you find yourself traveling to see him—caught up, transported.

On the sofa Mrs. Graves slept from weakness and medication and not without moans. It was cancer, Michael told Connie after the doctor went on his way. He had called him against her wishes. "But she was in too much pain."

Connie knew about mothers in pain. "Is someone helping you?"

Someone was. The neighbors on either side. Especially Claire, the daughter on the adjoining farm.

He had moved some of his work to the kitchen table to be close at hand when his mother needed him, and he showed it to Connie in the midday light, the illustrations he was doing for Syd. He was

all coolness and self-containment, which surprised her, yet as eager
to show himself as an orchid.

"You're beautiful," she said to him, looking at the skillful drawings.

"But I'm not going to succeed."

"Why do you say that?" Startled by his bleak tone, puzzled.

He got her letter from where it sat under the lamp on the kitchen
table, and she taught him the difference between *recede* and *succeed*.

Then his spirits lifted and he was no longer aloof. She would
have to tread more carefully, she realized.

Just as she was leaving, someone knocked on the door and came
in. In this way she met Claire, the girl he had mentioned, a strong-
boned, good-looking French Canadian, eighteen or so, with whom
he was clearly on easy and intimate terms.

A month later, she was walking with Syd Goodwin past the newly
completed war memorial downtown (neither of them cared for it,
although the foggy air of this unusually mild December gave it a
fleeting beauty), and he slipped his right hand through her arm.
"Marry me."

She saw he was serious and looked away and frowned. "You're
not expecting me to convert?"

His left forearm was in a cast, broken in three places from having
fallen on it with all his weight while playing hockey with his neighbor's sons. But he was happy. She hadn't said no.

"I'm not religious, Connie. I have no interest in synagogue."

"I love the Old Testament. Jacob and Esau, Samson and Delilah.
The Psalms." She was buying time. "I'm not religious either. I haven't
really read the Psalms."

"Don't think I want you to change in any way."

"I was engaged once, in France, until he said I had to give up
smoking. I broke it off."

"Smoke," he said.

His divorce was turning out to be less troublesome than he had
feared. They weren't going to stand in the way, his wife and her
lover. "I should have done it years ago."

"Why didn't you?" she said, and she turned her questioning eyes upon him and all he could do was shake his head.

"What happened to your anger?" she said.

"I still have it. But it didn't do me any good."

"It did *me* good. It was wonderful to see you lose your temper."

That week there were the kind of dark, intense, festering skies that reminded her of a full range of blues in a child's box of colors. She felt a great urge to see the water. On Lady Gray Drive, overlooking the Ottawa River, they stood watching the gulls on the ice moving and forming below, and marveled at how they kept their feet warm. She told Syd she wasn't sure she was made for marriage, for being tied down to one person, although she thought the world of him. He had his good arm around her shoulders. He didn't want to tie her down, he said, it wasn't in his nature. That's what he admired about Judaism. Everything was open to question, at least in theory. In practice, of course, his father had been rigid and punitive, overbearing. He himself hadn't been inside a temple since he was twenty-five, the year his mother died.

"What am I getting myself into?" she said to herself.

He laughed his rich and gentle laugh. "We have to embrace life. Take it on. You can't run from it."

On Sunday they went for a drive on the Gatineau highway all the way to the stretch between Kazabazua and Gracefield, where not so long ago a magnificent grove of spruce and pine had lined the road for a mile or so on both sides. Connie was behind the wheel of Syd's Plymouth, a newer model than hers, and Syd navigated. "It was a lovely bit of road," he told her, "the joy of the beholder. Then the cutters came on the scene a couple of years ago and today half the wood is gone. It's a great pity."

He was thinking, and so was she, of all the hand-planted trees on the prairies, carefully watered and cherished. Here, in this forested world of hills and sheltered valleys, they hated trees. Every so often they passed a rickety blueberry stand left to the winter elements, BLEUETS, one said, and below that, BLEUBARRYS, and he told her about the berry picking he had done as a child in Manitoba, and that his mother had done. In her old age she collapsed between the rows of strawberries from extended exertion in the full sun and they had to carry her home, but the next day she was back picking more quarts for more jam. Once, driving through Manyberries, Alberta, he had stopped and written a note home about the saskatoonberries in abundance, and about seeing a Siberian husky with pale icy-blue eyes ease the dark-blue berries off the twigs with his long wet tongue.

Syd was one of the men she loved. With his ink-stained fingers he pulled out the tree book he kept in his glove compartment in among the road maps. Anchoring it with his cast, he riffled the pages with his right hand and stopped on White Pine and read aloud, "'Especially in dense woods, old trees have straight clear trunks bearing crowns of graceful plume-like branches. According to Josselyn, an early English writer, "the distilled water of the green cones taketh away wrinkles in the face, being laid on with cloths."'"

The passage took her back to the single pine at the confluence of the Bow and Saskatchewan Rivers, and she told him about One Pine—the tree, and the man who reminded her of the tree. Strange Parley Burns. And in talking about him, the story of Susan Graves came out, and he was hearing it for the first time.

He looked out of the passenger window and didn't speak, until finally she asked him what he was thinking.

"I'm thinking that men like that are crippled inside."

"Perverse men."

"Enforcers."

He went on to say that if you were to meet a man as crippled in body as some men are crippled in spirit, you would reach out and help.

"He helped himself," she said. "He's doing all right."

They parked in the sun and ate their winter picnic of sandwiches and tea, their breaths visible, their hands cold. Syd had seen the face of Streicher the Nazi Jew-baiter in a news magazine and his face reminded him of someone, he couldn't think who, and then it came—the public executioner in the old silent film *The Hunchback of Notre Dame.* In Streicher's face, he said, was the secret of the pogroms. "He started out as a schoolteacher. I wish I found that harder to believe than I do."

"The secret of the pogroms."

"Arrogance. Unintelligence. Brute power."

Kristallnacht was barely a month old. "Goebbels," Connie said, "is not unintelligent. He's very educated, very smart. Insane, I think."

"He knows what he's doing. Stupid-shrewd, my grandfather would say. A profoundly unintelligent man."

He sat beside her with his ruined arm, movingly stalwart and full of abundant life.

On their way back to Ottawa, they passed the turn in the road that led to Michael's place and she felt her heart slide sideways in her chest. She glanced back for a fraction of a second, then gazed ahead.

"Syd, I want to ask you something."

"Ask."

"How would you describe me? I mean as a person."

"You're an open book."

She knew what he meant. He trusted her, he thought the world of her, too. But in thinking the world of her, he wasn't giving her a lot of thought.

"Which open book? Am I *Bleak House*?"

He smiled.

"*Winnie-the-Pooh?*"

"Point taken."

"*The Decline and Fall of the Roman Empire?*"

"You're not an open book," he said.

"You wouldn't describe *yourself* as an open book."

"I wouldn't mind if you did."

They were passing a stand of birch and poplar close to the road. Such slender, graceful trees. And she said, "How would you describe Michael?"

"Michael is a deep well."

She couldn't say *Michael* or hear it without a little landmine going off in her body.

"He took my eye the first time I saw him."

"He's too young for you, Connie."

"He's too *moody.*" Overstating, and she knew it.

They passed another berry stand abandoned to winter. "There were two old women in Jewel," she said, "who stuffed newspapers down their stockings when they went berry picking." She darted him a quick look, amused, pensive. "To avoid getting scratched by the brambles."

He reached across with his good arm to rub her gently on the shoulder.

"Don't be afraid, Connie."

With Michael, she would get a lot of Michael. She was grown up enough to know that. With Syd, she would get the wide world.

Mrs. Graves died on New Year's Day, and the next afternoon Connie and Syd drove out to see Michael with gifts of cake and whiskey. They sat in his kitchen and talked. Most of what Michael said he directed to Syd, but whenever he looked her way his glance was so pointed that it felled her.

At the end of the visit, as they were putting on their coats, Syd told him that he and Connie were going to be married.

Michael said, "Well, well, well." He smiled and gave Syd's hand a firm and vigorous shake.

"What about me?"

"You." He put his hands on her shoulders and gave her a quick kiss on the cheek.

He didn't meet her eyes again until he held the car door open for her and she swung her legs inside. Then he leaned down and looked intently at her bundled up in her coat. "Those gloves aren't warm enough."

"You're looking out for me."

"I am."

*   *   *

I have a picture of their wedding. The two of them holding hands, Syd with a white carnation in the buttonhole of his dark suit, fourteen years older than Connie, and Connie like a model from France, her dark hair parted in the middle and pulled back, a style only an oval-faced woman can wear. She's not in white but in a close-fitting knee-length dress that I might have guessed was blue had I not been told it was rose-red. The small wedding party includes my mother and father: Connie's youngest brother is meeting my mother at last, and he's as well groomed as Connie (that was her doing), and my mother so fresh-faced and pretty that I have tears in my eyes looking at her. Her famous head of curls is a shapely heap above her round and comely face; her eyebrows are plucked. She and my father are both nineteen. But the person my eye dwells on most is Michael. He could be a movie star with his brooding, self-involved looks.

The wedding took place on May 10, 1939. They honeymooned for a week in Algonquin Park, not quite missing the onslaught of the blackflies, and sent my father a few black-and-white snapshots, and so I have those, too. Here is the country not in its Sunday best but in its old clothes, unpaved, unfenced, full of character, ungroomed, unvisited, barely penetrable. My favorite of these photos is the one of Connie bronzed by the sun, bare-shouldered, a kerchief wrapped round her head, her face gleaming as she spurts water out of her mouth in a long, insolent gush.

They came back to the royal visit of George VI and Queen Elizabeth, pages and pages of it in the newspapers, and then, a couple of weeks later, three paragraphs about the *St. Louis,* with its cargo of 907 German Jewish refugees who had been denied entry to Cuba. One of the refugees, a forty-eight-year-old lawyer, had slashed his wrists and leapt into the sea.

That night she woke up before dawn and Syd was lying awake beside her, his mind full of Germany and its Jews.

"You asked what happened to my anger."

"Yes."

"I'm older," he said quietly. "And anger doesn't help when the worst is happening."

She was listening to him and listening to the stillness. There's going to be a war, she thought. And Hitler will beat us. And what then?

"I used to think education helped," he said.

"The right education does. The right teachers. You should be back in the classroom. No, you should be running education for the province. If the world were different, you would be."

"I've been lucky, Connie." They were holding hands. "I try not to fool myself," he said.

That was a true summer, the summer of 1939, its long warmth underpinned by the widespread belief that war had been averted and would keep being averted. Even Syd and Connie believed it so from time to time. They hatched the idea of a traveling school, and Michael was their sounding board; they were something of a threesome for a while, congratulating themselves on their mutual affection. The one who was most clear-eyed was the odd man out, Michael. But he was always knowing when it came to love and education. The school was to be modeled on the information-packed vehicles that used to pull into towns and farms on the prairies, bringing the latest ways to fight drought, rust, grasshoppers.

"We'll be nomads," Connie said, imagining a book-filled automobile going into remote parts of Northern Ontario and teaching children in a week what it took months to teach them at school.

The married couple lived in Connie's second-floor apartment on Cooper Street. Now and again the three of them talked so late that Michael stayed over in the spare room down the hall. One night, in the middle of July, Connie made coffee for Michael as Syd headed to bed; their room was directly off the kitchen, hers and Syd's. Michael was planning to drink his coffee and then drive home. "But if you change your mind," Connie said, "the spare room is yours." They talked for a few more minutes and then she followed Syd to bed, leaving Michael to let himself out.

Syd was already asleep. She undressed and got in beside him. He snuggled against her and soon he was aroused. It was quiet beyond the door—Michael had left. She and Syd made love as they usually did, that is to say, satisfactorily for Syd, but not for her: a fast and loving grapple followed by a deep snore. She lay still for a few minutes, then went out into the kitchen, and Michael was at the table smoking a cigarette.

Now it was her turn to feel as mortified as he must have felt at having his failures on full view at school. Her lovemaking overheard and less than stellar. She took herself to the bathroom and relived the sounds that would have reached Michael's ears, the pitifully short rustle and flurry and creak that produced only one cry of rapture. She was an orchard ready to be picked and Syd could not find the fruit.

Michael was still at the table when she came back. He reached for her hand.

"You're shivering," he said.

The murmur and rustle of leaves through the window screen, the wisp of smoke rising from the ashtray. He ran his finger up her bare arm. He knew how to make her happy, he insinuated, and *clang clang clang* went the trolley of her arm.

13

WRECK

They say the past goes on and on, but what I love about the past is that it's over. The past is on its own, just as your children in some essential way are on their own, and your parents, no matter how dependent they might have become, are still on their own. I suppose what I love is independent life and independent lives, and that includes independent love. Brave, unsanctioned, amorous love. And then when that's over, what's even harder: becoming yourself again.

What began between Connie and Michael didn't end. They couldn't stay away from each other. I don't think they tried. There was an evening in late July, during that first summer of her only marriage, when she left Michael's place near Wakefield under gathering clouds and drove home into the darkest sky, black but greenish, like army fatigues. Once she crossed the rumbling boards of the Alexandra Bridge, she turned left and followed Sussex to where it joined Lady Gray Drive, which dipped below the Mint, and down there she parked. Then she walked over to the same spot from which she and Syd had watched the gulls and the ice in December, and took in the huge drama in the summer sky. A French couple watched, too. The wife addressed Connie, telling her about urging her husband on as he drove. "But you hit every red light," she said, turning on him. "And we've missed most of it."

The darkness passed to the east, skirting the city, but around midnight rains hit. Connie was in bed by this time. She got up and lowered windows and watched the thrashing of trees caught in the walloping and windy thunderstorm. When she slipped back into bed, Syd pulled her into his arms.

"It's wild out there," she said to him.

"I hear it."

She was thinking of the French couple, the wife's palpable disappointment and the husband who couldn't do anything right. So far she and Syd had been very careful: what he asked, and what she said, hadn't scratched the smooth yet precarious surface between them.

In the morning she heard on the radio about a campsite in Quebec where pine trees had toppled, falling on a woman and crushing her legs. And she remembered lying on the ground in Michael's woods, looking up at feathery boughs, each gleaming needle a many-sided surface for refracting light. The bruise on her left upper thigh, the colors of a summer storm, had happened on her way out of his bedroom when she walked too close to the corner of his dresser.

"What's this?" Syd said one night, bending over the bruise.

"I don't even remember it happening."

"It's huge."

"I must have whammed into a table on my way by."

"Where?"

"In the kitchen," she said, after a pause.

Syd lay back against his pillow and said nothing. In that long moment she knew that he had guessed and decided not to make an issue of it for now.

*   *   *

On August 2 it was cool enough that Michael burned wood in his cookstove first thing in the morning. The stove was a Forest Beauty built by the Findlay Brothers in Carleton Place; it had a large front cooking surface and a bread oven at the rear. The day seemed to mark a turning point in the season, but then it got warm again and stayed warm.

Connie had awakened beside Syd from a morning dream in which a vicious dog had her right hand in its mouth and wouldn't let go. Its owner was in among the trees. She told Syd about her dream, and he told her about his boyhood dog, who lay on her back to have her belly rubbed and would move his hand with her paw to the spot she wanted stroked. They went for an early-morning walk and sniffed fall in the air. Her sandaled feet were cold, monarch butterflies swanned about. One of them flirted repeatedly with Syd as he talked to it tenderly, asking it if it was on its way to Mexico.

Then a few weeks later, on August 23, came the numbing shock of the Hitler–Stalin pact, and they knew it was all over, the summer of 1939. From then on, Connie worked long hours at the paper. The moment she learned about the invasion of Poland, she called Syd, and they listened together two days later, the third of September, when Neville Chamberlain's sad voice came over the radio declaring war. Syd, who had read *Mein Kampf*, was calmer than she was, but he was always calm in the early stages of a catastrophe. Michael was with them, too, on that Sunday. They walked to Sparks Street after the broadcast, and all the talk around them was of war and how it would be fought. Michael was keyed up and silent. At the end of September, he enlisted.

During the war, many young couples married hastily, urgently, before the young man was sent overseas. They often did so against the advice of their elders. "There was opposition," my father told me once, referring to his own wedding. His father had written to him, counseling him to wait until the war was over, but my father ignored the advice. He married my mother as soon as he graduated,

in May of 1942, and then he enlisted. Connie was teaching in Boston
by then and couldn't make it to the wedding. She joined them for
Christmas at my grandmother's instead. My grandmother was not
an easy person to visit, but Connie knew that—she knew her to be
snobbish, critical, fretful about money, adept at making everybody
feel bad by being blunt and cutting and oblivious. The visit worked
because it was brief. Her gift to my grandmother was a big canister
of tea, rationed in Canada but not in Boston. She gave my parents
a detailed atlas of the world and a handsome magnifying glass to
locate Singapore, Sumatra, Java, Moscow, Guadalcanal.

During that Christmas in Argyle, Connie learned about Parley's breakdown, how he had been given a leave of absence from
school and was at home recovering from nervous exhaustion. It had
become embarrassing, my grandmother said. He had taken to talking to himself in the school hallways, his breath reeked, whatever
he picked up he dropped. Now he couldn't get out of bed. Connie
said she wasn't surprised, but she was. It was like hearing about the
death of someone terminally ill: a shock of a special kind. She didn't
tell the story of Susan Graves. Not then. Certain things we keep to
ourselves for a long time. (Others we spill, as if our minds are brim-
ming bowls that slop over from time to time.) Mental illness ran in
his family, my grandmother said.

Two days after Christmas, Connie packed her bags for her journey back to Boston. My parents went with her to the station at the
end of my grandmother's street. The evening local was running
late, a longer train than usual due to heavy holiday traffic. Amid
all the bustle my mother saw her childhood friend Bess Macswain.
Bess was even taller than Connie, a gangly young woman with a
memorable grin, two years younger than my mother and heading
back to Kingston with a friend.

Passengers boarded at the rear of the train. Connie made her
way to the end of one car and continued on to the next, looking
for a window seat, and then the next, because Parley Burns and his
wife were sitting side by side and she pretended not to see them.
She recognized others, too: the short, aggressive housewife who five

years earlier had noticed John Coyle hanging out a pair of pants and a shirt when she stepped outside to empty coffee grounds onto her flower bed at 7:30 in the morning; and Miss Ivey, who had been searching in the bush and calling out Ethel's name when Johnny joined her, and whose opinion that terrible things were afoot in the world had been more than amply justified.

The train pulled out twenty minutes late. A light rain was freezing as it fell, and they continued to lose time. At every stop in the valley more and more passengers got on, until by Arnprior they were standing in the aisles. The train approached the town of Almonte forty minutes late. Mist rose from the river over which ran the trestle bridge that brought them curving into the station. A few passengers got off, and upward of sixty got on.

Connie stood up to stretch her legs. She caught Miss Ivey's eye and went forward to speak to her. Rosamond Ivey had a limp, not pronounced like Johnny's—she was not in need of a cane but had a slight lameness, an in-turned foot. Connie remembered thinking at the time how odd it was that the two searchers who found Ethel were both lame. Rosamond was a single woman in her thirties, intelligent looking, dressed in a new winter coat. She told Connie that she had noticed her name in the paper a few months ago as the sister of the man who married Hannah Soper; she herself was on her way to Ottawa to spend a week with her brother's family. The train was about to pull out. Connie wished her well and worked her way back to her seat, where her book was waiting for her.

H. L. Mencken's *Newspaper Days*. She opened it and was slammed backward against her seat. The lights went out. Then grinding steel, and another jolt, which flung her into the air, after which she seemed to be falling all the time, grasping on vacancy. She landed on her backside on the station platform, shaken up and bruised, but in one piece when she picked herself up. In front of her was chaos—wreckage and moaning and billowing steam. The cars had splintered into bits, but she was standing like a tenpin that hadn't been toppled. Men were running by and she called out, "What happened?" and one of them threw back, "Struck from behind." All the general noise had fallen away and particular sounds stood out, hanging in the air. A little girl covered in blood, except for her long yellow curls, was wailing out a Montreal address. Connie went to take her by the hand, but a trainman holding a lantern got to her first. Then came a distant siren, the fire brigade was on its way, and it occurred to her that the wreck might burst into flames.

I was just opening my book and then there was carnage. She said these words in her head to Michael.

It started to snow as she stood there. Damp, heavy flakes, just this side of rain. They melted on her face and on the ground. She turned in a circle and saw her handbag upright amid the rubble like an unbroken wineglass; she picked it up and clutched it to her chest. Then she recognized a voice asking for help and went toward it and saw a woman lying on the ground, her legs clearly broken, and it was Rosamond. She knelt beside her and put her handbag under her head. Rosamond's face glittered and Connie wiped the tears with her fingers but they were bits of broken glass.

Soldiers came with stretchers and Connie stepped back. They lifted Rosamond up as if she weighed nothing at all and carried her away. She retrieved her handbag, by now tromped on by pairs of boots, and stood for a moment wiping it with her ungloved hand. Then she was being led across the street into a stone house and given a blanket. Other passengers were there, all of them in shock. Parley Burns was standing next to his wife. He was patting her head like a boy patting a strange dog.

Connie went over to them, and since he didn't appear to recognize her, she reminded him who she was.

He said, "You avoided me on the train."

His breath smelled so bad that she took a step back. It smelled of rotten meat, gross decay. She took a further step to the side to get out of range.

His wife reached for his hand and held it. There was a sympathy between them that Connie hadn't imagined, and perhaps it was new.

A boy of about eight drew her attention. He was saying that he was awfully tired and couldn't he stay here for the night. And just beyond him, sitting on the floor, was a man with broken glasses and blood on his forehead. Someone gave Connie a cup of tea, scalding, bitter, and as she drank it, the journalist in her came back to life. *I should be at the station asking questions.* In her handbag she had a small notebook and pencil. She went back across the street to the station and began to collect the information that she would feed by phone to the night editor at the *Journal.*

It turned out that a solid-steel troop train from Petawawa had plowed into their passenger train from behind, driving right through two of the ten wooden cars and halfway through a third, scattering bodies into the night. Some of the injured were being taken to the local hospital, others to the theater just down the street from the train station, where they were given first aid. The dead were being carried to the old guardroom downstairs in the town hall. Connie made her way over there, following the downhill slope, treacherous in the wet snow. On the stone floor in the basement, she counted nine bodies laid out under gray blankets, and more were being brought in. A young doctor, nervous, overtalkative, told her that the male victims were fairly easily identified from the cards and licenses in their wallets or pockets, except for one man, who had been stripped of his clothing, even his socks, by the force of the impact. But the women's handbags had been thrown about in the snow on all sides of the train. He said it was going to take a lot of work to remove the slivers of glass and bits of lace and silk from the cuts and gashes in their mangled faces. He was referring to the injured, she realized, not the dead.

Relatives began to stream in. They came by car from all over the Ottawa Valley, having heard the news by radio or phone. They entered the temporary morgue, and provincial policemen turned back the blankets as they went up the long row. Connie heard a man say he was an undertaker looking for his niece. He said his name was Macswain. She saw him kneel beside one of the bodies and knew by his stillness that he had found Bess, my mother's friend.

Then word came that the undamaged part of the train would be leaving before long to make room for the hospital train coming in from Smiths Falls, and Connie returned to the commotion of the station. She dug coins out of her purse and used a pay phone, and the operator put her through to the *Journal*. She couldn't remember the night editor's name, but he remembered her. She told him she was in Almonte and he sucked in his breath, already aware of the wreck, thrilled to get anything firsthand. After that call, she made another, and Syd picked up the phone.

She had left him after a year of marriage, after they celebrated their anniversary in the Wakefield Hotel, where he reached across the table and took her hand and said, "Here's to our life together, love." His vulnerable, trusting, knowing face made her feel so fraudulent and so pained for him and so trapped that all she could do was hold his hand and stare at the white tablecloth. She knew a woman in Boston, someone she had met in Paris, who had contacts in education, and she obtained a teaching job in a Boston private school.

She and Michael were writing to each other. On paper he was bashful and sweet and unpunctuated. *Well I've outshone myself here I am on my third page.* He was on a bomber base in England, a parachute rigger with the R.C.A.F., part of the ground crew and relatively safe. *I'm about all washed up as far as talk goes so I'll say so long Sweetheart for now.*

She told Syd, "I'm all right. I'm perfectly all right, but there's been a train crash."

A few hours later, when her shortened train of six cars pulled into Ottawa's Union Station, Syd was waiting for her with a Thermos of coffee, a flask of brandy, an orange, cold sausages, boiled eggs, apples; also, mittens, a hat, a scarf, a sweater. He had hoped to take her home with him, but she refused, and he kept her company instead until her connecting train left, shepherding her through the tunnel under Rideau Street to the Château Laurier's lower level, then up into the hotel's grand lobby, where he claimed two deep armchairs next to a small table.

Her head was splitting and she asked if he might have some aspirin. From one of his pockets, he fished out a pillbox. Watching him fiddle the tiny box open with his big fingers, she thought her heart might burst as well as her head. He was the same prince of a man in the same tweed jacket, two years older than the last time she had seen him. From another pocket he pulled out a deck of cards. They played rummy for an hour and she beat him soundly. She loved to win at cards.

"I saw Parley Burns," she said. "He and his wife were on the train. They weren't hurt. He still has his Hitler mustache. Well, he's lost his mind, they say."

They sat back and regarded each other with love and sadness. She had thought of him in the midst of calamity, which meant a great deal to him. He was still happy to see her, and that was an enormous relief. She wanted to know how things were with him. He answered as he peeled the orange for her and refilled the Thermos cup, lacing the coffee with brandy. He missed Putman, he said, and she nodded, remembering his old boss at the school board, an irresistible character with a face like a stump, who had died two years ago, and perhaps it was just as well, Syd was saying. Everything the two of them believed in, the child-centered learning they had fought for in the thirties, was sliding away in the face of the new drift toward discipline, patriotism. He was thinking more and more about moving into adult education, probably in Toronto with the Workers' Educational Association; he admired Drummond Wren. And as for the war, he felt more hopeful now that the thought of defeat was eating into Hitler's brain.

He stopped talking. "You look radiant," he said.

"Syd."

"I would not lie to you."

They didn't speak of Michael.

Two days later, it started to rain in the valley. It rained for twenty-two hours. Then came a blizzard that covered every surface with snow and crystal ice. In Ottawa all the trams stopped running. New

Year's Eve, the quiet was broken by the sound of bells on horse-drawn sleighs pulled out of retirement as a teacher might be when midway through the year a colleague cracks up. At the beginning of January, the investigation into the wreck got under way. Thirty-six passengers were dead; 207 others were injured. On the second day of the inquiry, the conductor of the troop train committed suicide.

During that first week of January, Parley Burns went out on a supervised walk with several other inmates from the mental asylum on the St. Lawrence River, where he had been deposited by his wife. They passed ice-thickened hedges that looked like great masses of steel wool, they passed a maple tree that had a dozen birds frozen to its limbs.

A January thaw melted everything. Wrapped in a blanket, he sat outside against the south wall and absorbed the sun. Birds flitted from branch to branch. A deer came out of the woods and nibbled at grasses exposed by the thaw. The deer took note of the man in the fur hat and bedcovers, and discerned that he was no danger at all.

14

FLOODS

I didn't know any of this for a long time. Connie we seldom saw because we were in Ontario and she lived in Boston. Years went by. She sent us books, she wrote excellent letters. It's easy to fall in love with someone who writes excellent letters. Sometimes, unforgettably, she came for Christmas.

There is such intricate movement in things as they happen and such stiffness and resistance when you go back and try to reconstruct them. Conversations, a series of thoughts—their light-footed routes are untraceable after the fact. But I remember it was 1982 and the day after Christmas, a day always conducive to discoveries as we undergo a letdown so intolerable that by early afternoon the children and uncles and fathers finally expel themselves into the snow. The few who remain indoors breathe a deep sigh of relief and the house relaxes and stories emerge. And so it was on this day. I was in the kitchen with Connie and my mother, leaning my backside against the oven that was heating up the dinner I had prepared ahead of time; nothing else needed to be done. The house was quiet. My daughter had a fever and was lying on the chesterfield. My father, who wasn't feeling well either, was asleep in his wing chair among the African violets. For some reason my mother repeated something her high school principal used to say with cutting sarcasm to certain students. "Sometimes I sits and thinks," she said, "and sometimes *I just sits.*"

"Parley Burns," Connie said, and a world of meaning passed between them. They began to reminisce for my benefit, since I was hearing about Parley for the first time. He had married one of the two daughters of the previous principal, my mother said, and since the other daughter lived with them, he might as well have married both. I asked her what the two women were like, and she said they were tall, bony, lifeless. So was his stepdaughter, "Doris the Brain."

"He might have married me," Connie said. "He asked me to once, in a way."

"But he was *strange.*"

"He was unbalanced and dangerous."

My mother's eyes widened, but she didn't dispute it.

I hung on every word, amazed that I had never heard of him before, this man with the singular name: Parley Burns, the principal who taught French. But so many things are never discussed at all, never mentioned, never asked. It takes a certain mood, a certain time of day. The room empties out and in the welcome stillness we find the stray crumbs of our own thoughts.

"I would be reading on the veranda," my mother said, "and he would walk by our house. We would see each other out of the corner of our eyes, but give no sign of recognition."

She leaned forward a little as she confided in us, though she wasn't confiding so much as reliving a childhood I couldn't get enough of. Her cat would have been draped across her shoulders. Mickey. He rode on her shoulders even when she walked the two blocks to get the paper.

"There was something between him and Miss O'Connor, the Latin teacher," she said. "Whenever he came to the door of her classroom, she blushed a violent crimson from her throat to the roots of her hair."

"Like Mary Miller." Connie's interjection was a dry aside. She was standing close to the window, above which sat a fine old mahogany clock on a small shelf, a clock that had been passed down from one Flood to another. It was a great mystery to me how so confident and sociable a sister could have such a blustery, taciturn brother. He was a fact one room away, my father, the former high school principal. (Recently, in the grip of making dinner one night, it occurred to me to wonder if my mother was afraid of him too. I had realized suddenly how alarmed I was, how alarmed I always was, that dinner would be late. I was my mother at the stove, pots rattling, blood pressure rising, face flushed with steam.)

My mother went on describing Miss O'Connor. "She lived around the corner from Parley Burns and he lived on my street," she said. "Every day at lunch he walked her home, and every day after school he did the same. But she was a devout Roman Catholic, who advised her students to read as much as possible, since we would never have so much free time again, but cautioned us *not* to read *Anthony Adverse* because the author had been married three times in a cave."

I was still absorbing the marriages in the cave when my mother said, "Once, the elastic in her knickers gave way and they fell to the floor."

Perhaps elastic was less well made in those days. Or else women wore their underwear long after someone nowadays would have thrown it out. That seems most likely. "And what did she do?" I asked, delighted by these glimpses into an uncensored, unofficial past.

"She scooped them up and stuffed them in her book and continued on, blushing like mad."

I asked if Miss O'Connor was pretty. Ever on the lookout for romantic possibilities.

She was not. But she took pride in her appearance, as did Miss Wood, the secretary who was also in love with Parley and who wasn't pretty either, but who had the distinction of owning a genuine Harris tweed coat.

"Parley stood sentry in the hallway," my mother said, "and more than once I had the bad luck to walk the length of the hall alone and under his eye. He watched my progress the whole way and it made my skin crawl."

Connie nodded with complete understanding, and my mother continued, her face smoother, younger, ruminative. "He must have had a voice, but I have trouble giving him a voice. Can I say he had a gray voice?"

"You can," Connie said. "That's perfect."

"His one joke was to say to a student without an answer, 'Please go away and let me sleep. I would rather sleep than eat.' Which may or may not *be* a joke."

Still looking for the larger story, I wanted to know if there were certain students he persecuted, and she said that generally he directed his sarcasm at the big louts in the back. "Not at one of them in particular," she said, raising her hands (the thumbs of which curved backward into impressive reverse Cs, sculptor thumbs, like Henry Moore's) and letting them drop slowly, expressively. "Just a canopy of derision that settled over everyone in the room."

The past made my mother eloquent. It still does.

Connie was wearing a dress of black wool, simple, elegant, as all her clothes were. You have to have the body, the height, the narrowness of hips, the hair. The dress was fitted yet loose and made by a seamstress, one of three articles of clothing that cost a small fortune but were worth it, she said, because you needed nothing else when you traveled.

She was the easiest person in the world to be with, thanks to her knack of getting attention without asking for it and of conversing in an informed way about any subject, thereby earning my father's hard-to-win respect. But he was putty in her hands, my father. And because he loved and admired his big sister so much, my mother did too, and Connie became an endless source of fascination to me.

I said to her, "What did you mean before? You said Parley asked you to marry him in a way."

A wave of something crossed her face, old embarrassment, perhaps, something indescribable, but she didn't look away from me. She said, "We didn't like each other."

"Then why?"

"I don't know. It's not the sort of thing." She stopped. "I might have been the only one who talked to him. Maybe he thought I forgave him."

I was aware of the light outside and the peacefulness inside, the afternoon hours of a Sunday that held no terrors because school wasn't about to begin tomorrow.

"Forgave him for what?"

She explained for what, and as she did so her voice filled with grief. She told the story she had not told anyone since telling Syd. For a long moment we were silent, stricken. The walls of the past had blown away and we were in the unprotected fields of memory.

"Then when young Ethel Weir was raped and murdered, I wondered," she said.

My mother's eyes locked on hers. "I thought of him, too. But the hair in her fist was blond."

Independently, without even knowing his past.

"Such a strange man," my mother said again. "One day, when he and some other inmates at the asylum were taken for a walk, he committed suicide by throwing himself in front of a truck."

The heat from the oven pressed into the back of my upper thighs, my bottom. I waited for her to go on.

"I suppose it happened during the war," she said. "I'd moved away from Argyle."

"It was 1943," Connie said. "Six months after he went into the asylum. He was forty-nine."

"The Brockville asylum," my mother added. "Argyle didn't have one."

"Not the one in Brockville," said Connie. "A rest home, closer to Cornwall. A sanatorium. But he's buried in Argyle. I went to see his grave."

One of the things I most admired about my aunt was that she never apologized for her curiosity, ever.

"He's in a large impressive plot with his wife's family, about two hundred feet from Ethel Weir. It took me a while to find Ethel. There's just a grave marker in the long grass."

"And the girl who burned alive," I said.

"Susan Graves. Well, what was left of her would have blown away in the wind."

Her name is her grave, I thought, as if I were studying *Hamlet* again.

We went outside, leaving my father and my daughter asleep in the living room. A light snow was falling and no one else was about. We took the street to the corner, turned left, and made our way past the old farmhouse of pale-yellow brick, the original house in a neighborhood that used to be an orchard and now is choked with mega-houses and three-car garages. "Travesties," my mother called them, "godawful travesties." She was looking at them with the eye of someone who had grown up poor, a girl for whom Christmas dessert was either red Jell-O or green Jell-O. Every year it alternated. If it had been red at her mother's, then it was green at Aunt Em's. Every year, no matter who carved the bird, as the youngest child, my mother got the neck. She claimed she didn't mind. "It was turkey and it was good," she said.

We were making our way to Reservoir Park and soon we were there, walking under trees and past the occasional person out with a dog. At the small sliding hill we caught up with the rest of the family, and my mother was distracted away from her life and into their lives, a great loss, it seemed to me, since now she put on a concerted show of good nature and good fun. I wanted her to myself, that's all. Instead, her attention shifted toward my brother Ted, who had been so ill. He was frolicking with his children and his nephews, including my small son, and the sight of them delighted her. Connie and I watched for a few minutes. Then because she was cold, and I wanted to check on my daughter, the two of us walked home.

On Christmas Eve my father had seemed very tired, standing in the kitchen between the counter and the door that led to the dining room. He said he had been thinking a lot about his father. I asked him why.

"Because I'm afraid I'm getting more and more like him. More like him, less like my sister. He was quiet and I'm getting quieter."

He was coming down with the flu, although he didn't mention it, and although he got sick, he wouldn't get as sick as my daughter; he didn't miss a meal.

"We never got along," he said. "We tolerated each other. He wasn't any good at sports. He couldn't catch a ball if you gave it to him on a silver platter. I was disgusted with him, to tell the truth."

An honest man, my father. I love that about him. "You've always been quiet," I said. "There's nothing wrong with that. You move between being quiet and being the center of things."

He shrugged. His eyes—the pouches under them—were as soft as petals. Or pastry after it's been in the oven ten minutes or so, a certain shininess to those soft, thick folds.

"He was a rotten farmer, too. And why he married Zoe." My father shook his head and stared at the floor. "She was a terrible stepmother. After that, Connie stopped coming home."

He looked not only tired but much older, as did my mother.

The next morning Connie had pulled into the driveway, and my father was transformed. Her methods were invisible. She didn't make overt efforts to question him or include him in conversation, but he said more in an hour with her than in a month with anyone else. She was the only one who called him Jimmy.

Outside, as I write, a slow blush is working its way down the maple tree next door. Over the course of two weeks it has descended from forehead to cheeks, face, neck, shoulders, knees: the reverse of what happened to Miss O'Connor and Mary Miller. With some people the dead giveaway is the blush. With others it's the teeth, the telltale teeth nervously clicked or strenuously sucked. In my family it's the eyes. We have no control over our eyes. You would think we were all heart, the way we cry.

After our walk in the snowy woods, and before my Boxing Day dinner was served, we gathered in the living room with the poems we had written to my oldest brother, who had turned forty in the fall. I have a picture of Connie from that evening. She was seventy-one, and the expression on her face is calm, aware, inviting. I knew none of the intricacies of her romantic life, not then, except that she had been married once and briefly to a Jewish man, and had not converted, which might have been part of the problem, my parents thought.

This was the first time all of us had managed to get together since my brother's birthday in October. He sat in the rocking chair and we gathered around. My mother began first with her poem, and after two lines her eyes filled and her face quivered, an uncontrol-lable working of mouth and jaw. "Here, Daddy," she said. "I can't."

My father took my mother's poem, but read his own. He got to the end of his. My mother's effort he passed on to my sister, who passed it on to me, and I handed it to Connie, barely equal to read-ing my own verses, let alone my mother's. We leaked and dabbed and quivered and choked up, while my brother listened with embar-rassment and pleasure. The poems were not sentimental, let me hasten to say. But there was something about trying to express our love for my sweet-tempered oldest brother, even humorously, that made us dissolve.

"Thank you, Daddy," my mother would say at the end of a long car trip, when my father had brought us safely home. "You're a hero." She would pat his arm, having over the course of the long drive rested the back of her hand, palm up, on his knee. On hot summer days, eating our lunch on the back piazza, as my parents called the flat outcropping of rock at the far side of the house, my father would run his hand up her dress and stroke her upper thighs. She had a series of sounds for that, low warbling purrs of acquiescence and contentment. Just as she had a series of sounds whenever tension and irritability left their moorings and floated freely about the room. Then her throat would turn into a babbling brook that relied upon a dry near cough and the beginnings of a soft laugh merging with a hum. Awkward silence or conflict or too much feeling of any kind, and she would run to the piano in her throat and play a tune.

On the night of the birthday celebration, she stopped her eyes from overflowing by raising her hand and whacking herself on the side of the head. Whack, whack. First one side, then the other.

Connie read my mother's poem. She got to the end without shedding a tear, then she gave my brother a hip flask engraved with his name.

She represented everything that was worldly, relaxed, at ease with itself. It's rare to meet anyone with such presence, and a gift when the person is your aunt and therefore a part of your being, but the better part, the part you aspire to.

While everyone else did the dishes, my mother went to my six-year-old daughter, who was lying under blankets on the chesterfield, to take her temperature. She had been too busy to give her much attention until now. My mother loved Christmas, but it drove her out of herself because there was so much to do and she did everything. I can't say I appreciated this at the time. I was too taken up by the contrast between my mother and Connie, who had arranged her life to be free of such tonnage.

"I'll have you know," my mother said, shaking down the thermometer, "that I am a registered nurse. Past tense." And my daughter giggled, very pale against the pillows. My mother perched beside her on the edge of the chesterfield. "Under the tongue," she said, and slipped in the thermometer, as gentle as she always was with our dogs, and sometimes was with children if they weren't making any demands. "You, my dear, have a temperature of 102."

"Is that bad?" my daughter said.

"No, that's good. It means your body temperature has risen to kill all those germs. When it gets to 105, then we'll call the ambulance."

My daughter smiled. Her grandmother's voice was playful and full of knowledge.

"Shall I do this properly and take your pulse?" My mother took my daughter's wrist between her fingers. "Uh-oh. No pulse. Get me a feather . . . get me a feather, as King Lear said."

My daughter giggled again, and I explained that years ago they would hold a feather over your mouth to determine if you were still breathing, still alive.

My mother went on in the same musing, gentle, heartbreakingly gentle tone, "Poor King Lear. He lost his favorite daughter."

And then my other brother came into the room, the brother who had been so ill. The brother who had always been the star of the family with his clever poems and easy wit and high marks and remarkable smile. Ted came into the room and I realized how much my parents had aged and why. My mother didn't move from the side of her grandchild, but she turned with a different kind of worry to look at her son, and I saw her there holding her life in her hands—a childhood when she lost her beloved father and always received the neck, a youth when she had to share the bed of a fretful mother, a marriage in which she maneuvered and mothered and finally made time for herself, an old age so diffident she didn't know how to ask Ted without offending him, how to ask without seeming to pester, if he was feeling better or worse, this son, my brother. I saw her life spill out of her hands like water. The quality of her love washed away all questions, not just hers, but mine.

The next day the doorbell rang and someone answered it, my father, perhaps. At the sound of the visitor's voice, Connie stood up and sat down again. She stood a second time and went to the top of the stairs—in my parents' house the living room was on the second floor. She looked down at the figure below and I saw her center of gravity shift: she was still with us, but she had entered another room.

She put her hand on the railing and descended, moving easily and looking twenty years younger than she was. It's fat that packs on the years and makes us unrecognizable. Fat, stiffness, hair loss, brain loss. And child-bearing. Connie had no children.

I went to the top of the stairs and looked down. She was speaking to a man no taller than she was, but he seemed taller. His voice was outsized, too—a carrying, open-air, woodsy voice, unlike any other. He raised his eyes and held my glance. I was startled by his good looks. He was in his sixties, I would learn, yet he seemed to be in his prime, and not only to me.

Connie brought him upstairs and introduced him as her friend Michael Graves.

"Graves," I said.

He had been shaking my mother's hand and now he reached for mine.

"The name of the girl in the fire," I said.

"You mean my sister."

"Susan Graves." Since either you back away from a faux pas or you stare it down.

He held on to my hand, and his blue eyes, more faded than a young man's, took me in. Then he let my hand go and said to all of us, "I was Connie's worst student."

"Don't boast," she said.

I had never seen sex mow everything down before. His eyes stayed on her face, assessing, measuring, saying everything for her benefit, waiting. She was like a moonrise in her black dress—her wavy hair like silver, her unperturbed skin.

Years before, she had used my bedroom to change her blouse and revealed in the process a black lace brassiere and ample, spilling breasts. Such things were foreign to my mother's chest of drawers (and chest).

She was silver and ivory. He was dark hair and ruddy cheeks. (My mother's father was almost the same age when he lay in his coffin, not a gray hair on his sixty-three-year-old head.) They were two halves of something tremendously exciting. Her composure and his youthfulness. Her chaste raciness, and his blue eyes and manly charm.

Questions are an erotic tool, I was going to say. But even as I have the thought and write the words, I wonder whether I know what I'm talking about. I suppose I mean that the right question opens the other person up, and sometimes the right question is the one no one else will touch. A bit later, when Connie and my mother were in the kitchen, and Michael and I were alone in one corner of the living room, I asked him how his father had lived with himself after the fire. It was brazen of me, even more than I realized, but the story was so fresh in my mind and I was full of questions.

"My father." He narrowed his eyes. He had taken the armchair beside the fireplace and he was sitting forward, almost on the edge of the seat. I was on the sofa a couple of feet away, close enough that I could imagine no one else heard me.

He said, "The key to her room was in his pocket, and he was in the store."

It sounded like a nursery rhyme. His small laugh was bitter, and he began a slow rocking of his upper body. Strong-looking shoulders and arms, something of a belly.

"She had an oil lamp in her room," he said. Then, "You don't know what I'm talking about."

"We have them at the lake."

"My father believed she set the fire. He blamed *her* as much as himself. Then ten years later, he was dead. Highway 60. Don't drive when you're drunk. And so on and so forth."

"Michael."

"Connie, Connie, Connie. I should take my own advice."

She was hovering a few feet away and now she steered the talk to safer ground. But I gathered from what Michael had just said that he was fond of the bottle, too.

My father would say afterward that Michael wasn't good enough for Connie. A woman can't marry a man less educated and younger than herself. But you fall in love with someone who welcomes every question. Michael took a run at whatever you asked him, and he had a way of seeing things and putting them, a turn of phrase, that you didn't forget. He called our dog Professor and scratched his ears until Jet's arthritic old bones melted into the carpet. Our dog reminded him of a dog he remembered very well, an old black Lab named Professor, who had slept on a rug near the woodstove when he was small. "The thing is, the dog died before I was born."

"Then what were you remembering," I said into the long silence, "when you remembered the old dog?"

"Well, now, there's an easy explanation, but you have to be a little loose in your thinking." His smile was infectious. "My uncle had a dog named Professor, and I was named after my uncle. I was having my uncle's memory."

I began to understand Connie's interest in past lives.

I thought of my grandmother in me. I had her name and, according to my mother, her wretched personality; we were never a twosome, my mother and I, but a threesome, since I reminded her of a mother she couldn't abide. Now I digested the possibility that it wasn't always me who was remembering, it was me as namesake having my grandmother's curdled reactions to the people and situations in her life.

"Show her," Connie said to Michael. "Go on."

He raised his pant leg on a long, purple, irregularly shaped birthmark. His uncle had died in a bar fight, it turned out, knifed in the chest and the leg. Michael said there was a theory afoot that birthmarks were wounds incurred in a previous life.

I told him we had competing birthmarks. I raised my pant leg and showed the big brown saucer on my knee.

"I *thought* we had a special bond," he said, making himself even more irresistible.

"Michael, don't you think she looks like Susan?"

He studied my face. And even though I wanted to hear what he might say, I said to Connie, "You're making that up."

The truth is I was probably too intrigued. Even though I was in my thirties, married and with two children, I was as suggestible as a child.

But she wasn't making it up, she said. Other cultures were more open to such possibilities. She had heard about an Inuit child who refused to fly, terrified he would never manage to get out of the plane; at the time he was too young to know that he had been named after an uncle who died in a plane crash and was found inside the aircraft, directly in front of the door. "Syd told me that," she said to Michael.

"Syd?" I said.

"My ex."

"The sweetest man alive," Michael said.

He stayed for lunch, but couldn't be persuaded to stay for dinner, and during the time he was with us he rose to a fine pitch of sociability as solitary people often do. Over lunch we talked about northern summers, since my sister was about to return to her life in Mexico. She fondly described her childhood swing attached to the elm tree, the red currant bushes so close she could grab a handful of berries as she swung by, and the little summer house with its latticed walls deep in the woods where she had played and had tea parties with sugar water for tea. Michael went on a little riff about how summers end in the north—how the blue jay's call gets harsher, how flies and insects come inside on currents of warm air, how the shade of green in the woods takes on an older, weatherbeaten look, and foxes sit under streetlights in the country and snap up the bugs and moths that get fried and fall.

We took to him and he to us. He remarked upon our large, admirably close family and said he was a loner. He sounded rueful, proud. That's when I lifted the framed photograph of a family reunion off the wall to show to him, and he delighted in identifying Connie. "There she is," he said. She was standing on the left, slightly apart, slim, stylish, wearing a turtleneck and slacks, her head high and aware of itself, her posture excellent. The rest of us looked scruffy, gangly, or squat.

I went to rehang the photograph—he and I were standing side by side—and he offered to do it for me. Then, "You're as tall as I am." And he stood back and let me do it.

All that amusement and chivalry in his eyes.

Something else about him. He commented upon my mother's paintings. He asked who had done the big canvases, four feet by five, of arctic lichens on rock, splashes of bold, intricate color— jewels. Then he went right up to them and said, "They're beautiful, mysterious and full of meaning."

15

MAINE

I was a loner, too, as a girl, given to solitary walks and drawn to berry patches, as patient with them as with the slowest-moving book. I had no patience at all with my family. I used to imagine myself as a cheering orphan heading to Boston to live with my aunt. My loyalties then were a mesh of simplicities and complications, and only understandable in the shade of my mother's oak-like loyalty to my stern father and her expectation that I would be a good sport in all ways and at all times, and helpful besides. It has taken me a long time to reconstruct my loyalties, to redirect them toward my mother and my father, and to rest in that hard-won place. The first triangle in one's life is always the father, mother, child. It sets the troubled tone.

Eight months after the Christmas I've just described, I left my husband and two small children in Montreal, where they stayed with my mother-in-law, and took a run down to Connie's summer cottage in Maine, an island house with veranda, sleeping porch, wild roses with huge hips. In those days I used to visit her every summer. This time I stayed only the weekend, and one night we didn't go to bed at all, one of those warm August nights when your hands are full of what's slipping through your fingers, namely, summer in all its glory.

My visit overlapped for an hour or two a visit by one of her former students, a freckled, adoring young woman with a steady laugh and a scanty top, who told me that Connie used to bring the woods into school with her and take her classes into the woods. She recalled one March day when, in their enthusiasm, a few small pupils, she among them, brought Connie a handful of bluish-pink baby mice they had found in a nest in the snow. The mice were warm in the palm of her hand, squeaking, soft, *breathing*. She felt the pounding hearts, stroked the velvety skin. "Ah," Connie had said to them. "Well, now, we'll have to put them back or they will die."

Nancy was the young woman's name. She told me that my aunt was the best teacher she had ever had. "I read newspapers because of you," she said to Connie. "I read poets. Do you remember taking us into a farmer's field to study the stars? I've never looked at the sky the same way. You opened up the universe to me."

After Nancy drove away, heading back to Boston, Connie told me she worried about her. She was a promising girl from an unpromising family. Her parents hadn't armed her with enough knowledge to know how to say no, and that made her easy pickings for the kind of man who cruises around targeting vulnerable girls.

"Vulnerable girls," I said, thinking of my daughter, thinking of myself.

"Girls who aren't especially popular and will be flattered by their attentions and sucked in and used for sex."

We were sitting at the square wooden table in her kitchen. "And how do you say no?" I asked.

"Repeatedly, firmly, looking them in the eye. You don't vacillate."

"Vacillation." I dwelled on that word too, applying it to my own recent circumstances. "But you vacillate because you're vacillating in your mind."

"I know."

Then looking down at the table, I said to her, "This summer I became very attracted to a man." And, just once or twice raising my eyes to her wise and lovely face, I told the story. How he had called me and said I had made a strong impression on him. That he was much older than I was. He had other women in his life, I was sure of that. I was glad he was so old, it was a lot easier to dismiss a man who had hairs growing out of his nose. But I couldn't stop thinking about him. I thought of little else.

"Obsession." Connie said the word as if she understood it all too well.

I said with a smile, "Passion." Mocking myself, but serious. Passion goes further back than obsession. Much further back than the current neediness. (As if calling something *neediness* should make it easier to get over. It has nothing to do with anything that is easy to get over.) I had been reading Homer and those passionate Greek playwrights I can never keep straight.

"You would pay such a price," she said to me. "You have so much to lose. And you have to think of the effect on your children."

I agreed with her. "But the behavior that seems unforgivable to a third person doesn't seem unforgivable when you're *in* it. Hurting someone? It doesn't matter."

"I know. We become children again. It's the 'I' wanting what it wants."

Her kitchen was my favorite room in the house. It had the original dark pine paneling and large cupboards with multipaned doors. I toyed with the salt shaker on the table, while she sat across from me, her measured self.

"I thought something was weighing on you," she said.

"It could be any number of things. It doesn't take much for me to feel weighed down."

"What is the need in you that makes you respond to him?"

I considered this. She was having none of passion, she was boiling things down.

"Romance?" I ventured, although identifying a single need seemed impossible and beside the point. "Having someone attracted to me?"

"Couldn't you satisfy that need within yourself?"

"Masturbation?"

"But is it just a physical need?"

"It's not even a need I knew I had. It's inseparable from the man who ignited it. I just want to see him walking toward me. I just want to see him again. And when I see him, sometimes he bores me to death."

"So what does this man, who bores you and attracts you, what need in you does he fill?"

Here was the cautious amber of a seriously independent woman. But she was seventy-two and I was thirty-seven.

"Tell me about you and Michael," I said.

She shook her head a little, there was so much to say. But all she said was, "We couldn't stay away from each other. He's a very sexy man."

This last remark filled the room, and for a while we said nothing.

"But you're telling me to satisfy my need in some other way."

"He didn't make me happy, Anne."

It sounded as if he had made her very happy.

"I mean," she said, "he often made me happy. But he's too wrapped up in himself. And there were always other women, and sometimes he married them. The marriages didn't last very long." Then, reading my expression, no doubt, she said, "Who are we talking about?"

I felt the heat rise in my face. Not all love is incestuous, but a great deal of love has incestuous overtones or undertones or anti-tones as we find ourselves drawn to family resemblances, or the opposite, to men and women who bear no resemblance to any of our kin. Or to a man who has wooed the aunt you admire and wish you were. You want to be in the same atmosphere, to have the same effect, and failing that, to be so affected.

You can't compete, but you want to be a part of it.

"Anne."

It was a tone I hadn't heard before, a rather sharp classroom tone expressing disappointment. It brought me up short.

"You mind. You disapprove."

"How can I not mind?" She had turned her gaze on me, a level regard.

I saw myself with her eyes. I saw myself dropping a mouse at her feet, my derivative, copycat love. It was stupid of me to think she might have been pleased. I had taken admiration too far. It didn't matter that the love she had with Michael wasn't possessive or exclusive. It was theirs. It wasn't mine.

I had reconnected with him in May at a friend's party near Wakefield. It had been a warm and sunny afternoon, breezy enough to keep away the flies. I greeted my friend in her kitchen, then stepped onto the deck, and there he was, his hands resting on the railing on either side of him, his face in the sun, a man in his sixties, more youthful than most fifty-year-olds, yet no mistaking him for anything but a man getting old. He wore summer pants and a summer shirt and we recognized each other. He stretched out his hand to shake mine. "We met at Christmas. You're Connie's niece."

We talked until someone else, a woman I knew a little, addressed me. I turned to her as she spoke to me about writing and teaching, things unrelated to Michael. Nevertheless, he leaned toward us and added his own comment, and I felt his not impersonal interest in me. Later, he sought me out and told me about some of the nature books he had illustrated, and he asked me how I kept the creative process alive, which led us to the subject of memory.

"We forget nothing," he said. "It's all there, waiting to be triggered. By a death, for instance."

"If only we remembered what we learned," I said.

"But that doesn't matter. The facts don't matter." He swept his hands around. "It all blurs and merges and contributes to a way of seeing the world."

Someone else, a musician, joined in to say that we remember nothing unless it has an emotional context. He will ask girls in his choir to memorize a long piece of music and they'll profess their inability. Then he'll ask how many pairs of shoes they have. They'll think and say fourteen. "Describe them." They describe each pair in detail. "And why do you remember so well that blue pair with the strap at the back?" Oh, well, I wore them to a certain party.

It's true. I remember exactly what I wore that day: black sandals, light-blue cotton pants, and a checked shirt whose top three buttons weren't buttoned up.

He phoned a week later. "You remind me of Connie. I don't mean you look alike. But there's something."

Why was that so seductive? I felt folded into an area of amorousness, drawn in, because whatever he loved in her, I had an echo of. He said he and Connie had had a wonderful relationship that started when he was in his twenties and she was older, and lasted for many years, and they still sought each other out from time to time. She was a successful woman, he said, you could see it in the way she carried herself, and they had worked together on educational material for children with learning disabilities and so on and so forth.

I was very aware of his voice. He sounded his age. He sounded like a retired businessman accustomed to giving orders to the workmen outside. He was inviting me to visit, to bring my children to his place on the river, and my husband, too, if he was interested.

His property on the Gatineau wasn't far away from the farm he had rented for a long time. But this was his own—the remnants of an orchard, the frame house, the long, low log workshop in which he and two assistants made the boats, sleighs and summer furniture they were known for. The day we went to see him was a Saturday in June. He lent my husband a fishing rod. Then he took the children and me on the river in his rowboat and afterward gave them the run of an elaborate tree house he had built for his nephews, his sister's two boys. While they played, we sat on the veranda and he talked about the doubts he had about his business and his insecurities about the future, which ran deep. He didn't take his eyes off me, reading me, I thought, studying me. When my children bounded over, he gave them ice cream and lemonade.

*   *   *

In the days following, I looked at his phone number several times, thinking I should call to say we had enjoyed our visit, but I didn't call. I thought about him. I felt a little sorry for him and curious about him and disturbed. Then one day when I was buying milk at the corner store, I stepped into the pay phone and called the number I had apparently memorized. I got a gruff hello, then quite a different tone when he realized who it was. "I wish I could see you alone," he said, "without all the entourage. It's not that I have a hidden agenda, but there's so much I'd like to talk to you about."

"Why don't you drop by," I said. "The next time you happen to be in Ottawa." And I gave him our address.

"So *there* you are," my husband said when I came back through the screen door onto the side porch of our house.

The air was balmy, fragrant with rain fallen and still to come. We had our supper on the porch, grilled vegetables and steak. Our skin was smooth from humidity, from swimming in lakes. All summer I would walk barefoot down paths and across docks and up ladders onto rafts. I swam out toward loons and got to within ten feet of them, so absorbed were they in each other's posturing and aggressiveness—their wingspreads and chest-thrustings and wing-beats and calls. Then they went at it beak to beak. Three birds, and one of them an intruder.

I noticed my husband's handshake when Michael dropped by, assessing, deliberate.

He phoned every few days and I sat in a chair to listen and talk.

"I remember when you came up behind me and put your hand on my back," he said. "You came to say goodbye, and I felt this warm current run through me. Do you remember that?"

I remembered vaguely.

"At the party," he said. "But you're very tactile. I didn't know what to think. What to do with this strong attraction." He paused. "You don't have to say anything."

And so it went, lighting different parts of the fire, a fold of paper here, a bit of birchbark there.

"Your husband shouldn't mind if somebody else loves you. He should be flattered. But I don't want to make things difficult for you," he said.

I bought the big Saturday edition of the newspaper in the corner store and carried it home, the weight of it cradled in my arm, and as I turned into the back lane I flipped the sections with my free hand and the old whiff I had never thought to smell again came into my face. Newspapers of old smelled damp, inky, pungent. We would lie on the floor when we were kids, our noses inches above the paper, and devour the comic strips that were so glamorous in those days, the women and the men bewitching, all chiseled cheekbones and thick hair, full lips and swelling breasts. The damp wonder of sex and romance, and the excitement of the world out there awaiting us—it was all transmitted directly into our noses through newsprint and ink. I caught the smell, papers don't have it anymore, but I caught it and held the newspaper up to my face. Summer breezes moved in the trees, water-laden breezes, and at two in the morning I was still awake in the green armchair in the living room, in the angle of light from the street lamp outside, as the thought of him doubled me over at the waist, again and again.

How attraction works, making one's body almost painfully alive and one's thoughts concentrated, also painfully. And the truth of these powerful attractions—they have their own morality and nothing else matters.

It wasn't just the summer air reawakening the smell of newsprint as it used to be, but in my openness I was like a child again, susceptible to everything.

The next time I saw him we went for a walk, and a cat crossed his path and he called out with delight, "Pusser," and leaned sideways and with complete familiarity stopped it in its tracks by giving it a couple of firm, confident pats to head and back, "*with* the fur." Then with even greater familiarity, he lifted it by its tail several inches off the ground and set it back down. His happy grin. "It didn't expect that." Later, we heard two cats quarreling in the street, high-pitched toms, and he said it sounds worse than it is. He talked about the puddle of meaning that forms around an animal or a house or a boat or a book. About his liking for straight gin, sitting outside in the late afternoon with a glass of freezer-cold, unadulterated gin. About his awful years in school. About never taking sufficient risks in his life. About his workshop and the range of his work and the prices he charged and the sales he made and how he might make more, and how perhaps one day I might write about him.

He talked and talked, and when it was about real things, no one was more vivid, but whenever he turned philosophical he lost himself in abstractions. On the phone, it was different. Those moments opened wide. Do you remember putting your hand on my back when you said goodbye? And my own speechlessness.

After seeing him, I would think, Now it won't be hard. I can put him out of my mind. A day or two would pass, and once again the pressure would build, until either I called him or he called me, and then I would be out of my head with happiness. What could be wrong about feeling so alive? I came to see that what was easiest of all was throwing everything away. The husband disappears, and the absence of guilt (of feeling for him) is startling.

One morning when the kids were at camp, I went outside and sat in the car in the driveway. It was warm there behind the wheel, and I rolled down the window. The dashboard was dusty. The whole car, in fact, needed a good vacuuming. I turned the key in the ignition and at first I drove in subdued and fleeting sunshine, but soon it turned to rain and the rain was steady. A grader was out and I had to pull onto another road to let it go by. A glimpse of river on the right, then it disappeared from view and reappeared closer to the road. I turned into Michael's driveway and parked, and walked from the car into his kitchen, and for an hour or two we talked, keeping a safe, if charged, distance between us. As usual, he was talkative about himself, but also nervous, as nervous as I was, but his way of showing it was to fall into the exaggerated face-pulling that uneasy boys engage in. His voice was casual, a big voice that was light on its feet. I stood up from the table to leave and he stood up, too, and in that moment, to my surprise, since I didn't think it was ever going to happen, we stepped together and he put his arms around me. "You're lovely," he said. I kissed him on the corner of his mouth. Rain outside the window, soft dribbling off the eaves. We kissed again and the bucket inside me turned over and emptied its contents with a swoosh. "I want to lick you all over," he said.

The hours on the road to Maine helped, and the direction I was going helped, too, away from Michael. I had no plan. I just wanted, innocently, or not innocently at all, to spend a couple of days with Connie. It was a safe way of being close to him. I wasn't sure what I would tell her.

Once she realized who I was talking about, she stopped asking questions about the need in me. We went for a walk on the dirt road, past the yellowing raspberry bushes and down to the sailboats, one of which was hers. She promised to take me out the next day, but my husband was a fanatical sailor, with three sailboats, and I had had enough of sailing. We didn't speak for some time and the air between us grew more and more awkward.

"Tell me what you're thinking," I said.

"You've made me feel old, Annie. Old and jealous."

I reached for her arm and we stopped and faced each other. I said, "It's you he loves. He said I remind him of you."

She shook that off with a smile. "I don't blame you. I blame him a little. But why should I blame him? He's never been the only man in my life."

"But he's always been important."

"Yes." She looked away and was silent for a moment. "I don't know." And she shrugged. "That's life. People fall for each other. It's not hard to understand. Not hard at all."

She took my hand and we walked on until we came to a rocky high point with a view of the sea and the sunset. There was a weathered picnic table on the edge of the point, and we sat side by side facing the water. The air was sweet with wildflowers and the smell of the sea, and the sunset filled the sky from top to bottom with pink.

Then Connie led the way back to her house, and in talking about herself and Michael he came alive again in a new way, stronger than ever. She said that all of her teaching flowed from having tried to teach him how to read. (Her school in Boston specialized in dyslexia, a word she learned after the war.) And one of the things she had come to appreciate was ego. Michael wasn't the only one who was self-involved to a maddening degree. "When words avoid you, or continually cross you up, you have no escape from yourself."

In her kitchen she opened a bottle of wine and we cooked a late supper. She seemed to be almost amused in that weary way we have of being entertained by the unforeseeable workings of the world. "He's had a lot of darkness in his life," she said.

"Yes."

"But light, too. Lots of light." Her face became very expressive. She knew him through and through. "He's had to struggle so hard. He grew up believing he was stupid and he learned to keep going despite that. He throws himself at things."

I listened to her talk. She said he knew how to enchant, but running under the surface charm was touchiness, especially about being patronized. She smiled a little, and what she said next sounded less critical than affectionate. "He's so egocentric. But thoughtful. And, of course, he's one of the best-looking men around. But I couldn't spend even a month with him."

She was treating me as an equal fetched up on the rocky shores of foolishness.

"Tell me why."

"He's too solitary. Too frugal. Too cheap for me." Her familiar laugh pealed out the screen windows and across the garden and possibly down to the shore. "Your parents have a good marriage, Anne."

"My father is solitary and my mother is cheap."

"Your mother is loyal."

"My mother is solitary, too."

"That's the artist in her. I envy that. She's made herself into a serious artist."

These words soothed me, and I had to wipe my eyes.

Many hours later, we were eating blueberry pie fresh out of the oven and watching for first light. I heard tires on the gravel road and then footsteps went by, a boy delivering newspapers. Connie was telling me that the beginning with Michael was very subtle and secretive, and went on to be very conspicuous. Syd saw it all happening, and it had happened to him before, that's what made it so cruel. But he was always there when she came back from seeing Michael, he was always affectionate. After Michael enlisted, they didn't see him for several months. Then one night he dropped by in uniform and the three of them sat in the kitchen as they had in the past. "And suddenly I was the least important part of the triangle. They spent the time talking to each other. To hell with this, I thought, and I went to bed." Michael would tell her later that he had asked Syd to say goodbye for him. But Syd, of course, had said nothing. He didn't hide from her, however, the address Michael had written on a piece of paper and left on the table. He was at the Manning Depot in the Coliseum at the Canadian National Exhibition grounds in Toronto. *AC Graves Michael.*

"What became of Syd?" I asked.

She went to one of her many bookshelves and pulled down his eight books, including the history Michael had illustrated, and his skillful drawings gave me a stab of pleasure. The books included two volumes in a series for schools, *World History Made Simple* and *World Literature Made Simple.* I opened one and read the first sentence. "Much of history is the story of what *probably* happened in the remote and more recent past." And I looked away from those words and proceeded to tell Connie the rest of what had happened so recently between Michael and me.

He had called me in the morning after my husband left for work (this was the morning after I had driven to his house in the rain and stayed all day) to ask me how I was. I said I hadn't slept. He hadn't either. Then he got me laughing by telling me about an old hippie rogue he knew who gave an eighty-year-old woman a joint, which alleviated all her pain, but then her family arrived and they were mortified. And the old hippie said, "Don't worry. I'll talk Mrs. Drysdale down." He would talk me down, he said. And quite gently he told me that I would be scorned by everybody who knew me if I got involved with him at the expense of my marriage. "Call it old-school decency," he said.

I looked over at Connie as I told her this.

"I know," she said, understanding my predicament. "I know."

"What do you know?"

"He's going to break your heart."

In the early hours of that Maine morning, she had reached into the oven to pull out the blueberry pie, then reached in again to scrape up the juices that had spilled over, forgetting about the hot inside of the oven door. The burn was three inches long on the tenderest flesh, the inside of her bare forearm, but instead of whimpering, she sliced an onion and placed two thin slices over the length of the burn, then used two large bandages to hold them in place. The relief was immediate, I saw it in her face.

"Nature has everything we need," she said, "if only we pay attention. I learned that from Syd."

They were in touch by letter. He had remarried, a woman his own age, and a few years ago, moved by the memory of Jews being turned away from one port after another, they had adopted two children who were among the boat people fleeing Vietnam. He wrote to Connie several times a year. She showed me a recent letter, and it had that communing tone that counts for everything: *Monday morning now. August 1st and dense fog—can't see the bottom of the garden—a welcome change in a perverse sort of way. What we've had lately is lots of company and getting ready for them has put a strain on my usual equanimity.*

I borrowed *World History Made Simple,* eager to understand a few fundamental things from this knowledgeable man—like fascism and the Napoleonic Wars. But understanding takes you only so far, to the point where you don't want to understand, and this happens all too quickly.

* * *

I had resolved not to see Michael again after my flight to Maine. I took to heart all that Connie said. She had embraced me when we bid each other goodbye and asked me what I was going to do. I didn't know.

"Well, I'm going to lie down," she laughed. And then I saw how much I had exhausted her and how she couldn't wait to be by herself.

Soon after coming home, however, my thoughts became pliable again. The rise and fall of the urge to get in touch involves the complete overturn of your resolve. As if a giant leans down and plays with your pebbles of feeling—the rock of your conviction has become a mere pebble—and how easily the giant palms it, the giant of hankering that becomes the giant of need. Everything gives way to the desire to hear his voice—and it's not quite alcoholism, though it's certainly an addiction, since a mere drop, one gentle phone call, will satisfy.

16

LOVAT HALL

A year and a half ago, my mother lay in bed recovering from two serious operations, and very frail, her cup of coffee earning the world record for number of times reheated in the microwave. "Give it the one, two, three," she would say, their microwave being an old barge so slow that half a cup of coffee needed one minute and twenty-three seconds of reheating. Mind you, she liked things hot. What was left of her tongue, after a lifetime of repeated scaldings, liked things hot.

"Jealousies," she said, and she smiled and shook her head knowingly. "My brother Ken was a ladies' man."

In my mind I saw my uncle's lean, amused face as my mother finished her train of thought about the rivalry between her brothers. "He got a job at the bank through Parley Burns. I know he paid Mother a dollar a day room and board, and he liked clothes. He wore white pants when he golfed and when he worked in the garden. My brother David wasn't a ladies' man and he didn't care about clothes. He always maintained that when he and Ken worked in the garden, he did all the work."

David was the firstborn, famous for being the sole object of his mother's love. The day Ken reeled in the largest fish ever caught in the lake, he showed it to his mother in great excitement, and she had a picture taken of David holding the fish.

"Ken had my father's hands," my mother said. "Their steadiness. And his conciliatory ways. He could play pick-up sticks for hours without disturbing the pile."

"You have them, too," I said. "The same hands. The same conciliatory ways."

The previous week an intern in the hospital had remarked on the many veins in her narrow, tanned-looking, parchmenty old hand, and her retort, "Veins, but no vanity," passed over his busy head. Upon finding herself in the hospital, she had said, "There's only one word for this. Helldamnspit."

"Did Ken like Parley Burns?" I asked her.

She hesitated. She had such a soft spot for Ken. "I think he did. I know he went to his funeral."

For several summers before he entered the asylum, she told me, Parley Burns used to leave Argyle for weeks at a time. Among the social notices in the *Mercury*, there would be one saying that Mr. Ian Burns had gone to Toronto for two weeks, or three weeks; he went alone. In the summer of 1940, Connie happened to be in Toronto visiting my father when she passed a small theater on Berkeley Street and stopped to read the playbills posted behind glass. *What Is This Life?* A one-act play by Ian A. Burns.

That night Connie was in the audience of about fifty people, watching a short drama about the Welsh tramp-poet W. H. Davies, who had written the lines we all recognize from school: *What is this life if, full of care, / We have no time to stand and stare?* From the program notes she learned that on his way to the Klondike in 1899, and in the company of a fellow tramp called

Three-Fingered Jack, Davies jumped a freight train in Argyle, Ontario, and lost his grip. The wheels of the train crushed his right foot even as Three-Fingered Jack and the freight train disappeared into the night. In Parley's play, the poet lies in his hospital bed in Argyle, talking to a lame young man who brings him the newspaper and stays on to listen to his stories of gold, dancing girls, high adventure and escape. In the end the young man is arrested as he leaves the hospital, charged with murdering a schoolgirl.

Connie remembered her interview for the *Journal* with Johnny's gray-haired mother, heartbroken that the police had not done her family the simple courtesy of coming to the house to arrest her boy, but had plucked him off the street instead, depriving her of the chance to say goodbye.

Connie was acerbic when she told me years later about the favorable reviews Parley got for his play. She spoke with a kind of pain, salted pain. No matter that the wound was old, the salt had found its way in, and the salt was praise of someone she couldn't forgive and couldn't get out of her system. She admitted the premise of the play was good, that a boy who seems innocent might not be; the question was left open. "The play was better than I expected. I had to admire it. And yet there was something sour about everything he did."

When I listened to her describe the virtues of his play—the rapport between the poet and the boy, their lighthearted swagger—I didn't assume that Parley was, in fact, curious and kind and misunderstood. But his personality widened a little, a door in the house opened. Spaciousness entered. You wait for a moment when someone is different, even a little, from what you expect.

After the Almonte train crash, Connie had written to my grandmother thanking her for Christmas and mentioning that Parley and his wife, also on the train, had escaped unhurt. In her reply, my grandmother passed on the information that Parley had been on his way to the mental institution named Lovat Hall in Lancaster on the St. Lawrence River. He had been committed, but not against his will, so far as she knew.

This bit of news threw Connie's sighting of them into a much darker light.

At Easter 1943, when she made the long drive from Boston to Brockville to see my parents (my father was undergoing officer training and my mother was private nursing), she made a little detour to find out what had become of Parley Burns. She was more curious than my father, as well as more sociable, yet my father once spent two years tracking down former students, the several for whom he'd had the highest expectations and the several for whom he'd had the lowest, to find out what they had made of their lives; by no means the pursuit of an incurious man.

The village of Lancaster is close to the Ontario–Quebec border. Railway tracks run through the middle of it, crossing the short main street that in those days had shops, restaurants and a single hotel. Connie followed the hotel clerk's directions and drove to the long, curving driveway on the outskirts of town that led through extensive grounds to an impressive brick mansion on a knoll: this was mental care for the moneyed. Inside, a wall of south-facing glass overlooked the wide and tempting waters of the St. Lawrence. A huge fireplace filled one wall, and nearby an elaborate spiral staircase led up to the second floor. The staircase had a double banister, she noticed, one on top of the other, to prevent the inmates from pitching themselves over the side.

Parley was in his room on the second floor, in an upholstered armchair, staring into space. He didn't grimace when he saw her, or brighten. He knew who she was. And because Connie couldn't explain even to herself why she had come, except to satisfy personal curiosity, she soon ran out of things to say. She reached into her handbag and pulled out the book she was returning after all these years. "You will have forgotten you lent it to me."

He had not forgotten. Not forgotten the book she had lugged around from place to place like a punishment.

"Shall I read a few pages?"

She read the opening of *Jude the Obscure* to Parley, who stared at the floor and gave no indication that the story meant anything to him at all. But the words hit her as if for the first time, about the schoolmaster leaving the village and everyone being sorry, especially the boy named Jude, and she read very slowly, her skin prickling. After a few paragraphs she stopped and sat with the book open in her lap. Parley looked at her with his pale, brown, bloodshot eyes. Behind him and on top of his chest of drawers, in a hinged double frame, were photographs of his wife and stepdaughter, the bony wife and brainy child. They had the high foreheads of intelligence and the furtive non-smiles of the emotionally reserved. And it was driven in upon her again that he worked on the insecurity and the generosity of girls and women—his attentions a balm and an irritant; a distressing excitement. For him, too, distress and excitement.

She put Hardy on his bedside table and went over to the window. A tree-lined driveway led down to the river that flowed all the way to the Atlantic. "You must enjoy taking walks. The grounds go on forever."

He didn't answer, and she turned around and looked at him. He wore a cardigan and a shirt without a tie. He was ill-shaven. He was thinner. She saw the worry scab on his lip and the bitten nails.

"They take us in groups," he said finally, with a sigh, and his breath didn't smell nearly so bad as it had before.

"I'm teaching again," she said.

"I couldn't do it anymore. So you got your way."

She knew what he meant. *You're unfit to teach children.* She had been on his trail ever since, not intentionally, but it must have seemed so to him.

There was an Olivetti typewriter on the small desk beside the window and a sheet of foolscap beside it covered in tiny but fierce-looking handwriting.

"You were writing," she said.

"Something came to me."

She thought he was referring to his work, but he reached for an envelope. "It's for somebody else," he said.

She took the envelope from his outstretched hand and saw that it was addressed to *Andrew Burns.* "It's probably meant for you," she said. "They got your first name wrong, that's all. You can open it."

"There are things a man of honor can't do. If I'm given a letter that's not addressed to me, I'm not going to open it."

He had found a plank to cling to inside the wreckage of himself. A way to give himself a high moral grade.

"You're doing some writing," she said again.

"Every word is bad. Every sentiment is maladroit." *Jude the Obscure* had loosened his tongue after all. "But we are who we are, no matter how much it complicates our lives."

"And the lives of others," she said.

"Have I complicated your life?" His gaze was forthright and his voice was quiet. He seemed in that moment more self-aware than she had imagined.

"I wasn't thinking of me, but I suppose you have."

"For that I'm truly sorry." He said it quite sincerely and life flooded in. Complexity that was very simple flooded in. He was sorry.

She would always be careful around people like Parley Burns, tricky people who are thin-skinned and punitive and intelligent and surprisingly honest.

The smell of the place stayed with her. When she arrived in Brockville to see my parents, she carried something clinical and medicinal on her clothes and hair—the vase itself, emptied of old flowers, but smelling of them, unrinsed.

In the library I found Parley's obituary, and a death I was aware of finally registered with the force of a tolling bell. He threw himself under the wheels of a passing truck on May 24, 1943, and that was the end of him.

In his obituary he was Ian A. Burns, the principal of a collegiate highly praised by inspectors, a man who had given generously of his time and energy to maintain its fine traditions of scholarship and service, a man whose devotion to duty had led him to overtax his strength and impair his health. A past president of the Rotary Club, chairman of the public library board, member of the curling club and "a patient at Lovat Hall since early this year, for the benefit of his nervous system."

I left the library and bicycled home through a city full of tulips, thanks to a grateful Dutch queen. Every year they bloom, then lose their heads to an army of black squirrels that go about like little guillotines, decapitating, decapitating. Tulips have so much more personality than other flowers—cut and arranged, each stem bends and swings low or wide or high, and the flower opens like a plate and comes right out to greet you as if it were a schoolgirl and Parley a squirrel.

A sentence bears the weight of the world. *The emotional girl set about baptizing her child.* Tess took her dying baby from her bed in the middle of the night and christened him in the presence of her small and sleepy brothers and sisters. Words weigh nothing at all, yet they carry so much on their shoulders over and over and over again.

The long shadow of school falls across the rest of our lives. I draw *Tess* forward, year after year, a novel I studied in grade ten, then taught with limited success for many years. It's a novel that works better as poetry, although it's the bare bones of plot I can't forget.

Last spring, I drove to Lancaster looking for traces of Lovat Hall, and the train came whistling through, barely slowing down. In a coffee shop, from a clutch of white-haired Anglicans gathered after church, I learned that the sanatorium had been torn down and turned into parkland some years ago, its stone fireplace so monumental the dismantling of it required dynamite. One elderly woman, her large face lively and eager, confessed that as a child she had worried about them coming close, the inmates, since they weren't quite right in the head. She couldn't stop imagining bodies washing up on shore after one of them, a young woman, drowned herself in the river.

I went down to the wide river. Its waters here extended far enough to be called a lake, Lake St. Francis, a breeding ground for redhead ducks, least bitterns, great egrets, black terns. The mighty St. Lawrence. I remembered a letter of Connie's in which she told of attending a conference of educators in Montreal, at which the guest speaker, a punctual professor from Kingston who was expected at ten in the morning, didn't arrive until four in the afternoon. On his way he had seen cranes lifting houses out of the path of the seaway and watched, mesmerized, for hours. He was seeing the creation of the lost villages, the lost schools, the lost schoolchildren who were put on buses and transported to larger schools before the man-made flood raised the river and drowned its rapids and islands, fashioning a new shoreline with a new view of enormous tankers plying its length.

Standing there, I thought about Connie's view that we carry the past forward even when things and people are obliterated. But surely you need a very long memory for that to happen.

It was late afternoon, overcast, peaceful. Not another soul in sight. I could hear her voice admitting that Parley had a certain dignity, twisted though he was.

I didn't expect to learn anything more about him. It was the spring of 2007. Everyone who had known him was dead, except for my mother, and her memory was in tatters. But I stood there for quite a while. I felt like a pilgrim, having traveled to the place where he died.

I began to think of my name, the name I shared with Connie, my parents, the flooded world. In her last years Connie was compiling a genealogy and promised to send me a copy when she finished, but she never did finish it. The wide river was comforting, the long view, the smooth waters. Nothing to get caught up on, no twigs and branches of learning, no stones to stumble over. I thought of other villages gone back to grass, wooden sidewalks hidden by weeds, and then I wondered if perhaps Connie was right and my fascination with Parley came not just from the obvious, his ruinous connection to people I loved, but from something more submerged.

17

MICHAEL

The phone would ring in the evening and his voice would change, drop a notch, become intimate, and he would settle into long conversations as if he still lived alone.

There were other women—at least two, possibly three. One he had known for years, the other more recently. In time I met them both, and neither held a candle to Connie, although they were much younger than she was, of course. Thérèse was buxom and burly, in her forties, a woman made for stooking hay in the fields, a goodhearted nurse in the throes of leaving her husband. Cathy was fifty-eight, ten years younger than Michael. She was built like a bird and rode horses. When I asked him once what kind of woman attracted him, he said, "My taste changes. It's all over the place. I like strong women."

"Physically strong?"

"Strong in every way."

In those two years or so of being with Michael, when I lost a
husband and half lost an aunt, my thoughts turned more and more
to women on their own. In my family I had always had Connie's
example, but also my grandmother's, the one as exciting as the
other was cautionary. After the death of her husband, my grandmother expected my mother, seven years old, to sleep with her,
which meant lying on her dead father's side of the bed and listening
to her mother's fingernails fret the seam of the pillowcase all night
long. Side by side, they were sleepless souls, my mother missing the
father she never stopped missing, and my grandmother wild with
worry about money. Picturing them, I recall something else, something very different, the time my mother and I shared a bed after I
took up with Michael. It was in December, right after my husband
had moved out, quick to decide that everything was over between
us the moment he knew I was having an affair. Our children would
remain with me, except for weekends with their father; deceptively
sturdy, both of them. We had put the house up for sale, and the sign
on the winter lawn was grim. My parents in their concern came to
visit. One look at me and that night my mother lay beside me in the
double bed, on my husband's side, and massaged my shoulders and
stroked my hair until I slept. In the middle of the night, aware of
me lying awake, she rubbed my back with those great hands of hers
and I slept again.

She must have done that for her mother, that is, comforted her
mother with her presence. But her mother did not comfort her.

The first Christmas after her father's death, when she was eight,
my mother and her brother Ken decorated the Christmas tree
while their mother worked in the store. It was a small tree, matching their reduced circumstances, set up on a table in the dining
room. The two nimble-fingered children worked long and com-
panionably, placing all the decorations on the little tree, deeply
pleased with the effect. My grandmother saw it and exploded.
Tired though she was, she removed every single decoration, so
lovingly hung, before redoing the tree "properly," she sputtered,
"appropriate for a tree that size."

It's not hard to imagine the seething anxiety and fatigue that swept away every other consideration, or the children who said nothing, but remembered.

I think back to what drew me to Michael, and what held me, and remember an afternoon in August charged with late-summer warmth rather than burning heat, when he taught my children not to be afraid of snakes. They were seven and five, my daughter and son. Michael lay on his belly on the sun-baked rock and they lay beside him, all three of them watching intently as two water snakes slid through the water and up onto a nearby rock, black and coiling. He was deft at slipping his hand under the upper body, gently lifting, then grasping the lower body with his other hand and getting my children to reach out and touch the black suppleness, the creepy undulation. "These wild creatures have such a different rhythm," he said.

He could mimic a raven's call, the gurgle in the throat, the little popping and ponging sounds that accompany the croak. He could mimic the sound of crickets. "They're sharpening their scythes to cut the grass," he told my children. He taught them how to build a campfire, and he was meticulous, fanatical, about the proper use of matches, the danger of wind. I read his past into his precautions. Next to the rapids, we found a family of snakes in among the grass and the rocks, alerted by one brown tail and one brown head poking out from beneath a rock—and then there were many and they were all wriggling on bellies that were almost orange. Copper bellies, Michael said. Garter snakes proliferated; their bellies were the color of lima beans.

I loved how he hoisted himself effortlessly out of the river onto the raft—the strength of his arms and shoulders, his dexterity, his physical confidence—yet he wasn't a good swimmer: too many years on the prairie. I was the better swimmer. My children loved to splash him, loved to be around him. He was the least straitlaced, most playful of men. But he didn't have a lot of time for them, and then he had less. When his playfulness disappeared, the verbose, unlistening Michael would appear, and my children and I would drift away.

I read to him. He liked poetry. We worked our way through Ted Hughes, which sort of amused me. Both men were catnip to women, but their true loves were not women, it seemed to me, but animals trying to sneak past the human storm. Michael lay with his head in my lap, listening closely and gradually falling asleep.

He wore dollar-store reading glasses whenever he read to himself. He followed the lines down the page with his forefinger, then returned to the top and inched his finger down the page a second time like a student reading Hegel. His handwriting was spidery and loose. He watched in simple wonder as my daughter learned to read, reminded of his early agonies, of lying on his back after a day of school, looking at the treetops and the clouds and recovering some sense of his right to exist.

"You don't get over it," he said, "failure in elementary school. Other sorrows you might get over, but not that."

And once he asked me, "I imagine you were good at school?"

It was the most wistful question I had ever heard.

I was always aware when I was with him that I was in the presence of a sad and intricate story, his misery at school, his rescue by Connie, the tragedy of his sister's death, his hatred of his father and his love of his mother. He told me that his mother had read to him, but she stopped "after my sister burned alive."

"What was that day like?" I said, after a pause, fully expecting him to change the subject. But in an even tone, without emotion, he said he remembered how she came home sobbing in a yellow dress and stood in the doorway. The hem of her dress was torn, she had chalk on her forehead. It flashed through his mind that she had been cleaning the blackboards and fallen somehow, or had a fight in the schoolyard. But then she stuttered out the words, "Mr. Burns." That week he saw the man at school. He watched him and hated him for going after his sister and hurting her, but the one he really despised was his father who did nothing—nothing, that is, except punish Susan, and for what? For *embarrassing* him. He paused in his recounting, and I thought he had stopped and wasn't going to talk about the fire itself. But then he picked up the thread again. On the night she died, he said, people came up to them afterward as they stood staring at the smoking ruins—he and his mother and his father and his little sister—to say they were sorry. "They shook my father's hand."

I was watching him. He was still speaking in a low, flat voice, but his face had darkened as the story welled up and suddenly the even delivery was gone. "I wanted to kill him," he said, "even if he was my father. I grew up wishing he'd drop dead. But this was something else. Killing him. Making him suffer like Susan did." He looked at me then. "I saw her in the window, you know."

I put my hand on his. He didn't seem to notice.

He said, "That night all I did was turn my back on him. I don't think he cared. Or even knew." He drew his hand away from mine. "My father was the kind of guy who'd come home in a foul mood and strike me on the side of the head. 'That's for nothing. Do something and see what you get.'"

He paused again. He bit at the side of his index finger, tearing off dry skin. "I just wish I knew how it happened. It wouldn't have taken much—a candle too close to the curtain, or the wind knocking over the lamp."

He seemed about to say something else.

"What is it?"

He shook his head. "Nothing."

His sister came with her sons for a week in July during the only full summer we were together. I liked Evie. She indulged Michael by cooking for him, by mending his clothes, but not necessarily by listening to him talk about himself. "He tries too hard," she once said to me when he left us to go upstairs. "He always tries too hard when he wants to impress."

"Not always," I said.

She didn't look like him, being stocky, fair-haired, pale. I assumed she looked like her father.

She said, "I didn't see Michael for years, not until after Dad died. I was living in Toronto with Dad's sister and he showed up one day in his uniform."

I knew this from Michael, but hearing a story retold has its own power. I asked her how old she had been.

"It was right after the war. I was nineteen. I remember him eating a banana, how thrilled he was, his first banana in six years."

She and I would have been sitting in the screened-in porch and it would have been late, since we were night owls in the summer. Aware of how different she and Michael were, I asked her how *she* felt about her father.

I can still see the expression on her face, unapologetic, forthright.

She said, "I loved Dad and felt loved by him. Michael doesn't understand it. But then Dad was horrible to him. We all knew that. Always putting him down, treating him like he was stupid."

It took me a moment to absorb how firm yet clear-eyed she was in her loyalty to her father.

She looked away from me. "He never forgave himself for what happened to Susan. That's what all his drinking was about." She sighed. "But he was good to me. Always."

She had been his favorite. I've never met a favorite child who wasn't forgiving of the parent. Either they see more generously or can live happily with their blindness.

"Maybe in being good to you," I said, "he was making up for past sins."

She didn't disagree. She acknowledged that he had been harsh to her mother, too. "But then my mother fought back and left him. There's a lot of sadness in my family. Michael should be a father, he's wonderful with children. But he has a harem instead."

I laughed because it was so true. She wasn't trying to hurt me. She was just alerting me to the lie of the land.

Michael also drank too much. He was a tortured sleeper, rocking, twisting, jerking, coughing, scratching. But his touch remained unhurried and skillful, intuitive, as it was with any animal within reach, even if he could no longer always depend on his equipment, he said, gesturing toward his groin. He kissed my neck not high and on the side, but lower down and toward the back, calling me baby, and had me eating out of his hand every time I turned around.

About four months after that last visit to Maine, I had phoned Connie to tell her that I was moving in with Michael. "Maybe he's told you himself," I said, hoping he had. But no.

She was quiet at her end.

"The kids are with me," I said, "except on the weekends. Their father is talking about moving to Toronto."

"It must be hard to see everything come apart." Her voice was less itself, as if she were holding herself away from me.

"Men are quick to adjust. He's angry, but he's already making a new life for himself. Men are good at that."

"Hard on you, too, Anne. And on the children," she said. "Just don't stop writing. Don't lose that."

I did lose it for the better part of a year. My productivity had always been slim, some poems, a few stories, but now it stopped altogether. It's something you can get used to, inactive, unmoving air inside, as we do when we shut ourselves up in an air-conditioned house during an endless heat wave. In a photograph you might very well look happy, and no doubt your descendants would assume you *were* happy, but you are not exactly happy.

I imagined phoning Connie dozens of times as the months passed, but I didn't call and neither did she. I took her silence as a rebuke, of course. (Now I would say that it was nothing more than natural.) When finally I dialed her number, she responded with such pleasure (saying she was better already now that she was talking to me) that I had to dry my cheeks with the back of my hand. I told her I had been picking the second crop of raspberries, my fingers were bright red. It was interesting, I said, talking too much, to see how raspberries ripen, one perfect berry on a cane of otherwise green berries, like members of a family, one beauty and the rest runts.

"Annie, how are you?"

"I'm exhausted. I can't sleep. I don't make him happy either."

"I think you do."

"Why?"

"He told me your times together are an utter joy."

"An utter joy. He said that?"

"Don't make me repeat it," she said with a short laugh.

"He must mean so long as there are big gaps in between."

"Well, that's who he is."

"That's who he is. Now who on earth am I?"

I wasn't Connie, who had trained herself to be self-sufficient in love. But I began to work at it.

I took to sleeping in another bed after we made love. I found an apartment in Ottawa and my children and I spent weekdays there—it was easier for them to go to school, and it was easier for me to work, to resume doing a little writing before the kids got up and before I headed across the city to teach English at Woodroffe High School. Even so, Michael referred more than once to the tar baby story, how in pulling one hand away, the other gets stuck, until before you know it, all of you is stuck.

"Am I tar?" I said, prodding his chest with my finger.

"Not in the last hour," he said with a smile.

The single time we went to see my parents, my mother took him into her studio to show him what she was working on, then out into the garden where she was grafting fruit trees: pear and plum to apple. Her father had grafted many trees in their big garden in Argyle; she had the knack. Michael's affection for my mother was something else that held me. He identified with her as a fellow experimenter in working by hand, with wood in his case, paint in hers. She told him something I had never heard before, about swimming as a girl and claiming the rock afterward: she and her brothers and their pals would come out of the lake, blue from the cold, and race to the glacial rock as big as a room that had soaked up the sun all afternoon. It had ledges like little thrones and they would claim their thrones, pressing their bare and shivering skin against the sun-beaten rock, and those who arrived last would climb to the top and crowd into whatever spot wasn't in the shade. By the time of this visit, my mother had moved from painting lichens on rock to painting rocks unadorned, and they would occupy her until she stopped painting altogether.

"Annie," she said to me on the phone later, "he's as old as I am."

"I know."

A moment passed. "My mother married a man twice her age," she said.

I considered this. "Did you ever know why?"

"I suppose she wanted what he had to offer. He had an established business. He was a fine-looking man. He gave her the admiration she craved."

"So he loved her."

"He did. He adored her. And he was very partial to me, and I was very partial to him. I don't know how much my mother reciprocated his feelings. I disliked her," she said, "vastly."

My grandmother never remarried. She didn't want to be bothered with another man, or so she told my mother. "Meaning sex," my mother said with scorn. "She didn't like to be touched. She wore her precious pince-nez and if you came within a foot of her, she'd cry, 'Watch my glasses! Watch my glasses!'"

I felt I'd slipped in my parents' estimation when I became involved with Michael. I'd slipped in Connie's estimation. And in Michael's. In everyone's, except my own. It had taken a lot for me to do something unconventional, and no matter how badly I had done it, I had done it. I felt stronger, less predictable to myself, and split a dozen ways. I can see now that I was trying to say goodbye to certain over-influences, weaning myself off Connie with the tender ruthlessness that governs so much love; we admire, we move on. Except that doesn't begin to capture the strain of it or the emotional price that everyone pays. Connie and I were in touch, but carefully so. We phoned each other a couple of times a year and skirted many topics. Theft is aggressive,

and I had taken up with Michael, not stolen him so much as borrowed him through the back door.

His dance card became full. I would wait for him to phone me, to
confirm that he wanted us to come out for the weekend, and he
wouldn't call. I would call him and find out more than I wanted to
know, about some woman who hoped he would father her child,
for example. I imagined a calendar in which I marked off each day
I resisted phoning him. Imagined a story where the suspense is
whether she can resist calling and whether he will call. I wrote the
story. He called. I took up the Buddhist strategy of letting your heart
break, breathing in the pain, then letting it go as relief and compas-
sion in this groundless world. What was happening was in a way
what I had hoped for, that his behavior would let me off the hook I
was on. But there is pain in being removed from a hook.

He insisted every time we spoke that I was happy. "You sound
happy."

"Do I?"

For a while I was able to carry it all inside me, like a big bouquet
of peonies, and then I couldn't anymore. The moist, plump peony
heads got to be too heavy. They were like pounds of raw hamburger
hanging upside down.

I moved to the other side of the country and took my children with
me. They spent parts of every summer with their father, who was
well ensconced in Toronto by then. The pleasure of being in Vancouver came from the shift to a milder climate within the same country.
You lived without any need of storm windows against the cold, or
screens against mosquitoes, in a land that offered a complete transformation but gently, naturally, without any shock.

The difficulties were on another level. My children entered classrooms where friendships were fixed and they never really found a
way in. I worked as a teacher, but I had never been a good teacher.
There is a special confidence, a strength of character all good teachers have. They enter a classroom and you feel their power. They

aren't (at least in the classroom) divided against themselves. They love their material. And the best of them make their students almost forget themselves in favor of the subject at hand. But I wanted to be a writer, not a teacher. Just as my mother had wanted to be a painter, not a nurse.

Connie passed through Vancouver just once. She had booked herself on a boat trip up the west coast to Alaska. It was September of 1991 and we were to meet for a late lunch; we hadn't seen each other in eight years. I walked down Robson Street and there she was, standing on the sidewalk outside a small café. She welcomed me with open arms, engulfed me in a hug, and said she had been afraid that I had written her off. She had even lost sleep over it.

I was moved and didn't know what to say. It's true that I hadn't initiated a phone call in a long time. It was she who had called the night before to see if I was free for lunch.

"My life is different now," I said in lame apology.

"I know, but you are brave, and years from now you will look back and be glad you broke away and came out here."

I admired everything about her, as always. Her hair was completely white and cut short. She wore a silver bracelet and, almost invisible, a hearing aid in each ear. She was eighty-one.

"I miss the East," I confessed once we were seated and I had collected myself a little. Her generosity had shaken me. Is that really how she saw me? Brave?

"Come home."

"Mountains. I want to look at little things."

"'Little objects for the soul.'"

I nodded, looking into her eyes. "You're quoting someone."

"That's what Michael calls stones and shells and feathers and so on and so forth. Things he picks up and puts in his pocket."

His name felt like a small punch. She reached across and took my hand when I stared at the floor. I could tell by the firm way she grasped my fingers and then released them that she wanted me to buck up. *You are brave.*

"How is he?"

"I'm sure he's fine. I haven't spoken to him in quite a while." Then she leaned forward. "Get on with *your* life, Annie." And she asked about my children, my writing, my personal life. I told her that I had been careful to find a man several years younger than myself. "You would like Leo. He teaches history. He loves the woods. He's learning to play the piano." I paused. "I think of you all the time, Connie, even if I don't phone."

"It's all right. I understand."

Awkwardness kept us company no matter what we talked about. She told me about a new interest of hers that had started as curiosity then expanded into a serious project. She pulled a few pages from her handbag and introduced me to the many branches of her mother's family—the Douglas line of descent went back centuries to the Black Douglases of the Scottish borderlands, she said. In Alaska she would be meeting for the first time a distant cousin who would fill in some of the blanks.

I looked at the diagrams of generation upon generation and found them impossible to follow. You needed a degree in physics, it seemed to me, to keep all the names and connections straight.

"But what about *your* personal life?" I said.

"I'm not lonely, Anne."

She spent most of the year in her house in Maine, and winters in New York, staying with a close friend. They were out nearly every evening at one thing or another.

"Who is the close friend?"

"If you think I'm going to introduce you," she said, "you can forget it."

It was a relief to laugh, even if darker feelings lay behind the quip. What I saw in her face was mostly affection—affection laced with wit and self-respect and the same assertive spirit that I had always seen in her. Before, I would have teased her about taking up genealogy, and asked if bridge was next. Now I kept the thought to myself. Was it because she had no children, I wondered.

It was while we were having our coffee that we talked about my parents. I told her I had been having many dreams about my mother.

"I'm sorry she hasn't been all that well," she said.

This stopped me. "We talked on the phone on Saturday. She said she was fine."

Connie immediately said, "She wouldn't have wanted to worry you. The pain in her shoulder was really getting her down, but it's under control now. She's back in her studio, as productive as ever."

"They don't *tell* me. They always say they're *fine*." I set down my coffee cup. By not worrying me, they were excluding me. It made me angry. And it hurt.

Connie looked at me for a moment. "You're so lucky to have your mother still alive. I can't imagine what that would be like."

We said goodbye outside the café. Our leave-taking was tender-hearted, almost too effusive. The sort of effort you then have to recover from. You take a long walk and ponder your failings. I thought about how much I loved Connie and how little we had to say to each other. I thought about her search through the dry genealogical past for traces of her mother, while mine was a living creative force on the other side of the country.

Halfway home, I passed a flower bed that spilled over onto the sidewalk and I stopped to examine the delicate, bluish-purple blossoms inhabited by a few bees. I asked the man who was walking across the lawn if he knew what they were. Lavender, he said, which surprised me. I thought I knew lavender.

It was five in the afternoon by the time I got home. I felt uncommonly tired, worked over and sad, as if a death had occurred.

18

ONTARIO

My thoughts turned more and more toward home, toward Ontario and my aging mother and father, and after seven years in Vancouver I moved back with my teenage children. After a few months Leo followed me, and we have been together ever since, my piano player and I. I'm not like Connie, I do get lonely. We found this house in Old Ottawa South and took over a garden that was like a cemetery full of white wooden stakes bearing the Latin names of the old botanist's various plantings; some of the stakes were readable, some too faded. From neighbors I learned that the former owner had been a big man, white-haired and stoop-shouldered, garrulous, opinionated and abrupt, who worked in suspenders and slippers as he documented everything that crossed his path, not just the thousands of plants he collected and labeled and sent to herbaria around the world but features of his daily life. He liked to smoke at the table beside the kitchen window and sometimes cigarette butts fell on the floor; he wrote the date beside each scorch mark.

With almost the same accuracy, I can date the moment when my life came into focus for the first time since falling in love with Michael. It was late July of 1993. We had driven up the Ottawa Valley, turning off the highway at Argyle and picking up the road toward Algonquin Park. Near Golden Lake we parked and proceeded to hike up Blueberry Mountain, a steep and shady climb crowned by a view of the Bonnechere River valley, its fields and glistening lakes a part of the larger Ottawa Valley. The hilltop was covered with blueberries. The ones in the sun were very small and warm to the touch, the ones in the shade were big and worthwhile, and all of them had the dusky bloom that's like the film of chalk after a blackboard has been erased.

I knelt down. The berry-heavy twigs were low to the ground, and I lifted them up like tangled hair off the back of one's neck and combed the berries into a pot. Under the small green leaves and small dry twigs, they hung unblemished, seamless, their sheen disturbed by my warm fingers moving like my mother's, and I was with her in a new way, feeling an old and deep emotion, the rapport I had been looking for all my life.

So much of coming home is wondering why. You make a long journey *for* something and what is it once you have it in your hands? It's a series of second thoughts. A bundle of doubts. A nest with no eggs. And so you look at the nest and think about the missing eggs. You look at this nothingness and after many months start to see the intricate basket, the catch basin for your empty guts, the twigs, the leaves, the undersides of the leaves, and the beautiful, beautiful berries.

I picked, relaxed at first and careless of results, then more feverishly and more possessively once I heard the voices of other pickers deep in the woods, and in the back of my mind was my mother's first memory, of being carried up Blimkie's Mountain by her father and set down among the blueberries that she picked and ate all afternoon—a memory of love, color, abundance, on the ground and in her father's arms.

I was back in the land of her wounded childhood, and the land fascinated me and so did the childhood. It seemed to me that going deeper into my mother's past would help me understand all the life that was blocked up inside me, that is blocked up inside each of us.

And so on a Thursday afternoon in March of 1994, about half past three, I sat down at a long white table in the Ottawa Room of the Ottawa Public Library and began to go through abstracts of births, marriages and deaths from the Argyle *Mercury*. As I read I imagined Connie doing similar research and I felt closer to her, too. In the first abstract I found my grandmother's birth, and a quiver went through me. *1884—April 13, Mrs. Thomas Stewart, a dau., Easter Sunday Morning.* Then I turned to the Deaths and saw the mother listed five days later, *wife of Thomas Stewart, aged 25 yrs.* I paused, considering all the consequences that poured out of that birth and that death. Sifting through more pages, I discovered the record of my grandmother's marriage in 1908 and then I came to my mother's birth in 1919. *Soper, Nov. 26, a dau.*

I used to brush my mother's hair when I was a girl. I learned texture, thickness, solidity, scalp smell, scalp color: the pallid blue-grayness under her thick brown hair like a broken piece of china, the view you have when a plate breaks in half. My mother's patience in this one regard. She liked to have me stand behind her chair after dinner and brush and brush and brush her hair.

In the mornings it was her turn. I sat on a stool beside the kitchen window and looked out at the snow as birds flew by, arrows of red, arrows of blue, while my mother brushed and combed and braided and quizzed. She had me spell *wear, were, where. There, they're, their. Where were the birds going in their finery? They're over there wearing their feathers.* I learned hard little words as my hair was tugged into French braids by rapid, relentlessly competent fingers. Later, when I read in Lévi-Strauss about language arriving from heaven on a long braid of hair, I felt I had known this all along.

Her merciless fingers were undistractible. *Never waste a moment,* they drummed into my skull; the world is a slate and you must have some further inch of learning to show for yourself at the end of each day. Words were synonymous with insistence, short jabs of pain, stoicism, my mother's moods.

She inherited her father's hands, as I've said, his bony, capable hands that planted gardens and grafted fruit trees and worked with furniture and corpses. Unhappy undertaker. He had no choice, my mother believed, but to take over the family business, though what he really wanted was to go West and be a farmer. He left uncollected bills worth thousands of dollars when he died and no life insurance, but seventeen bushels of gladiola bulbs.

These details I discovered in my Uncle David's photocopied memoir, my mother's oldest brother, an inveterate note-taker and chronicler of his own life. I learned more when a cousin sent me her father's brief but revealing account of his ancestors. Much of it was nothing my mother knew, despite her lively memory, and nothing she was interested in. "You can't imagine my *un*interest," she said to me once, "in all those Sopers."

I was discovering a past ruined for her by her father's early death and her mother's bile, a past that was coming into leaf for me and never would for her. But the leafiness contained her, whether she knew it or not, cared or not.

They had been piano and cabinet makers in England, my grandfather's people, coming to Canada in 1860 with some means, but little in the way of luck or savvy. They bought a cabinet-making business in a small Quebec town in decline and the business was so unprofitable they had to abandon it after a year. They moved across the Ottawa River to Ontario and took up land on the Opeongo Road in Admaston Township precisely when deep snow concealed the abundant rocks and general unfitness for settlement. They built a commodious house, which contained the most valuable collection of books in the district—a detail that touched me to the core—only to see it burn to the ground in 1864, thanks to a fit of helpfulness on the part of the father, who set fire to the brush piles in the clearing and the house went up, too. See where helpfulness gets you. By this time the son had married a young woman, eighteen years old.

Hannah, after whom my mother was named, stayed in the rebuilt house and raised the first several of what would be eleven children. She managed the cows and chickens and garden and children, while father and son opened a furniture and undertaking business in Argyle, traveling back and forth, the two of them, between country and town.

In 1869, while Hannah was still on the farm, snow fell without interruption for nearly six weeks. It began falling on the morning of February 11 in a slow obliteration that coincided with one more sudden, for that same morning a crowd of five thousand had gathered outside Ottawa's Nicholas Street jail to watch Patrick Whelan, who had been convicted of murdering Thomas D'Arcy McGee, hang by the neck until he was dead. It was the last public execution in Canada. By noon, a raging blizzard enveloped the city and the surrounding countryside. Many of those heading back to their homesteads on the concession lines had to seek shelter with friends or relatives or strangers, and there they remained, marooned for weeks. Drifts twenty feet high stopped trains in their tracks, and cattle died lowing in their stalls.

Hannah had a book of fairy tales rescued from the fire, tales of magic cloaks and yearned-for wealth and small children who lose their way in the woods. She read the stories to her children and then stepped outside into the spellbound Year of the Deep Snow. She used snowshoes to get around, cutting up fences for fuel, shoveling her way to the barn, tunneling her way to the woodpile, working in the moonlight: a figure of surpassing stamina. My grandfather, her second child, would become the tenderest of fathers. These are the stories my mother tells, that when she was small, she sat in her high chair beside him and held his hand while they ate their supper. At bedtime, he would give her a piggyback ride upstairs and half a dozen somersaults on the big bed beside her crib before they knelt together on the floor to say, "Now I lay me down to sleep." He settled her in her crib and kissed her good night, but as soon as his foot hit the landing she would call out, "Daddy, I need a drink of water," and back without fail he would come.

On April 19 of that legendary winter, it started to rain and it kept raining until all the rivers flooded and the countryside was under water. When the roads were finally passable, Hannah went into town with her four children, including my grandfather, and moved into the apartment above the store and refused to return to the wilds. She slept in a big bed known to her offspring as the funeral bed for the carved plumes on the dark headboard and foot-board that resembled the purple-feathered plumes on the family's horse-drawn hearse.

Loosen the reins and our personalities take us back to childhood; loosen them more and they take us back to our parents as children. Back to the horses themselves that drew the hearse in the flu epidemic of 1918–19. My mother was born in a flurry of death, her undertaker father unable to get to bed for two weeks, so busy was he burying the dead.

In his furniture store on Argyle Street, they kept the caskets on door panels that swung up into the wall like stowaway beds. Over the years, my grandfather in his workshop also put hundreds of solid-rubber tires on wagons and baby buggies, pressing the wheels between the pit of his stomach and the workbench, then using a round wooden handle to work the tire and its double-twisted wires into place. Some who knew him, like my Uncle David, believed that the continual pressure and irritation to his lower stomach was the cause of the cancer that made him drop in weight from 145 to 98 pounds. At the Royal Victoria Hospital in Montreal, they cut out the tumor and sewed the bowel to the stomach, and this permit-ted him to eat again, but he continued to fail, and in July of 1927 he died at the age of sixty-three, breaking my mother's seven-year-old heart.

My mother has always said that he died in the spring, but here it is in black and white in the *Mercury*. A summer death. In her mind she carries the clear image of her father lying comatose in bed, the spring breezes lifting the curtains at the open window as a semi-circle of solid, dark Soper bodies sit around him, waiting for him to die. It was too much. She began to cry, and one of her uncles, a minister, resolutely took her by the hand and led her downstairs to the summer kitchen, where he left her.

In her own short and vivid account of her life, which I typed out for her about five years ago, she wrote, *I took an instant and permanent dislike to that man, which I have, to a lesser degree, extended to all ministers.* She refers to her father as the youngest of the nine Soper children. In fact, he was the second-oldest of eleven. I'm reminded of what Michael said about memory: the facts don't matter; everything you learn blurs and merges and contributes to a way of seeing the world. My mother sees herself in the springtime of her young life losing the person who meant everything to her, and he was the youngest in his family, just like her.

The *Mercury* tells me that the day after he died hailstones the size of plums fell at the lake six miles away, which he had been instrumental in stocking with pickerel. Moments before the storm, a fishing party caught a string of seven pickerel and six black bass, one of the bass weighing three and a half pounds. When I informed my mother of these events with their otherworldly implications, her face lit up as if her father had just walked into the room.

I told Michael about it, too. I had phoned him when I returned to Ottawa, an impulsive call triggered by the sight of children trooping bravely back to school at the beginning of September. He was almost eighty by this time. I was in no great danger. I learned that he was still managing to hang on in the country, thanks to his self-reliance, his appetite for solitude, and the women who went in and out of his life. Every so often the urge to tell him something would come over me and I would pick up the phone. Like my mother, like me, he appreciated the notion that the lake had observed my grandfather's passing. Perhaps my grandfather had orchestrated the weather. Or come back as a pickerel.

One summer I spent a week alone in a borrowed cabin on the same lake, just down the shore from my mother's childhood cabin, which was still there, though fully rebuilt. The nights were full of

mice and wind, skitterings under and across wood, the odd mos-
quito, and on several occasions—storms. The days were divided
between berry picking and writing. I took to haunting a neighbor's
raspberry patch, the raspberry season nearly over and no one about.
My mother's voice was in my head. We went out all day, she said. We
carried pails and took our lunches. It was so hot. We had to walk
and climb for the berries, hike for them. We wore old straw hats and
long-sleeved shirts and afterward we threw ourselves into the lake
and oh, how our scratches stung in the water.

This was the place where she was happy, this lake six miles from
Argyle with its main arm reaching east toward the surrounding
hills. Now here I was in the same spot, fascinated with the jittery,
nervous shaking, the incessant movement of a chipmunk's hind-
quarters. It would sit poised on a log, ten feet from the picnic table
where I was writing, and remind me of the tiny black-and-white
snapshot in which a chipmunk ate out of my mother's sixteen-year-
old hand. The benign delight on her face was not unlike her expression in her wedding photograph, and similar to the look her face
acquired after two weeks away from housework.

It happened several times when I was a child that she would go
away for two weeks to a summer art school in Doon, near Toronto.
There she would be taught by more experienced painters and not
cook a single meal. When we picked her up at the end of those times,
years had fallen away. Her face was softer, without irritation, and
her bosom was fuller. Into her brassiere she had slipped those wonderful falsies women used to wear, endowing herself by hand with
what nature had failed to provide. Anyone who saw the relaxed,
eager face and the round swelling of the summer blouse would have
concluded that here was someone in love.

She stood under trees—apple, pear, plum, birch—at the end of a
grassy driveway and greeted us, her family, with abundant delight
as we clambered toward her. She was in love with us and we with
her, not having seen each other for days and days, but she was more
in love with what she had been doing and who she had been with:
they were the source of the transformation that was unforgettable

and thought-provoking, especially to a daughter of eight, nine, ten. She turned her laughing, welcoming face on us as if she were turning her head on a pillow, and her eyes were full of deep, womanly satisfaction.

The memories came back during that week at the lake as I jotted down loose thoughts about my mother and the valley—the woods and weather and split-rail fences of this rougher, less finished part of the world. I knew that despite her endless accommodation of my father and her dogged approach to domestic life, she was creative to the tips of her fingers. She was the touchstone, the springboard, the key but overshadowed influence in my life. I intended to write a book about her, but nothing came of it for a long time. It's inexplicable, the pause between the clear intent and the actual doing of the work. It can last for decades. In this case, my parents were still alive and I felt constrained when I tried to write about them, and so I put it off. But that doesn't account for all of my reluctance (or for my willingness now, since they are still alive). It doesn't account for how, when I finally returned to the material of my mother's life, I came at it sideways, through the story of Parley Burns, which led me to Connie and to Michael. It's rather like what happens when you go to visit a certain place in the general vicinity of an old lover's house. You have no intention of seeing the old lover, you have something entirely different in mind. But then you allow yourself just to drive by.

19

AFTER CONNIE

When I remember it, I think of waiting for him to arrive. The air is hot, especially inside the house, and in the late afternoon shrubs and bushes start to toss their heads, the sky darkens, the winds drop, and the rain begins.

I see history passing me by. I am standing on the sidelines and it is whirling past, and the people who come after will see it one way and it won't be my way. Liquid wax takes the shape of a candle. But I see the liquid and they will see the candle. His old Buick pulls up across the street. I am watching from the window. The rain has stopped and the heat has eased off. It occurs to me that I have never seen him in a hurry. He moves deliberately, at his own pace, and I am as grateful for that as I am for people not lowering their blinds or drawing their curtains, so that when I walk by I can see into their rooms and know how they live without having to share their lives. I move away from the window and feel him closing in, this man who turned my life upside down, this heavily romanced and romancing man. I have never been entirely myself with him, not for a single minute, partly because he is so much older and partly because that's how attraction works.

He still has a big voice, the sort of voice that calls to you across a stream and asks if you've caught any trout. His way of phrasing things, his broken heart.

"She was my first love," he says, leaning forward in the summer chair, bringing himself a foot closer to me on the back porch, "and my greatest love."

At the funeral in Maine the week before, he had sat apart. Then as soon as it was over, he made a round of rapid goodbyes. He embraced my children, who were thrilled to see him again, and embraced me and shook my husband's hand, but he was determined to get away. He said he would call me. It was May of 1995.

My father had collapsed during the final hymn. Not a heart attack, it turned out, but a sudden drop in blood pressure brought on by dehydration and nervous strain. Soon he was sitting up, taking sips of water, which he loathed, and adamant that he would not go to the hospital.

Death and sex. They smash through the walls and sit like tanks in the living room.

My parents went back to their hotel, very tired, eager to be alone. The rest of us returned to Connie's house—in her will she had left it to her old school as an island retreat—and we had a little supper together, and then songs and poems. How beautiful my children were as they sat across from Syd Goodwin, who stood and sang, battling with his memory, "But I had it a moment ago," pulling the lyrics out of the crack into which they had fallen, and delivering robustly, grandly, wonderfully, "Almost Like Being in Love" from *Brigadoon*. My daughter sang "Blackbird," her hands dancing and diving and searching for lost words. My son read "The Fish" by Elizabeth Bishop after we ate the sole.

Had my parents been at the table, nothing of the sort would have happened. We would have been too formal and careful around my father's grief.

Syd was in his nineties, still vigorous, with the muscled forearms and enlarged hands of old and dedicated gardeners. He traced his passion for flowers back to a childhood summer in Scotland when his widowed grandfather had taken him back for company and he experienced roses in dappled sunlight. "Old men have to fall in love with something," he said. His garden on the Ottawa River was a teaching garden for nearby schools, and in her will Connie had left it a considerable sum.

On my back porch, Michael was saying that she always had a tremendous glow about her, kids used to follow her around like blackflies following a cyclist. He remembered a day when she rescued a monarch butterfly. She lifted it half-drowned out of a puddle and held it in her palm, then thought to set it down on the cherry pits, the residue of the cherries they were eating, and after half an hour it revived and flew away. He said she was uninhibited, shameless, principled. She shimmied her hips in a way that kept him happy all day.

He was wearing old pants, dark gray, an old sweater, dark blue. Even his way of sitting was loose and relaxed. Brown face and neck. Out in the sun. He remembered a man whistling at her in the street as she took off her sweater, and her instant comeback that he was a little big not to have grown up. "She was schoolteacherish in her deadpan humor, her elegance."

I followed the evening light fading on his face. He still looked much younger than he was; he became more handsome than I remembered. The life of an attraction. Like a pear in the sun. And then the shadows lengthened and he was as old as the hills.

Soon it was dark enough that I went in search of candles, and when I came back onto the porch I learned why Connie had stayed in the same school for thirty-five years. Something kept her there, someone she loved, a married man she loved.

"She was more bohemian than you are." He leaned back, studying me with his blue-bleak eyes. I was Connie in diluted form.

Neither was I getting him at his best. He was dented and well used.

"You're conservative." His voice sounded so husky and cool and aged. "Yes. You are. You're ready to break through the fence, but you don't."

"I'm perfect," I laughed, "and don't you forget it."

I had broken through a fence and fallen into a ditch named Michael. But he was right. I knew he was right, although I hated hearing it.

My daughter rescued us. She arrived home from her summer job at the Ritz Café and sat with us for a while. Her arrival reanimated Michael, and his presence surprised and delighted her. She had forgiven me more easily for separating from her father than for putting half a continent between Michael and us. Responding to him, she looked rested and lovely. Her skin was perfect, free of birthmarks, moles, freckles. I say this gratefully. Grateful for the fresh start in front of my eyes. She was nineteen.

Just the three of us, there on the porch overlooking the garden. My husband was away for a few days, my son was staying overnight with a friend. In the darkness the white lilacs came forward, big and splendid, deeply fragrant.

Michael said with emotion, "There's such *opera* in those flowers. When you look at them, they live and die at the same time."

Connie indulged Michael the way mothers indulge their sons, so I've come to believe. The mothers can't help it. And the reverse is true. Daughters quicken a mother's critical faculties. None of this is deliberate or thought out—it's on the level of the physical. And so sons bask. And daughters fume. And women brood. And men move on. And yet they don't move on either.

At midnight I was making him coffee. We were in the kitchen, he was leaning against the counter.

"She often drove up to see me," he said.

"In the summers."

"Whenever the spirit moved her. She was impulsive. She never thought she did enough with her life. I told her to start her own school. She could have."

"The teacher she was involved with. The married teacher."

"He taught history and economics. I never met him."

"He would have come to the funeral." I was trying to picture who he might have been and assuming that this was the close friend in New York, the one she went out with every winter evening to one thing or another.

"I imagine so."

Michael held out his mug for more coffee and I filled it. The kitchen light was unforgiving. I kept looking at him, the way you gaze into a mirror, half convinced that if you look long enough you won't seem so terribly old, and after a while it works, you resurrect your younger self.

Seeing Michael again was natural and not painful, yet it would keep me awake for nights.

At the funeral, Syd had taken the stairs cautiously. He was still erect in his bearing, but he needed a cane. He had a fine, big head and a ready mouth out of which came one surprising, casual remark after another. He said how much he liked a wild garden, not French gardens, "which are like barbershops. Versailles. But gardens in which plants are free, not restrained. Anti-military gardens." He proceeded from plant to plant, not with energy but with intensity, noticing the lovage, mint, chives, and confessing to a new craving for onions, of all things, following a mild heart attack. "It's like you work beside someone for twenty-five years without noticing her, and then one day you discover she is the apple of your eye."

We came to Connie's view of the sea and stood there breathing in the sea air and watching the sailboats in the distance. I was full of sorrow for not having made the effort to see her again before she died. She was supposed to live longer. Eighty-four didn't seem very old to me, not when I was standing next to Syd who was closing in on a hundred.

He said, "A tender, tender thing comes over you when you get this old. It's a marvelous thing when you learn how to live. As my mother said, you give over."

I learned that he had spent years collecting and cultivating early-spring flowers, trilliums and snowdrops especially, developing as many strains as possible. He described how snowdrops struggle out of the ground without any appearance of struggle, suddenly there, small, white, drooping—simple; the first flowers after a long winter. One strain of snowdrop, *Galanthus plicatus,* he had named 'Susan Graves.'

You think you are paying attention and then someone says something and you snap awake.

A dead child becomes a flower. A gardener weaves her back into the tapestry of life. It doesn't lessen the tragedy, it makes it resurface every spring, a little shock to the heart.

"A bit of lonesomeness," Michael had confessed on the porch, "is far better than the anguish caused by a woman's expectations. I've cut off all the girlfriends."

He was like that. He needed solitude until he needed its opposite. He binged; he cut himself off; he binged.

I remembered something he had said to me when we were together. "It's like musical chairs. We'll see which woman is left at the end."

20

2008

Children tend to know so little about themselves and are so inclined to believe the worst, so inclined to agree they are no good, that they grow up confused and lost and at odds with themselves without knowing why. It's only with great effort that they overcome this emptiness in themselves, this terrible sense of emptiness.

I was ugly enough at birth that my mother threatened to send me back. She joked with the doctor about it. Another woman would have been in tears over my mashed and flattened face and the size of my nose and the overwhelming number of birthmarks, the small islands of dark brown and red on my chest that formed the Outer Hebrides to the mainland of my discolored left knee and elbow, and the river of scalded red across the back of my neck that echoed the same mark in the same place on my dreaded grandmother. Some prenatal happening, an accident in the sea of the womb, had knocked me about, and I carried the evidence with me into this life, where it was mute, one of those untold stories that hover about us and tantalize.

A few years ago, urged on by my mother saying it was the best book she had ever read, I made my way through *Moby-Dick* and came upon these words about Ahab: "he found himself hard by the very latitude and longitude where his tormenting wound had been inflicted." In this house, I am hard by the nursing home on Powell Avenue where my grandmother lived out her final years and died at eighty-eight, virtually abandoned, after inflicting the wounds that still torment my mother.

It took me years before I bicycled past the home. I had been on my way to the National Library to do more research about the trial of Johnny Coyle for the rape and murder of Ethel Weir, and instead of noting the name of the street and continuing on as I always did, I turned right and bicycled its length, looking for the house number I knew from an old letter, a place we had visited when I was growing up, but not often, once every few years when we drove here from southwestern Ontario. My grandmother would light up at the sight of us, then manage to undo her welcome by letting us know we had neglected her, and we had.

I recognized the three-story house with the wheelchair ramp, the place my grandmother called jail. More rundown, perhaps, but it had looked rundown when she lived there. It had the force of an anti-magnet, pulling me even as it pushed me away. I felt my grandmother's deep loneliness and deep touchiness. I felt it as an ache and a pressure, the scabbed-over relationship she had with my mother. By *pressure* I mean something moral and close to the bone that's hard to put into words, but begging to be put into words.

Living here, immersed in my mother's and grandmother's past, is more like living in old bathwater than in Melville's ocean, except for the waves of feeling. Even now, if I want to unsettle my mother, all I have to do is raise the subject of *her* mother. I asked her once what year Granny died, and immediately the air was awkward. She couldn't remember. She didn't want to be reminded of the aggrieved figure in the nursing home who found fault with everything she did.

"She was never loved as a child," my mother said. Then couldn't help adding from her store of bitterness, "Another person would have overcome that."

My mother meant overcome her tragic beginnings and then overcome the tragic middle of her life, too. Instead, she continued all the way to the tragic end.

My grandmother was only forty-three when she became a widow. She was a hard worker, my mother readily acknowledged, a seamstress whose life began with a cut thread. Her mother's death, five days after she was born, came from puerperal fever, the "childbed fever" caused when germs enter the womb and lead to blood poisoning, something that could have been avoided so easily by simple cleanliness.

My grandmother was drastically unmothered as a child, read to only once. On the recommendation of others, her father bought a copy of *Alice in Wonderland,* which he opened in their farm kitchen on the Opeongo Road in 1892. He read three pages to her before he got up from his chair in high dudgeon, walked to the kitchen stove, lifted the black lid, and stuffed the book into the fire. He laughed out loud exactly once, at the sight of a dog spinning around in the kitchen chasing its tail. My grandmother went on to marry the peace-loving man who was old enough to be her father, then after he died she was forced to construct her living in a variety of ways, including selling Spirella corsets door-to-door, or as her three-line ad in the *Mercury* had it, "Spirella Training Garments. Latest models, attractive material. Prices ranging from $6.50. Mrs. E. N. Soper. 48 Argyle Street. Phone 316."

She took in boarders, male boarders, with the exception of Connie. She did not like women. When she gave birth to my mother, having already produced three sons, she held her up and said, "It's a girl. What do I do with *it*?"

And yet my mother named me after her.

For years I cherished this grievance, that in calling me Anne, my mother had set me up for the day when she would stand at the head of the stairs and scream down at me that I was the most selfish person she had ever known, even more selfish than *her mother*. Much later, when I was a young mother myself and apprised Connie of this stinging part of my history, she looked at me thoughtfully. "Maybe your mother was hoping to have a different relationship with you."

Then I was set back on my heels and the whole of my life looked different.

When I was small, my mother used to paint in the summer kitchen of our old house on the hill. Our beloved dog had his beloved armchair in the corner. My mother had her easel. Of her early paintings I recall a close rendering of the pattern on an oriole's egg, the dark lines like calligraphy on a pale greenish-blue surface. And certain portraits. She painted all four of her children. She painted her mother and sculpted her head in clay. This last came into my possession when we emptied out my parents' house. My brothers found it shoved to the back of a topmost cupboard in the laundry room, where it had been hidden from view for nearly forty years.

When I take it in my hands, I am holding something severed at the neck that refuses to die. My fingers follow my mother's working into being the deeply furrowed forehead, the scornful eyes and flared nostrils, the peevish mouth that drags down at one side, and the coiled braids arranged in two figure-eights at the back of her head and held in place by a hairnet. My mother discovered a stash of these hairnets after her mother died, dozens upon dozens of unopened paper packages in her bedside table. "She must have thought she was going to live forever," my mother said to me and, characteristically, she kept them. Years later, when my young daughter took ballet lessons and needed to hold her bun in place, we found a use for them. I have a package on my desk as I write. "Intimate hairnets, the un-see-able nets, one size fits all hair do's, neutral. 59 cents." I lift the torn envelope to my nose and unbelievably I can smell the nursing home's bad breath.

The home is a twenty-minute walk northeast of here, almost directly across the canal from the retirement residence where my mother and father have ended up—a coincidence that surprises me anew every day. It's possible that a hidden symmetry is often at work as we stumble our way through life.

One oppressively hot afternoon in early August, coming back from the archives, I stopped by the residence to see my parents and bring them breaking news of 1937.

"This is the day that Ethel Weir was murdered seventy years ago. I've been reading about her."

My mother's face became thoughtful and expressive. "What times those were." She had a sweater on and another sweater over her knees.

She told me that she and her brothers had disagreed about Johnny Coyle. "I thought he was guilty. Well, the papers were full of it, and it was simpler and less upsetting to pin it on someone." Her brothers, on the other hand, had thought anyone passing by could have done it, alone as she was in the woods.

A lucid conversation. More typically, my mother has to close her eyes in a furious effort to remember. "Damn," and she'll give her head a shake, "*nation.*"

I washed her hair. We set up a heater on the bathroom floor to keep her warm. Then she took off her vest and shirt. Her skin hung like silken parchment. She was skin and bone. She bent over the sink and I poured cupfuls of warm water over her head, then I shampooed and smoothed and rubbed, then worked her scalp with my fingertips, the good scrubbing she wanted, feeling the wens on her scalp like tiny hard nipples; rinsed, conditioned, rinsed; then emptied the sink, wiped up all the water, and lifted the heater onto the counter and trained it in her direction as she sat on the toilet, combing and brushing her still-impressive silvery-white hair.

The child I'd been reading about in the *Mercury* had an old woman's name: Ethel. And now my mother was like an old, old girl. How was it possible for similar lives to diverge so completely and then become similar again? One day recently, I had rolled up my mother's pant legs to check on her swollen ankles and knee, and was shocked to see that she had painted her lower legs yellow. In my dismay I thought of Ethel Weir, not just the little palette of color-makings and blood in her clenched fist but the bruises all over her body.

The last summer in her studio, when she was eighty-seven, my mother asked me to help with her last big painting, four feet by five feet. All it needed was the final application of the beeswax sealant over the finished image. We used long brushes to apply the sealant, then moved a heating lamp inch by inch over the surface until none of the brushstrokes were visible—all slick, like flooding a rink to get smooth ice. Unhappily, in showing me how to do it, how to cook it, as she said, and in taking a turn, she aggravated the compression fracture in her back. Pain pill, hot-water bottle; unable to eat her dinner. The painting was of the stone, one of three, she had picked up at Lake Tuborg on Ellesmere Island in the High Arctic when she was there with a group of scientists, living in a tent, sketching and taking photographs for future work; she was in her early seventies then and having the time of her life. A week after she came home, the face of the glacier gave way, slid down and took out the scientific instruments in the streambed and buried the streambed itself from which she had taken the stones. The ice slide lasted a minute and changed everything. My mother got the news a week later, and it was borne in upon her how lucky she was, and how precious the three stones were: they had almost vanished from sight for another million years. After that, they became the soul of her work, sandstone and quartz melted and run together into such interesting lines and colors and shapes that they never stopped feeding her imagination.

Now the stones are in a shoebox on a table in their small living quarters and my mother is stymied, unable to work.

At dinnertime, I accompanied her and my father downstairs to their table in the dining room and sat with them while they had their dinner. My mother emptied her tiny paper cup of pills onto the table and made compositions with them, like Cézanne arranging his peaches. My father pointed out various inmates, as

"My mother talks about your stepfather. Mr. Burns."

"I have good memories of him." She wasn't defiant, she was firm. "We read plays together. We dressed up in costume." She said it again, "Good memories. Of course the poor man was mad. He had himself committed and then he put an end to himself."

I sat down beside her on the bench. "Tell me more," I said.

"I remember your mother. She doesn't remember me. I invited her to a Halloween party once. She refused to bob for apples. Didn't want to get her hair wet. Or perhaps she felt intimidated by my step-father. Everyone did."

The sun shone in our faces and I turned sideways to get it out of my eyes and to see her better. They are their own breed, these capable spinster-teachers of old. A handkerchief poked out of the cuff of her brown cardigan.

I said, "I know your stepfather as Parley. That's what my mother called him, and my aunt. My aunt taught with him in Saskatchewan."

"He wrote a play about Saskatchewan."

The sun went behind the clouds. I had no trouble at all seeing her face.

"He didn't finish it," she said. "A lot of things he didn't finish. He was a hugely frustrated man. I think that's what drove him out of his head."

I touched her arm. "But you read it as far as it went. This play about Saskatchewan."

"It was among his papers. I kept them for a long time. I had to get rid of a lot of things when I moved in here." She sighed. "It was such a grim play, unforgettably grim."

"Tell me."

"Oh, it was about a teacher who goes mad."

"Parley was the teacher." The words escaped me, but she didn't react; a little deaf, I thought.

She said, "I think he heard the story when he lived there. I think it haunted him."

Crows had set up a racket in the tall spruce on the other side of the driveway. I became aware of them as I waited for her to continue.

he liked to call them: a small, alert woman who used to
Minister Diefenbaker's secretary; a retired English pro
hundred years old, who was rereading Milton; a forme
man whose fingers were severed at the knuckle by a
but still he managed to play the piano. "That woman,"
said of someone petite and ancient and pushing a
very proud of her legs." Her short skirt revealed daint
dainty knees.

At one of the tables sat a monotone of old woman with
in a book.

"Your mother knows who that is," he said.

My mother smiled and I tensed a little, knowing she h
ten, as my father was about to point out.

"Who is it?" my father said to her.

My mother kept smiling, having perfected an adroit
his teacherly interrogations. "Oh, some tagalong."

"She's from Argyle," my father said.

"She *is*." My mother nodded brightly.

"She taught French at the collegiate." Always quick, my
connect with another teacher.

But neither of them could remember her name.

I happened upon the same woman as I was leaving. She v
on a bench in the sunshine with her book. "You're from
I said to her, "like my mother. You taught French." And I
was the daughter of Hannah and James Flood.

Her name, she said, was Doris Burns.

I nearly said, *I thought you were dead,* I was so astonis
meeting Doris "the Brain" Burns.

She indicated the small volume of French poetry she
ing. "My stepfather gave it to me. He taught French, too."

I took the book from her hands, feeling almost ligh
dropped straight down into the eerie pattern of human lif

She was ninety-four years old, she confessed. "Isn't tha
ing? It's awful." Her horror had both of us laughing.

"The teacher was female," she corrected me. (Not deaf at all, then.) "She falls in love with one of her students and the boy sets fire to the school. The boy is backward. He can't read."

Michael.

"He's playing with matches at the side of the school. The grass catches and the wind takes it and the flames spread and leap to the house across the road."

I was back with Michael showing my children how to light a fire, how never to let it run away with itself. I was seeing him on that sultry windy night in May somewhere in the vicinity of his big frame house, matches in hand, setting a fire in the grass, then thinking he had put it out and going off, only to return to a house in flames. But I knew the fire had started in Susan's room. I knew that.

And yet how much did I really know, especially about the worries of a traumatized boy? Perhaps Parley, with his experience of schoolboys and with his own morose imaginings to draw on, had touched upon some kind of truth about Michael's fears.

Doris Burns was repeating that she had held on to his papers for a long time. "But then they went into the recycling bin. Who would have been interested?"

"*I* would have been interested."

She patted my knee. "He was a great diary writer for a time. That was sad reading, too, those diaries."

"Because he was so . . ." And with my finger I made a circling motion at my temple.

"He was smitten and knew his feelings weren't returned. He saw her every day because she taught in the same school."

"Connie."

"My names have gone," she said.

We sat on without speaking, side by side on the bench, until I stirred and asked if there was nothing in the play about the boy's sister dying in the fire.

"I don't recall it."

"You wouldn't forget," I said. "A girl screaming in an upstairs window and no one able to reach her."

She didn't recall anything like that.

"Not even in his diary?"

"No."

It seemed to me the final injustice, even though I understood what it is not to be able to face something or find the words for it.

I thanked her and said how good it was to meet her, assuring her, when she apologized for her memory, that I had learned a great deal.

Parley was revealed to me as a failed writer, a smitten and rejected man, haunted, as she had said, by what happened in Jewel. He worked with the material as every writer does, removing himself by submerging himself in others. And so he assigned his madness to Connie and his self-condemnation to Michael, and he couldn't even begin to write about Susan. Whatever he invented was beggared by reality, and he couldn't write about reality.

I didn't think to ask Doris Burns what she remembered about Ethel Weir and John Coyle until I was halfway home. But the next time I saw her, I produced their names and she had no trouble. She told me that her stepfather and Johnny had kept in touch, and that Johnny was one of the pallbearers at his funeral.

It's early September again, and in time with the first yellow school buses comes a new urgency, almost like pain, to the flashing, shrill cries of blue jays in the woods. For Michael it was the sound of the closing down of a better season, the rising of panic. He remembered being so much in tears, he told me once. He would sit and look out the classroom window. He was going to be scrutinized and judged. He was going to fail. And then Connie came along, he said, and saved him.

He died three years ago, ten years after Connie. It was Evie who phoned me to say he was in the hospital in Wakefield following a heart attack. The sister, it turned out, was looking after the big brother. We were in November and snow had fallen, but not in quantity. In the hospital, coming down the corridor, I heard his voice, flirting with the nurses, and thought he was bound to recover. I stopped to listen. His voice still worked on me. But then I entered his room and he was so shrunken and spent. He reached for my hand. He asked about me and my children and my mother, and when I told him my mother was still in her studio every day, he said that was good, he wasn't ready to die either. "Are you in pain?" I said. He had been. But drugs had taken care of that. "Tell me your news, Annie. Talk to me." I began to describe my trips to the archives and to Argyle, and as I talked his eyes closed and he slept.

I had forgotten to bring a book with me and there were no books, no reading materials in his room. Watching him sleep, I remembered him telling me how he learned to distinguish the letter *b* from *d*. Imagine a bed, the *b* is the foot of the bed and the *d* is the pillow. I remembered our conversation about the courage of schoolchildren. "Brave and trusting," he said, "poor little suckers."

His clothes were folded neatly on a chair. I lifted his sweater and smelled it. It was Michael, a combination of woodsmoke, outdoors, animals and boy.

In the hallway Evie told me quietly that he wouldn't be going home again, she was searching out a nursing home for him. But he died in the hospital four days later at about one in the morning, and alone.

I walk into my parents' rooms in the late afternoon, the door unlocked, and my mother is sitting by herself in a chair beside my father's desk, head down like a castigated schoolgirl.

I tell her so, and she looks up at me and laughs and agrees. She says she can't put five words together. Her brains are gone.

Words escape her, and the chronology of her life and the whereabouts of the elevator down the hall. Without my father she is lost.

A few weeks later, when we drive across the Ottawa River and into the Gatineau Hills, she comes alive. She reaches behind her for my father's hand and they hold hands, she in the front of the car and he in the back. They say repeatedly what a splendid day it is, enchanted by the colors. We are in Quebec on the old River Road, flush with the Gatineau River, a low and bumpy way familiar to me from the many times I drove out to see Michael.

He filled my dreams one night recently, and in the morning I woke up refreshed and content. Then the dreams proceeded to wash across the day, surfacing and catching me off guard, until I thought something had actually happened—something significant was astir. What had ended by day had found a way to live on at night, the reverse of its earlier self, when it occupied every waking thought and disappeared at night, for in the actual living of it I never dreamt about him. It would seem our past lives have dyslexic minds of their own.

At Wakefield, beyond the covered bridge, we veer east for a bit, then leave the highway and head deeper into the countryside on a back road that turns and twists and takes my mother back in her mind to the six miles of road that led from Argyle to the lake. She is so much more lucid in the woods. Twice, she says how amazing it is to think that everything we are seeing was once under frozen water, miles of it. She means the last ice age, the two-mile-thick glacier that began to retreat twelve thousand years ago. She hasn't forgotten that the earth is recent in this particular manifestation, its beauty a form of recovery from a great, cold weight.

My husband is driving. My father and I share the backseat. Rather late in the day, but not too late, I've come to appreciate the crusty humor and intelligence and melancholy thoughtfulness of this former principal, who at exam time would drive my brothers and me to his high school on Saturday morning and put each of us in a separate classroom to study until noon. Alone in the classroom, I felt undefended and my stomach hurt. Exams loomed, as did my father in his office down the hall, working away and expecting his children to do the same. Sometimes there would be a rap on the window from a brother on the loose savoring a moment of rebellious escape.

We are almost there. We roll down the windows to smell the trees and the breeze and the water coming close.

No excitement compares with arriving at a lake in the woods. You leave the highway behind in favor of a gravel road that eventually turns into a dirt road and becomes so quiet, the dirt covered with pine needles, the smell of pine, the trees enclosing you, and then the sudden lake.

Down by the water, my mother talks about her father, how he would drive the horse-drawn buggy to the lake on Saturday nights after he closed the store, then return to Argyle very early Monday morning. They slept in two big tents behind the cabin, she says, which was just a converted, outsize boathouse. But no swimming on Sunday, no matter how hot, because her father was a strict Methodist. With him she used to drive to his plot of garden, eight acres, on Thompson Hill. He let her handle the reins once they got off the main road. She had no fear of horses and found it thrilling that if she pulled on the right rein old Maude went right, and if she pulled on the left rein the mare went left. "I really miss that man," she says.

Her father's garden was just down the road from the cemetery where he was soon to be buried, and where so many of the people I've been writing about lie buried, too.

The day I went to the cemetery, about three years ago, I wasn't even looking for Bess Macswain, my mother's childhood friend who died in the Almonte train crash. I left the car at the side of the narrow road and entered through a wide swing gate and soon I was among the Sopers. Two long rows of ground markers, seven in each row, led up to a big Soper tombstone. My grandfather and grandmother were beside each other at the end of one row. It wasn't hard to find Parley either. He was with his wife's family inside an enclosure marked off by a low wrought-iron fence, a shaded and darker spot, set apart.

After that, I wandered. I came down a grassy slope and discovered the large headstone for the Coyle family, father, mother and two sons, including John, who died in 1989. Then I looked back up the slope and there was Bess Macswain's headstone. I was seeing her full name for the first time: Anne Elizabeth. And it was my own name. I felt like Pip in *Great Expectations*, understanding who he is from the words on a tombstone. What I had known about collided with what I had never been told, and what I had never been told and had almost missed was crucial to my life. I was named as much for a beloved friend as for a behated mother, even if it was unconscious on my mother's part. I could see that everything is accidental to some degree. The right hand isn't aware of the left, the melody is picked out while the left hand is idle, then suddenly my two hands were together and playing the same tune, the right hand on the present and the left on the past. This music is something we gravitate toward, no matter how distant it is and how hard of hearing we are.

And then I stumbled over Ethel's gravestone, and more stories flew up like birds.

On Parley Burns's grave, growing in patches, was the pale bluish-green lichen that appears in my mother's paintings. I scraped some of it free and have it in a little box on my desk where it sits like pale jade.

Acknowledgments

I would like to thank my family for sharing stories and knowledge, especially my brothers Stuart and Alex, my sister Jean and my sister-in-law Christiane Morisset. Above all, my parents, the dear old flesh-and-blood, as P. G. Wodehouse would say.

My thanks to the many others who answered my questions, in particular, Anne Taylor, Philip Stiles, John Eaton, the late Gladys Arnold, Betty Flower, Norman Hillmer, Anne-Marie Demers, Robert Fox, Carl Christie, Stephen Harris, Bob Gidney, Wyn Millar, Sara Burke, Ann Beauregard, Nina and the late Tom Phillips, David and Nancy Currie, Lois Sweet, Bob Coltri, Bill Terry, Daphne Marlatt and Sheila McCook.

Grateful love to my husband, Mark Fried, who is my first reader and a fine editor. Special thanks to my agents Bella Pomer and Jackie Kaiser. Ongoing thanks to my publicist, Ashley Dunn. Thanks as well to Leah Ringwald and Kendra Ward, and to Shaun Oakey for his keen editorial eye. Deep and abiding gratitude to my indispensable editor and publisher, Ellen Seligman, for once again seeing what I miss and knowing what is needed.

Some small parts of this book appeared in slightly different form in *The New Quarterly* and *Canadian Geographic*. My thanks to their editors.

Finally, sincere thanks to two excellent libraries: Library and Archives Canada and the Ottawa Public Library, including its Ottawa Room. Without them I would be a lost soul.

ELIZABETH HAY's previous novels are the Giller Prize–winning *Late Nights on Air, A Student of Weather,* which was a Giller Prize finalist, and *Garbo Laughs,* which won the Ottawa Book Award and was a finalist for the Governor General's Award. She is also the author of two books of nonfiction and two collections of short stories, including *Small Change.* In 2002 she received the prestigious Marian Engel Award for her body of work. She lives in Ottawa, Canada.